MY HUSBAND'S
Sweethearts

BRIDGET ASHER

MY HUSBAND'S
Sweethearts

A NOVEL

DELACORTE PRESS

MY HUSBAND'S SWEETHEARTS
A Delacorte Press Book / September 2008

Published by Bantam Dell
A Division of Random House, Inc.
New York, New York

Book design by Catherine Leonardo

Delacorte Press is a registered trademark of Random House, Inc.,
and the colophon is a trademark of Random House, Inc.

Library of Congress Cataloging in Publication Data
Asher, Bridget.
My husband's sweethearts / Bridget Asher.
    p.   cm.
ISBN 978-0-385-34189-9 (hardcover)
1. Spouses—Fiction.   2. Adultery—Fiction.
3. Terminally ill—Fiction.   I. Title.
PS3601.S54M9 2008
813'.6—dc22   2008013502

Printed in the United States of America
Published simultaneously in Canada

www.bantamdell.com

10   9   8   7   6   5   4   3   2   1
BVG

For Davi, my sweetheart

Contents

(Sayings Your Mother Never Cross-Stitched into a Pillow)

Chapter One

Don't Try to Define Love Unless
You Need a Lesson in Futility

Careening past airline counters toward the security check-in, I'm explaining love and its various forms of failure to Lindsay, my assistant. Amid the hive of travelers—retirees in Bermuda shorts, cats in carry-on boxes perforated with air holes, hassled corporate stiffs—I find myself in the middle of a grand oration on love with a liberal dose of rationalizations. I've fallen in love with lovable cheats. I've adored the wrong men for the wrong reasons. I'm culpable. I've suffered an unruly heart and more than my share of prolonged bouts of poor judgment. I have lacked some basics in the area of control. For example: I had no control over the fact that I fell in love with Artie Shoreman—a man eighteen years my senior. I had no control over the fact that I am still in love with him even after I found out, in one fell swoop, that he had three affairs during our four-year marriage. Two were lovers he'd had before we got married, but had kept in touch with—held on to, really, like parting gifts from his bachelorhood, living memorabilia. Artie didn't want to call these *affairs* because they were spur-of-the-moment. They weren't *premeditated*. He trotted out terminology like *fling* and *dalliance*. The third affair he called *accidental*.

And I have no control over the fact that I am angry that Artie's gotten so sick—so deathbedish—in the midst of this and that I blame him for his dramatic flair. I have no control over the compulsion I feel to go back home to him right now, bailing out of a speech on convoluted SEC regulations—because my mother has told me in a middle-of-the-night, bad-news phone call that his health is grave. I have no control over the fact that I'm still furious at Artie for being a cheat just when one might, possibly, expect me to soften, at least a little.

I'm telling Lindsay how I left Artie shortly after I found out about the affairs and how that was the right thing to do six months ago. I tell her how all three affairs were revealed at once—like some awful game show.

Lindsay is petite. Her jacket sleeves are always a bit too long for her, as if she's wearing an older sister's hand-me-downs that she hasn't quite grown into. She has silky blond hair that swings around like she's trapped in a shampoo commercial, and she wears small glasses that slip down the bridge of a nose so perfect and narrow I'm not sure how she breathes through it. It's as if her nose were designed as an accent piece without regard to function. She knows this whole story, of course. She's nodding along in full agreement. I forge on.

I tell her that this hasn't been so bad, opting for business trip after business trip, a few months hunkered down with one client and then another, every convention opportunity—a life of short-term corporate rentals and hotel rooms. It was supposed to allow me some time and space to get my heart together. The plan was that when I saw Artie again, I'd be ready, but I'm not.

"Love can't be ordered around or even run by a nice-enough democracy," I tell Lindsay. My definition of a democracy consists of polling the only two people I've chosen to confide in—my anxiety-prone office assistant, Lindsay, who at this very moment is clipping along next to me through JFK airport's terminal, and my overwrought mother, who's got me on speed dial.

"Love refuses to barter," I say. "It won't haggle with you like that Turkish man with the fake Gucci bags." My mother insists I get her a fake Gucci bag each time I'm in New York on business; my carry-on is bulging with fake Gucci at this very moment.

"Love isn't logical," I insist. "It's immune to logic." In my case: my husband is a cheater and a liar, therefore I should move on or decide to forgive him, which is an option that I've heard some women actually choose in situations like this.

Lindsay says, "Of course, Lucy. No doubt about it!"

There's something about Lindsay's confident tone that rattles me. She's often overly positive, and sometimes her high-salaried agreement makes me double-think. I try to carry on with the speech. I say, "I have to stick by my mistakes, though, including the ones that I came by naturally through my mother." My mother—the Queen of Poor Judgment in Men. I flash on an image of her in a velour sweat suit, smiling at me with a mix of hopeful pride and pity. "I have to stick by my mistakes because they've made me who I am. And I'm someone that I've come to like—except when I get flustered ordering elaborate side dishes in sushi restaurants, in which case I'm completely overbearing, I know."

"No kidding," Lindsay agrees, a little too quickly.

And now I stop in the middle of the airport—my laptop swinging forward, my little carry-on suitcase wheels coming to a quick halt (I've only packed necessities— Lindsay will ship the rest of my things later). "I'm not ready to see him," I say.

"Artie needs you," my mother had told me during last night's phone call. "He is your husband still, after all. And it's very bad form to leave a dying husband, Lucy."

This was the first time that anyone had said that Artie was going to die—aloud, matter-of-factly. Until that moment it had been serious, surely, but he's still young—only fifty. He comes from a long line of men who died young, but that shouldn't mean anything—not with today's advances in medicine. "He's just being dramatic," I told my mother, trying to return to the old script, the one where we joke about Artie's dire attempts to get me back.

"But what if he isn't just being dramatic?" she said. "You need to be here. Your being away now, well, it's bad karma. You'll come back in your next life as a beetle."

"Since when do you talk about karma?" I asked.

"I'm dating a Buddhist now," my mother said. "Didn't I tell you that?"

Lindsay has grabbed my elbow. "Are you okay?"

"My mother is dating a Buddhist," I tell her, as if explaining how terribly wrong everything is. My eyes have filled with tears. The airport signs overhead go blurry. "Here." I hand her my pocketbook. "I won't be able to find my ID."

She leads me to a set of phones near an elevator and starts digging through my purse. I can't root through it right now. I can't because I know what's stuffed inside— all the little cards that I've pulled from little envelopes stuck in small plastic green forks accompanying the daily deliveries of flowers that Artie's ordered long distance. He's found me no matter what hotel room I'm in or apartment I'm put up in anywhere I happen to be in the continental U.S. (How does he know where I am? Who gives him my itinerary—my mother? I've always suspected her, but have never told her to stop. Secretly, I like Artie to know where I am. Secretly, I need the flowers, even though part of me hates them—and him.)

"I'm glad you kept all of these," Lindsay says. She's been in my hotel rooms. She's seen the flowers that collect until they're all in various stages of wilt. She hands me my license.

"I wish I hadn't kept them. I'm pretty sure it's a sign of weakness," I tell her.

She pulls one out. "I've always wondered," she says, "you know, what he has to say in all of those cards."

Suddenly I don't want to find my way into the line at security with a herd of strangers. The line is long, but still I have plenty of time—too much. In fact, I know I'll be restless on the other side, feel a little caged myself—like one of those cats in the carry-ons. I don't want to be alone. Go ahead.

"Are you sure?" She raises her thin eyebrows.

I think about it a moment longer. I don't really want to hear Artie's love notes. Part of me is desperate to grab the pocketbook out of her hands, tell her *sorry, changed my mind,* and get in line with everyone else. But another part of me wants her to read these cards, to see if they are as manipulative as I think they are. In fact, I think I need that right now. A little sisterly validation. "Yes," I tell her.

She plucks the note and reads aloud, "Number forty-seven: the way you think every dining room should have a sofa in it for people who want to lie down to digest, but still be part of the witty conversation." She glances at me.

"I like to lie down after I eat—like the Egyptians or something. The dining room sofa just makes good sense."

"Do you have one?"

"Artie bought me one for our first anniversary." I don't want to think of it now, but it's there in my mind—a long antique sofa reupholstered with a fabric of red poppies on a white background and dark wood trim that matches the dining room furniture. We made love on it that first night in the house, the boxy pillows sliding out from under us onto the floor, the aged springs creaking.

She pulls out another one and reads, "Number fifty-two: how the freckles on your chest can be connected to make an approximate constellation of Elvis."

A crew of flight attendants glides by in what seems to be the V formation of migrating geese. A few of Artie's old girlfriends were flight attendants. He made his money opening an Italian restaurant during his late twenties (despite a lack of any real Italian blood in him) and then launching a national chain. He traveled a lot. Flight attendants were plentiful. I watch them swish by in their nylons, the wheels on their suitcases rumbling. My stomach cinches up for a moment. "He actually did that once, connected the freckles, and documented it. We have the photos." I'm waiting for Lindsay's righteous anger to become apparent, but this doesn't seem to be the case. In fact, I notice that she's smiling a little.

She pulls out a third. "Number fifty-five: the way you're afraid that if you forgive your father—once and for all—he might really disappear in some way, even though he's been dead for years."

Lindsay raises her eyebrows at me again.

"Artie's a great listener. He remembers everything. What can I say? It doesn't mean that I should forgive his betrayal and go home to him." Here's one of the reasons I hate Artie. He is so fully and completely himself, his own person, but when I asked him why he cheated on me, he came up with a tired, worn-out response. He constantly falls in love. He thought he could stop when we got married, but he couldn't. He confessed that he fell in love with women all the time, all day, every day, that he adores everything about women—the way they sway when they walk, their fine necks—he even loves their imperfections. And he would get caught up. They confided in him, women did. Suddenly it seemed that a woman was telling him everything and then the next minute she was unbuttoning her blouse. He told me that he hated himself—of course—and that he didn't want to hurt me. At the same time, he loved the women he'd had affairs with—all in different ways for different reasons. But he didn't want to spend his life with them. He wanted to spend his life with me. I hate Artie for betraying me, yes, but I might hate him more for getting me caught up in such an embarrassing cliché.

I was too heartbroken to respond, too angry to do anything but leave.

"Do you think he'll be okay?" Lindsay asks, meaning his health.

"I know," I tell her. "I know. A good person would go home and forgive him because he's so sick. A good person probably would have stayed put and tried to sort it all out, in person, one way or the other and not just run around the country like I did. I know." I'm getting emotional. I take a moment to press the tears from my eyes. I wipe away some mascara. Why did I put on makeup at all? I realize that I'm dressed all wrong. I'm wearing a professional outfit—tan slacks, expensive shoes, a blazer. What was I thinking? I remember getting dressed while packing quickly. I was on autopilot—bumping around my hotel room amid the dying flowers. I'm an auditor—a partner in a firm, in fact—and I look like one—even now when I shouldn't. Trust me, I'm aware of the irony that it's my job to know when someone is cheating and that I was blind to Artie's infidelity for so long. "I'm supposed to know fraud, intimately. It's what I do for a living, Lindsay. How could I have not seen it?"

"Well, he wasn't really handling his risk of detection very well." Lindsay smiles, trying to cheer me. She's recently gone to a lecture on the risk of detection and is proud of herself in this moment. "You'll sort it out, Lucy. You sort everything out. It's what you do best!"

"At work," I tell her. "But my personal history doesn't bear that out exactly. Two different worlds."

Lindsay looks around the airport like she's a little confused—she's wearing her confusion on her face, *advertising* her confusion, as if she's just for the first time heard that there are actually two different worlds—a twilight zone moment. I've been grooming her for upward mobility. She's going to be taking over while I'm on leave and she'll have to work on her toughness if she's going to make it through. I've talked to her about trying not to display her emotions so readily. I'd give her a little lecture on that right now—but I'm no model of emotional discipline at present.

"You think I should forgive him, don't you? You think I should go home and that we should try to figure it out, don't you?"

She's not sure what to say. She looks side to side and then she gives in and nods.

"Because he deserves it or because he's sick?"

She shifts. "I'm not sure that this is the right reason or not, but, well, because I've never had a boyfriend who could get past three or, maybe, four reasons why he loved me. Not that I've asked for a list or anything, but, you know what I mean. Because Artie loves you like that."

Artie loves me like that—it seems true in this instant, as if she's stripped away all of the gestures that I've taken as manipulation and just seen them purely, as a manifestation of his love—for me. I'm shocked by this way of seeing it—the bareness of it all. I'm not certain how to reply. "I'm sure you'll do fine while I'm gone," I tell her. "I know you can do it."

She's a little caught off guard. She blushes—again, something she shouldn't do, but, in this case, I'm glad to see it. She gives a little bow. "Thanks for the vote of confidence." She hands me my pocketbook and looks at my bags. "Do you have everything?"

"I'll be fine."

"Okay then." She turns and walks into the crowd. She's all business now, her chin up, her arms swinging strongly. I'm proud of her.

And just then the elevator lets out a loud *ding!* and I think of Artie's #57—the one that arrived this morning and that has been eating at me ever since: *The way you love the sound of an elevator bell, and once said it was like a little note of hope, the idea that things are bound to change, that you are finally going to get to go somewhere and start over.*

The only problem is that I don't like elevators. I've

always felt they were little movable death boxes—if anything, the ding seems to me like an awfully chipper death knell. They've always made me feel claustrophobic, and, another thing, I don't particularly care for change—like, say, finding out your husband is cheating on you—and, despite all the recent travel, I've never really had the feeling that I was finally getting to go somewhere else and start anew. *A little note of hope?* I never said any of these things. Number 57 isn't mine. It belongs to some other woman. Number 57 belongs to some other woman the way my own life right now—my work life, my personal life—seems to belong to some other woman.

An elderly woman in a wheelchair is pushed out of the elevator by a young man—maybe her son? They move on by, and the stainless steel doors close. I see a dim fuzzy reflection of myself, and I feel like I am that other woman. As misappropriated as it seems, this life is mine.

Chapter Two

Happy Strangers Can Bring
Out the Worst in Anyone

When I step onto the plane, I wave the greeting flight attendant toward me. She's wearing extremely red lipstick so high gloss that she looks fishy—especially up close. "I'm going to need a gin and tonic, pretty much immediately," I whisper. "I'm right here, four-A."

She smiles, gives me a wink.

I've already decided to drink my way through the flight even before I look up and see the woman I'm to sit next to. She's my mother's age, giddy, freshly sunburned, overly smiley. I try not to make eye contact.

I used to be a nice person, I swear, I was. I used to say *Excuse me* and *No, you first.* I used to smile at strangers. I used to banter with overzealous seatmates. But not now. No, thank you. I'm not interested in the joy of others. I take offense at it. When I look at this woman, it crosses my mind to fake being foreign. I could muster a really sweet, "No English!" But this woman strikes me as the type to bully through a cultural difference like that—

to want to play charades and draw pictures—to really connect. She looks like a combination of overly cheery and prudish. Plus, I've already outed myself as American (a desperate American) to the flight attendant, and since she has the alcohol, I want to protect that relationship.

As I'm wrestling my borderline oversized luggage into the overhead, the woman blurts, "It's my first time!"

I'm not sure how to take this. It all sounds way too personal. "Excuse me?" I say, pretending I didn't hear her clearly, and hoping that a little communication speed bump will give her time to change her mind about revealing things to strangers on planes.

She shouts—maybe thinking I'm a little deaf, "My first time! In business class!"

"Congratulations," I say, not sure if this is the appropriate response. What is? *Bully for you?* I stand in the aisle, waiting for her to get up. But it seems she doesn't want to relinquish her seat, not for a second—as if she's afraid someone might horn in on her privilege. I have to negotiate around her to get the window seat. I decide to go by her butt-in-face—maybe a little passive aggression is what's needed.

It doesn't register. She says, "My son got me this business-class seat. 'Who needs a business-class to fly from New York to Philly?' I say to him. But he doesn't listen. He's a hotshot like that."

I'm pretty sure I'm supposed to say, "Oh and what does he do?" But I let my cue die. I rise up in my seat to see if the flight attendant noted the distress in my voice and is working on the drink order. I don't see her now and this jangles me. I look out the window at the ground crew. I'm jealous of their headphones filled with engine drone.

The woman is staring at me. I can feel it, and I also

happen to know, immediately, that she's the kind of woman my mother disapproves of—the kind who doesn't wear makeup or dye her hair or go to the gym. My mother would call her a "quitter," assuming that the woman once did all of these things, which may or may not be true. But my mother assumes that the quitters have given up on the fight. "What fight?" I've asked in the past. "The fight against looking your age." My mother is always fully dressed, often in a coordinated velour sweat suit—I call it the formal wear of sweat suits—and coifed, and overly made-up. She seems to wear so much makeup these days that she's no longer really trying to look more attractive, she's just hoping to disorient people while she safely hides behind it. I don't know if this is a fight that I want to be a part of, frankly. I almost feel tender toward the woman next to me, because she doesn't care what people think of her so very much. She hasn't quit the fight as much as she has, maybe, risen above it. But my tenderness doesn't last long.

She says, "Are you one of those high-powered female professionals they talk about these days?"

Who's they? I wonder. I lean toward her, conspiratorially. "I'm not a high-powered *male* professional," I admit.

She takes this as comedic. She rears and laughs up into the air nozzles overhead. She settles quickly though and asks her next question. "You're probably part of one of those high-powered couples with a baby that's learning Mozart. I've heard of those genius babies from high-powered couples. Am I right?" Her question has the air of someone on a game show.

"Sorry," I say. "I don't have a baby. No kids—genius or otherwise." This is an old wound. Artie and I had started talking about a family. We'd started reimagining the bedrooms to include a nursery. We'd taken up the habit of interrupting our own conversations to say, "Wait, that would be a good kid name." The names were always ridiculous—Ravenous, Cotillion, why Nathaniel and not Neanderthal? In the wake of the popular trend of place names for kids (London, Paris, Montana), we were compiling a list of our own: Düsseldorf, Antwerp, Hackensack. Artie had just sold off another chunk of stock in the Italian restaurant chain and had hired a young, tough, soon-to-be mogul type to take some of the pressure off. Our lives were calming down, and we'd started trying to have kids. I hated the term *trying*—as if we were two bodies flailing aimlessly at each other. It implies sexual incompetence and that was never one of Artie's problems. And then just two months later, I intercepted an e-mail from a woman with the screen name "Springbird." (Springbird! It didn't seem right to be duped by a woman self-named Springbird!) I'd come across good old Springbird when I was looking for Artie's travel info and mistook her for his agent. The e-mail asked if Artie's back was okay from "sleeping on that lumpy futon" and said that this woman "loved him" and "missed him achingly."

Achingly.

Then I went to Artie's partner's secretary. His own secretary is an austere, tight-lipped woman who'd never tell a thing. But his partner's secretary, Miranda, is a legendary gossip. I took her to lunch at her favorite place, the All U Can Eat King Chinese Food buffet, pretending to seek her advice, pretending to know a lot more than I did. She spilled the news over sweet-and-sour chicken and fried dumplings that Artie had someone on the side. She'd seen an e-mail or two herself and corroborated the name Springbird, but didn't have much beyond that. My fortune cookie read "You will visit the Nile." What's that supposed to mean? Was that supposed to be a metaphor?

When I got home, I confronted Artie while he was taking a shower. He stepped out and told me the truth, the whole truth, not just about the woman Miranda had mentioned, but he confessed to the two other flings—*dalliances.* He said he'd tell me anything I wanted to know. Full disclosure. He said, "I'll do anything to make this right." But I didn't want to know any details. He sat on the edge of our bed, a towel around his waist, shampoo still in his hair. At this very moment, sitting next to this woman in business class, staring at the upright tray table in front of me, I despise Artie as much as I did then. I despise him for what? Not so much the infidelity—this sometimes overwhelms me—but I despise him for his carelessness. How could he have been so careless with our marriage, with me?

"Well, now," the quitter muses aloud, "high-powered isn't right. Not exactly. That's more like what they call newfangled cell phones. What *do* they call them? Power couples? Is that right? What does your husband do?"

Finally the flight attendant is walking down the aisle, my drink in hand. She smiles. She bends down and hands it to me.

"What does my husband do?" I repeat the question. "Well, flight attendants are always a big favorite."

The older woman says, "Oh . . . well . . . that's not what I meant!"

The flight attendant isn't startled at all. She gives a sad, wry, guppy-lipped smile—as if to say, *You think it's easy being me?*

I shrug.

I've successfully shut this conversation down, and I didn't even have to pull out the great guns of *I'm an auditor,* which tends to clam people up. The older woman opens up a book that she's made a little cloth jacket for—to hide the cover. A bodice ripper? I'm not interested in her little jacket-wearing book.

I turn my head to the oval window. I fiddle with the plastic shade and I feel my throat tighten up, and I know that I'm about to cry. I don't like being emotionally messy. I try to distract myself with little mental notes about which partner to call to talk through how this necessary leave of absence from work will be sorted out, who will lead my team of managers, who will hold the hands of my clients. I decided to be an auditor because it sounded so sturdy. I was drawn to it for its tidy rows of numbers, for the way those numbers can be ordered around, for the emotionlessness of it. Auditor. It's the kind of job my father never could have held down. He was an "entrepreneur," but never discussed the details of what that meant. He was, in many ways, the first lovable cheat that I fell in love with. I went through a phase in college of being a lovable cheat myself, but I couldn't stomach hurting people. I tethered myself to the role of auditor to keep me steady. Auditors don't cry. They don't get emotional about your tax choices. They pore over digits. They calculate. They decide whether those numbers are accurate or fudged. I chose to be an auditor because I knew it would put me in stuffy room after stuffy room with other auditors—mostly men and none of them anything like my father. I imagined falling in love with a fellow auditor and leading a very well-ordered, emotionally tidy life. Auditing would toughen me up, shut me down. And maybe it did for a while. Maybe it did. But then I met Artie.

I stop fighting the crying jag. I just let the tears slip down my cheeks. I pull a tissue from my pocketbook—digging around Artie's love notes—and pinch my nose. I drink the gin and tonic straight down, order another before takeoff.

Chapter Three

There Is Barely a Blurry Line Between Love and Hate

With each exhale, I'm aware that I'm steaming up the shuttle van with gin fumes. I'd apologize to the driver, but I can hear my mother telling me not to apologize to those in the service industry. *It's so middle class.* The fact that we were middle class throughout my childhood never seems to matter. I decide not to apologize though because I don't want to make the driver uncomfortable. Apologizing for drunkenness is something that you shouldn't have to do while drunk—that's one of the benefits of being drunk, right? That you don't care if people know you're drunk. But the fact that I want to apologize is proof that the drunk is wearing off, sadly. I pop a few chocolate-covered cherries bought off an airport rack and make idle chatter.

"So, any hobbies?" I ask the driver. I've had drivers who were epic gamblers, brutal genocide survivors, fathers of fourteen. Sometimes I ask questions. Sometimes I don't.

"I give tennis lessons," he says. "It didn't used to be a hobby, but I guess it is now."

"You were good?"

"I've gone a few rounds with the best of them." He looks at me through the rearview mirror. "But I didn't have the last little bit it takes to push you to the next level. And I didn't take it well."

He looks like a tennis pro to me now. He's tan and his right forearm muscle is overdeveloped like Popeye's. "You didn't take it well?"

"I took to drink—as my grandmother would say."

This is alarming—he's at the wheel.

He must read my nervousness. "I'm in recovery," he adds quickly.

"Ah." I feel guilty for being drunk now—like the time Artie and I brought a bottle of wine to the new neighbors only to find out he was a recovering alcoholic. I'm sure the driver can tell I've had my fair share today. I want to make excuses for myself, but I try not to. More talking just means releasing more gin fumes—this is my drunken logic at the moment. In a fit of paranoia, I wonder if I'll become a drunk. Is that the way I'll go down? Will I be the type to stick out AA? I fret about my constitution, and then I burp, and I hate the stink of it so much that I know I'll never be much of an alcoholic. I lack some essential heartiness, and I'm relieved.

"Do you play?" he asks.

I look at him, confused.

"Tennis?"

Oh, right. I shrug, give him the sign for "just a little," by pinching my fingers together and squinting.

The van is winding through my neighborhood, past

the plush lawns of the Main Line. I've never really fit in here. There were barbecues and cocktail parties, and millions of those other little checkbook parties where women gather to drink wine, eat chocolate, and muster an unhealthy adoration for candles or wicker baskets or educational toys. There was one sex-toy party, but it's strange how, after enough stiff Main Line conversation, vibrating pearl dildos can seem as boring as vanilla-scented tea lights.

There are friends, still, but not the kind I ever wanted. In fact, when things started to go wrong, I was happy to leave before they started phoning in with their alarmed condolences. I didn't want their sincere sympathy and I certainly didn't want the fake sympathy designed to get me to hand over the inside scoop, which would then hiss around the neighborhood. I was angry at Artie. For the betrayal, but also for the wounded pride. I was the fool. I didn't appreciate having the role forced on me. I wondered what Artie told his women about me. I existed in those relationships he had, but I was absent, unable to defend myself. What version of me appeared? The obstacle, the shrew, the dimwit? There are only so many choices for the cheated-on wife to become—none of them good.

We round the corner and I know that if I look up I'll see the house. I'm not quite ready. Artie and I had gone halvsies on the house. He'd wanted to pay for it outright, but I'd insisted. It was my first house and I wanted to feel like it was really mine. My mother thought I was insane to storm off and leave Artie there. My mother has policies on how to divorce well. She told me, "When leading up to a divorce, the most important thing is to stay in the house—and it doesn't hurt to hide some of the expensive finery, either. If you can't find it, how can you divvy it up?

Become a squatter. I always stay and stay until the house is mine." I told her that I didn't want the house and I didn't want to hide finery. But she hushed me like I was being blasphemous—"Don't say things like that! I raised you better"—as if my reluctance to be a squatter in my own house were a social flaw, like not writing thank-you letters or wearing white shoes after Labor Day.

It's been almost six months now, and I'm not sure what kind of monumental change I'm expecting, but as the airport shuttle van pulls in the driveway, I'm surprised that I recognize the house at all. Did I expect it to fall into immediate disrepair? Artie had fallen into immediate disrepair, it seemed. The heart infection was detected just a few weeks after I left. The timing was suspicious from the get-go. I'd always thought it was a prank, a plea for sympathy, but now it seems more like his sickness is my fault. I lean forward in the van to pay the driver, and, despite the fact that we're strangers, I have the overwhelming urge to tell him *Artie broke my heart. I didn't break his.* I restrain myself.

The driver/ex-tennis-champion-hopeful/recovering alcoholic hands me his card, embossed with a racquet.

"If you ever want to work on your swing . . ." he says, winking.

My *swing* . . . Is my driver/ex-tennis-champion-hopeful/recovering alcoholic hitting on me? I do believe he is. I take the card, ignoring the wink. "Thanks." In the wake of Artie's cheating, I've been so austere, so tough, that no men have flirted with me—at all. Am I looking vulnerable? Am I losing my austerity just when I need it most? Or maybe it's the fact that I'm drunk in the afternoon . . . I tip, modestly. I don't want to give the wrong idea.

He offers to tote my suitcase.

"No, no. I'm fine." I'm one of those drinkers who stiffens up to compensate for the looseness. Artie called me a stilt-walking drunk. I stilt-walk over to my suitcase and stilt-walk up to the house, relieved to hear the van pull away without some sassy honk.

Someone's been keeping up the garden, weeding, trimming. I suspect my mother—she has compulsions of these sorts, always has. I make a mental note to tell her to cease and desist. I walk in the front door. It smells like my house—a mixture of sweet cleanser and Artie's aftershave and soap and garlic and the damp woodsy smell from the empty fireplace. And, for a moment, it feels good to be home.

Our wedding picture—the two of us in an old Cadillac convertible—still sits on the mantel. I poke through a pile of mail on the lowboy. I walk through the kitchen, the dining room—there I find the sofa, the one he had reupholstered for our anniversary—the bright poppies. My chest contracts with a sudden pang. I close my eyes and walk away.

I can hear a television in the den. I walk down the hall and find a young nurse wearing one of those uniform jackets with cartoon crayon drawings of kids printed on them. She's asleep in Artie's recliner. Did she have to be a young nurse? Couldn't she have been old and pruned? Did she have to be so blond? Sure, her presence was probably a random, computer-generated assignment, but still, it seems particularly, cosmically insulting.

I leave the nurse dozing and walk up the staircase, glancing at the photographs lining the wall. This is the spot you'd usually hang family photos, but these are artsy pictures I took before I met Artie, back during my artsy photographer phase: pictures of a dog with its head stuck out of a sunroof, speeding by; a girl in a frilly dress riding a pony at a fair, but crying hysterically; a Hare Krishna talking on his cell phone. These are my quasi-art moments. And I'm relieved they aren't the standard family shots right now. I couldn't take the fakeness of Sears renditions of a happy home life. And I'm relieved that they aren't old photos of our parents and grandparents—Artie and I both hail from scoundrels of one kind or another. We couldn't have ever made the convoluted decisions of which sets of families to include. For example, which of my mother's husbands would make it in a staged photo with her? My father, who abandoned us? Husband number four, who was by far the sweetest, but, while wrestling an ancient, bulky antenna, fell off the roof and died because, as my mother put it, *His tragic flaw was that he was too cheap for cable*? Or the most recent divorce, because she got the best settlement out of him? How to choose? No, I'm happy to see my old artwork. I was numb to them when I left, but now they strike me as, well, funny and sad, as I had intended, I guess, back when I had intentions of this sort.

But at the top of the stairs there's a new framed photo—one that Artie took, not me. I know it immediately. It's a picture of me looking down at the freckles on my chest—no obscene nudity—inked out to represent Elvis, midcroon. I'm looking away, laughing, my chin tilted back. I know now that Artie has been expecting me. He's planted this framed photograph as a way of buttering me up with nostalgia, and my heart responds. I can't help it. I miss that moment in our lives together, so intimate and so bound together. But I don't let myself dwell on that. I'm in no mood for manipulation. I march up the final stairs.

I walk down the hallway, quietly, toward the nearly closed door of our bedroom. The last time I saw Artie he was standing on the other side of airport security, staring at me, wide-eyed, his arms opened, frozen, as if in the middle of an important question. I was supposed to have taken it as a plea for forgiveness, I guess.

I place my hand on the door. I'm afraid to open it. He's been existing in my mind for so long that I can't imagine his body, his voice, his hands. I'm afraid, suddenly, that he'll look so sickly that I won't be able to bear it. I understand the *idea* of Artie's sickness. I'm not so sure I'm prepared for the *reality* of it. But I know that I have to.

I push the door open a crack and see Artie in bed. He's staring at the ceiling. He looks older. Is it just that I have this youthful image of Artie in my mind, one that some part of me refuses to update (probably because I'd have to update my own), or is it the sickness that has aged him? He's still beautiful. Have I mentioned that Artie is beautiful? Not traditionally. No. He was punched as a kid—yes, over some girl—and has an offset nose, but a gorgeous smile and a certain boyishness, a restlessness that gives him such ebullient energy, but also probably the same part of him that led him to other women. He has broad shoulders—a bulky manliness—but he's uncomfortable with them. He slouches. He has always looked best at the end of the day, loosened by a drink, when the light gives up and things fall into shadows. He has thick dark hair tinged gray and a way of pushing it roughly off his forehead, and blue eyes—soft, sexy dark eyes under heavy lids.

And now? Now. Artie's dying in our bed and it is still *our* bed, after all, and, although there is a knot of hatred in me, I want nothing more in this moment than to crawl into bed next to him, to lay my head on his chest while we take turns telling each other everything we've missed—my overly positive assistant, the lady on the plane—and in this way saying: *it's going to be all right. Everything's going to be all right.*

"What are you looking at up there?" I ask.

He turns his head and stares at me. He has a charming smile—a little cocky, but also affectionate and sweet. It's as if he predicted today was the day I'd come, and it had gotten late, but he'd remained confident, and then I actually showed up, proving him right. He smiles like he's won a gentleman's bet. "Lucy," he says. "It's you."

"Yep. Here I am."

"I planned on doing this some other way, you know."

"Doing what?"

"Winning you back," he says, eyes crinkling. "I mean, dying wasn't really what I had in mind. It lacks charm, frankly."

I don't know what to say. I don't want to talk about dying. "What was the other plan?" I ask.

"Reformation. Penance. I was going to make amends and become a new man," he says, tilting his head. "I wasn't against renting a white horse."

"I don't think I would have bought into the white horse." Artie has always loved a grand gesture. More than once my fortune cookies at Chinese restaurants were stuffed, behind the scenes, with more intimate notes. He once had a Pulitzer Prize–winning poet write a sonnet for my birthday. In a fit of nerves, I told a garish hostess how much I admired her necklace—a gaudy, spangled,

Liberace affair—and for my next birthday, there it sat in an enormous velvet box. I loved Artie's desire to surprise me, but I truly loved the quiet, unplanned moments—cooking pastries together, finding ourselves powdered with sugar or arguing about some principle of physics or the construction of aqueducts in ancient Rome—those things neither of us know anything about. I've always loved Artie most when he wasn't trying to be lovable.

"Well, the white horse might have been *my* little fantasy," he admits. "I envisioned a desert scene, you know, a little Lawrence of Arabia. But deserts are hard to come by here. And I don't think I'd have looked so great in eyeliner. Basically, I'd planned on avoiding death."

"Ah, *cheating* death. Now that is part of your pattern."

"Let's not start in with that so fast, okay?" His voice is tired. He is dying, after all. The exhaustion comes on quick. It's a quiet moment. I don't have anything else to say. And then he adds, "My heart's turned on me. I thought you'd appreciate the irony of me having a bad heart."

I don't say anything. My damn eyes well up with tears. I let them tour the bedroom like it's a gift shop. As I pick up curios and perfume bottles off the dresser, I inspect them absentmindedly. They're mine but they feel like someone else's things, someone else's life.

"You used to think I was funny," he says.

"You used to be funny."

"You should laugh at a dying man's jokes. It's only polite."

"I'm not interested in polite," I say.

"What are you interested in?"

What was I interested in? I look at the shoes I'm wearing. I paid too much for them. I can feel them fading out of fashion in this very instant. I am here, in these shoes, standing in my bedroom because my mother told me to come home. That's not all this is. I'm not simply a dutiful daughter who doesn't know what to do and so does what she's told. But I am a daughter—my father's daughter, the father who left my mother and me for another woman. I swore I'd never repeat my mother's mistakes, but hadn't I? Artie, the older man. Artie, the cheat. How could I have known he would cheat on me? Was I drawn to him subconsciously because I knew that he would? Did my subconscious dupe me? Did it force me to marry my father? Am I just playing out some twisted Freudian scene—now I'm required to play out my father's death? Required to tend to Artie?

"Do you have a round-the-clock nurse?" I ask.

"It makes me feel better to have someone else in the house. They don't stay all night. Marie is here now and she'll give one last call—like at a bar. Insurance doesn't cover it all, but now that you're here . . ."

"We'll keep the nurse," I tell him. "I'll be sleeping in the guest bedroom downstairs."

"You could play nurse," he says with this playfully sad expression. Irrepressible. My heart feels full, like there is a tide within me, and I steady myself with one hand on my bureau. This is Artie, the man I love, in spite of reason. I'm here because I love him—arrogant, cheating, busted-hearted Artie.

I can't quite look at him. I manage to focus on the bed-side table. It's overrun with pill bottles. Artie is dying. I'm going to be the one to hand him over to the mortician, to death. Alone. Regardless of those other women in their other lives, I'm his wife, and this strikes me, suddenly, as hugely unfair.

"I'd like to know where they all are now, Artie. Where are they?"

"Who?"

"Your other women. They were there for the good times," I say. "Where are they now?" I sit down on a chair next to the bed. I really look at Artie—our eyes meeting for the first time. His blue eyes are watery, darker because of it. "Am I supposed to go this alone?"

"*Are* you going to go this?" he asks.

"All I'm saying is that it doesn't seem right that I should have to. I didn't say whether I was going to or not."

He reaches out and tries to touch my face. *No, no, Artie Shoreman. Not so fast.* I jerk my head away, then stand up and begin to pace the room. I can feel him watch me pick up a photo of the two of us on the back of a ferryboat to Martha's Vineyard. Suddenly I remember holding hands as we toured the gingerbread-looking houses in Oak Bluffs, gazing out over the cliffs at Gay Head, and Artie praying for our future together, blessed by abundant blubber, at the Old Whaling Church in Edgartown. I look at his arms around me in the picture, and I remember that exact moment—how warm he felt against me, how cold the wind was on my arms, and the little, wizened old granny who snapped the shot for us and smiled that old patronizing smile. Now I know why she was smiling. *Just wait until he cheats on you and then dies on you.* I turn to face Artie. He's looking at the ceiling again.

"Call them," he says. "Call them up."

"Who?"

"My sweethearts. Call them up," he says. "You shouldn't have to be alone in this."

"Your *sweethearts*?" I hate this little euphemism. "Are you joking?" I ask, incredulous.

"No," he says. "I'm not joking. Maybe it'll be good for everyone. Maybe one of them would actually be helpful." He looks at me and smiles a little. "Maybe some of them would hate me so you don't have to."

"And what should I say? This is Artie Shoreman's wife? He's dying? Please call to schedule your turn at his deathbed?"

"That's good. Say that. Maybe I can still go with my old plan to win you back," he says.

"The one with the rented white horse in the desert?"

"I could still reform, do penance, make amends." With some effort, he pushes himself up onto his elbow and roots out an address book from a drawer in his side table. He hands it to me. "This book is filled with people I should make amends with." As I reach for it, he holds on to it for a moment, tightly, the way people sometimes stall for a bit just before handing over their shoddy accounting records for an audit. He looks worn—maybe my presence has weakened him. His face is completely serious now, pained, the lines deeper than before I left, his hair maybe a little grayer. I feel a deep ache in my chest. "I'd like to see my son, too," he says.

"You don't have a son," I remind him.

He lets go of the book so that it slips into my hands. "I've been meaning to tell you. I had him when I was just a kid—twenty. His mother and I never got married. He's grown now. His last name is Bessom. He's in the B's," he says.

I'm suddenly aware of heat in the room. It's rising up inside me. I know I couldn't murder Artie Shoreman on his deathbed (though surely wives have killed husbands on deathbeds before), but I wouldn't mind beating a couple of weeks out of him after this delicious little bombshell.

Couldn't he have told me in flower bundle #34? *I love you so much, you made me forget to tell you that I have a child with another woman.* I pick up the picture of us on Martha's Vineyard and, before I'm aware of the impulse, I throw it across the room. A corner of the frame catches on the wall and makes a solid dent. The glass shatters, littering the floor. I look at my empty hands.

I've never been the type to throw things. Artie gapes at me, completely surprised.

"I know that Bessom is in the B's, Artie. Jesus, you're an ass. A son, you tell me now after all of this time? That's lovely!"

I storm out of the room and almost knock over Artie's hot little nurse, who has been listening at the door. I can't tell who's more stunned, me or her.

"You're fired," I say. "And tell the agency only male nurses from now on. Got it? Ugly male nurses. The burlier and hairier the better."

Chapter Four

Your Mother Is a Woman You
Don't Have to Become

Marie left quickly, apologetically, and in a few hours a new nurse came to do Artie's late-night last call. The nurse is a man—though not as burly and hairy as I'd hoped. But he is a nurse—older and quiet—with one of those modern Toddish names that begins with the letter *T.*

He walks by the kitchen doorway and looks at me. He circles back the way he came. I eat a few crackers, then he appears again. He stalls in the doorway. "There's a woman in your yard. I think she's weeding. In the dark," he says, sounding more surprised by the dark than by the weeding.

I'm not surprised. I stand up and walk to the front door. And there is, in fact, a nicely dressed older woman pulling out some weeds at the base of our shrubbery. I turn on the outdoor light.

The woman stands up, holding the weeds, roots and all. It is, of course, my mother, wearing one of her velour sweat suits—royal blue, zippered only halfway up to show off some cleavage. "Lucy, dear! How are you? You look awful. Have you started smoking again?"

"I've never been a smoker. That's you," I tell my mother.

"I confuse you and me, sometimes. We're so similar."

"No we aren't."

"I've brought dinner," she says, placing the bundle of roots in a tidy pile on the ground.

She walks back to her car and lifts up a casserole dish in a canvas bag with the words *Hurray for Potluck* stitched onto it.

"Like that, for example. I don't even own a canvas bag, much less one that says Hurray for goddamn Potluck!"

"Don't cuss," she says, wagging her head. "Some women think it's sexy, but it's not."

I stare out the back window at the swimming pool while my mother, Joan, buzzes around the kitchen. She arranges plates on the kitchen island. She flutters around fixing the dishes, getting silverware, dishing up food. Did I mention that she's brought her dog, Bogie? Bogie is a well-endowed dachshund. He is so well endowed that her fourth husband called him the five-legged dog. The fifth leg is, however, a sad appendage. First of all, neutered and ball-less, it's been rendered pretty useless. Second of all, because of the dog's swayed back and four stumped legs, it had started to drag a bit on the ground—not so bad in shag carpeting but difficult when it came to, say, gravel. This was a problem. Eventually, the thing might get calloused from such dragging, and is that any way to live? Really? My mother decided it was *not* any way to live, that it was embarrassing, in fact, so a few years back she fashioned some penis supports for dear aged Bogie. A *doggie support lederhosen,* she called it. But Artie and I were quick to correct her: it's a doggie jockstrap. So that the most important protective gear stays in place, the doggie jockstrap is an elaborate harness system reaching around Bogie's hind legs, over his front shoulders and snapping midback. This would be fine, I suppose, if my mother didn't have such a fashion flair for doggie jockstraps—a hidden talent, really. She uses wide ribbon and bows, always color coordinated with holidays—orange in fall, red and green in winter, robin's egg blue in spring . . . As a result, Bogie always looks like he's dressed for some upcoming event. He's a handsome dog, nearly show-dog quality to begin with, as my mother is quick to point out.

And so here is Bogie, waddling around my mother's feet in his dapper jockstrap. He always holds his chin high, but can't ever shake the watery, worried look in his eyes that makes his cockiness seem like a fragile mask for deep insecurities. Of course he's insecure, and who can blame him, really?

"Bogie is looking good these days," I tell her.

"He's showing his age," she says. "Aren't we all?" She bends down and lifts up one of his small paws, bobbing it at me in a wave. "Hello, Lucy!" she says in this high fake voice that's supposed to be Bogie's. "I wanted to bring him along because he's missed you!" she says.

"And I've missed him," I say. Bogie, really, rarely enters my mind, although I have to admit that when certain subjects come up in conversation—like pervie stuff bought for a bachelorette party—I can't help but think of Bogie, whom Artie calls the oh-so-sad Marquis de Sade of the dog world.

My mother pours us both a stiff drink. She lifts it. "To Artie! Dear, dear Artie! May he pull through!" she chirps.

"He isn't going to pull through. You said so yourself."

"Yes, but that information doesn't make a good toast. Toasts are positive."

"And why are we eating like he's already dead?" I ask. My mother doesn't answer.

The *Hurray for Potluck* bag has reminded me of a running joke that Artie and I used to have. My mother went through a phase of cross-stitching every sappy saying known to man—of the *If you love something, set it free* variety—onto pillows, blankets, shirts, wall-hangings, pot holders, and trivets. Artie started pointing out some of my mother's philosophies that she'd neglected to cross-stitch for all of posterity—for example: *You should marry your first husband for his genes; the second for his money; the third (or fourth or so) for love.* "Where's the pillow with that sentiment?" Artie would ask. "Where's the pillow that says: *Never let thine ass give in to gravity*?" Artie loves my mother and, even though she was dead set against our marriage, she loves him, too.

My mother and I both take our swigs and set our glasses down. I pick at my food.

"I know he's hurt you but you have to forgive him," she says. "He's just like that. Put on the earth that way."

"I don't think he was an adulterous baby," I say.

"Don't be so literal. It's unbecoming. You know what I mean."

"I'm not sure I do know what you mean," I say.

"I mean, you know I was never crazy about your marrying Artie. I told you he'd probably make you a widow— I had no idea how young. But listen to me. I forgave my husband and it made me the bigger person."

"Which husband?"

"Your father, of course." She pauses while she flips

through her mental marital filing cabinet. "And husband number three."

"Neither of those men deserved to be forgiven." After my father left my mother, he moved to the West Coast and downgraded his role in our lives to one card on my birthday and one on Christmas with twenty bucks in it. He died of an aneurism, mowing his lawn.

Bogie's tags jingle as he chews one of his paws.

"But I was the bigger person," my mother says. "And that's what allows me to fall asleep at night."

"I thought you took drugs to fall asleep at night."

"*What helps me fall asleep at night*—that's an expression, dear. You really shouldn't be so literal all the time. It's bad for you."

I'm about to argue with her—because I think that there should be a measure of truth spoken here—but there's a knock at the door. I look at my mother. She looks at me. We aren't expecting anyone else.

The male nurse walks briskly into the kitchen. "That'll be the doctor. He said he'd stop by."

"The doctor?" my mother says enthusiastically, touching her hair.

"Please don't use this as a shopping opportunity to pick out husband number six."

"Don't be gauche."

The nurse walks to the front door, but stops shy of answering it. As I follow him down the hallway, I can hear my mother rustling and primping along after me.

"How's the Buddhist?" I ask, wondering if that relationship has flatlined. My mother is unfailingly loyal to her husbands and beaux, but once it's over, it's over. She'd never miss, for example, the opportunity to flirt with a handsome orderly wheeling husband number nineteen to the morgue or the dashing minister who presided over the graveside service of number twenty-one.

"He's been reincarnated," she replies with a certain amount of disinterest.

"Into someone else's boyfriend?"

She continues to primp, which means yes.

"So soon?"

"His karma will catch up with him."

I open the door.

The doctor is my mother's age—gray-haired, professionally concerned.

"Come on in," I say.

"So glad you're here!" My mother can't contain her glee. He's her hero. I want to remind her that Artie's still dying, but decide not to get in the way of a beautiful thing.

The doctor sees Bogie, who's motoring toward him to smell his shoes. I can tell he's about to ask about the jockstrap, but something in him stops him short—a good bedside manner? A hidden fear that the problem is medically related—why add the chronic medical conditions of a dachshund to his laundry list?

I usher the doctor upstairs, then my mother and I watch from the doorway as he examines Artie, asking questions, answering in hushed tones.

I hear the chime of ice on crystal and see my mother polishing off her vodka.

"Don't you want to be the bigger person here?" she asks.

"I don't know what that entails," I say.

"For better or for worse. You took a vow. *In sickness and in health,* you said."

"He has a son."

"Does he? Artie? Was he married before? Was this . . . *out of wedlock?*"

A few years ago my mother asked me to help her update her vocabulary so she wouldn't seem old. She said: *Just tell me when I say something that's dated. Promise?* "People don't really use the phrase *out of wedlock* anymore," I tell her.

"Oh," she says, "I knew that. I'm just so . . . scandalized by it."

I don't tell her that people are rarely scandalized either. We, as a culture, have gotten too used to scandal to be scandalized. "It happened when Artie was twenty. He and the woman never got married."

My mother regains her composure and reaches a hand out to touch my arm. "Are you okay? I'm so sorry. How old now?"

"He's a grown-up in his thirties. Artie wants to see him before . . ."

"That's overly dramatic. Why didn't he tell you earlier? I don't care for this kind of secrecy."

"I don't either," I say.

"See, we're so much alike." My mother raises her glass, gobbles an ice cube, and smiles at me sadly, out of half of her made-up face. "You'll get through all of this."

I'm not so convinced. I turn to walk back downstairs. My mother follows, slurping at her ice cube. "A son. Oh, no, I don't care for that at all."

Later, as the gray-haired doc is preparing to leave, my mother has recovered from her disgust for men. She gazes at him adoringly.

"I've finished up," he says, more like a coroner who's just done the embalming than someone paid to bring people back to health. My mother primps in the background, riding out her vodka buzz.

"Do you think he's in a lot of pain?" I ask.

"The pain should be under control. The infection has done its damage to his heart. He's weakening at a very quick rate. It won't be long now."

"How long?"

"He could hold on for a week or two. A month at the outside. I'm sorry."

I can feel blood rushing to my face. I want to slap the doctor. A month at the outside? It sounds like he's placing bets. And I don't want his sympathy either, not this kind so easily handed over. I know I'm not being rational, that the doctor is doing the best he can. I look at the floor and then back at him and it seems, now that I'm taking a moment to regard him, that he is genuinely sorry. I manage to say thank you.

My mother isn't saying anything either. She's turned her attention to me. I can feel her love for me; for the moment anyway, I'm the sole focus of her worry.

The doctor lets himself out while we stand there. It's too hard to fathom that Artie is upstairs now, breathing, shoving his hair across his forehead the way he does—and that soon he'll be gone.

I look at my mother.

"Oh, honey," she says.

"I'm still too angry to grieve." This isn't the life I expected with Artie. And what was that life? I can't even remember now. A good life. Some babies. Kids in the pool. Birthday parties. Artie coaching Little League. He could have managed a Little League team. Vacations at beaches.

Growing old together, wearing Bermuda shorts. Simple things. I feel a surge of anger. Artie and I have been robbed. The anger is flooded with helplessness.

"You can be angry," my mother says. "That's okay. The grieving will come. There's plenty of time."

I look at her—this small woman zipped into her tight velour sweat suit. She knows grief. "Okay," I say. That's all I can manage right now. "Okay."

Chapter Five

Is a Bad Decision—Which Changes Your Life
for the Better—a Good Decision in the End?
(Or: What's the Difference Between a Good Decision
and a Bad Decision? About Three Drinks)

I'm drunk again. I blame my mother and her endless toasting. Not long after the doctor left, she put her arm around me and steered me back down the hallway to the kitchen, poured us drinks, and let the toasting begin. She toasted the strength of women. She toasted mothers and daughters. She toasted Joanne Woodward and Paul Newman, just because. She toasted anger and sadness and hope. And now she's toasting love.

"To love!" she says. "It springs up in the middle of everything else where we least expect it!"

I can't remember a time in my life when I was ever drunk twice in one day. In college? Senior year of high school on spring break?

My mother falls asleep on the sofa in the dining room—the anniversary gift from Artie. I still have a hard time even looking at it. My mother will be up and gone before dawn.

I find myself in the first-floor guest bedroom and decide to settle in. I unzip my suitcase and then heft it onto the bed. But I should have hefted it first and unzipped it second because I fumble the heft a little and the clothes flop out onto the floor. I find my drawstring pajama bottoms and a Black Dog T-shirt from the Vineyard. I'm still sipping my last drink. I start sloppily shoving clothes into drawers, trying to force the overstuffed drawers shut. I shove so hard I get a little winded, then give up, letting them sit there, overstuffed.

I then see my pocketbook across the room. It looks innocent enough, but I know that all of the love notes are inside—the complete set, numbers one through fifty-seven.

I pick it up, grab a handful of notes, open the bedside table drawer, push them to the back of the drawer, then another handful, then another, until they're all there, messy, out of order, crumpled. The driver/ex-tennis-champion-hopeful/recovering alcoholic's card is there too. I could call him. I could take him up on his offer to improve my *swing*. For a moment this seems like the perfect revenge, but I don't even like the driver/ex-tennis-champion-hopeful/ recovering alcoholic. I rip up the card, thinking that I don't want this kind of revenge, but at the same time, knowing that I do want some kind of revenge—as horrible as that sounds.

And then I'm startled by a voice. "I'm taking off for the night." It's the male nurse.

I open the door, still holding my drink. I can see him in the hall light—my mother is snoring lightly in the distance.

"Is he asleep?" I ask.

"Soundly."

"Thanks for everything," I say, and it dawns on me that I *am* thankful. I'm flooded with gratitude, in that way you can so suddenly flood when drunk. "I don't think I could do it . . ."

The male nurse says, "I'm just here to take care of his physical needs so that you can concentrate on all of the important things, like his emotional needs."

This seems like an unfair division of labor. I'm annoyed. I stiffen up. "Is that my job? Am I supposed to be Artie Shoreman's emotional needs manager?"

Todd—let's call him Todd—says, "I don't know. I mean . . . not necessarily. I was just saying . . ."

"Don't worry about it," I tell him. I know I'm drunk. I have some self-awareness left.

"Good night, Mrs. Shoreman." He hustles to the door.

I mumble, "Good night," but it's too late. He doesn't hear me.

I shut the door and look around the guest room—the new mess I've made (record time!), my pocketbook on the bed, and on the bedside table (filled with Artie's love notes), Artie's address book (filled with Artie's old lovers and, somewhere in the mix, the three women he cheated on me with, a woman who loves elevators, and the address and phone number of the son he never mentioned—in the B's).

I pick up the address book and thumb through it. I notice small red marks beside some of the names—only by the women's names. Some are red X's; some are dots—a code. He's had the book for ages, the pages are worn at their edges, almost feathery. I know that most of these women came long before I ever knew Artie—some may even go back to high school. They knew Artie when I didn't. They have access to a version I will never be able to know. This seems cruel. Was he the same person then—in some deep unalterable way? Do we ever really change?

It's strange to see their names—Ellen, Heather, Cassandra. Who are these women anyway? I realize that I've fully envisioned Springbird—the one name that I've had for months now, albeit only a screen name. She's short, blond. She's perky, but when the perk fades, she's quick to whine. But this is all imagination. Of course I won't find her screen name in the book. I keep flipping forward. The names come at me as I turn the pages—Markie, Allison, Liz . . . I don't want to read another name, but I can't stop myself either. The ache is deep in my chest.

I hear myself say, "I don't want to be Artie Shoreman's emotional needs manager."

I sit down on the edge of the bed. I finish my drink and look up at the ceiling where, above, Artie is sleeping soundly, where Artie is dying. And it dawns on me that he knows that I would never call up one of his *sweethearts,* that I haven't wanted to know anything about the three of them from our marriage, the other ones from his past. I get up and pace. "Artie, you son of a bitch. You don't think I'll do it, do you? You think I'm just going to play my role here. Forgive you. Be the good wife. Pretend nothing ever happened. Go it alone. Be the bigger person."

I open to the A's, let my finger cruise down to a name with a red dot. Kathy Anderson. I take another drink. I dial. It's long distance—one state away—after midnight. The phone rings twice, and then the machine kicks in, a woman's voice with New Agey wind chimes in the background. I immediately hate the woman. After the beep, I go ahead as planned. "Artie Shoreman is dying. Please call to schedule your turn at his deathbed."

I slam down the phone. But this feels strangely good. I call the next number with a red dot. This time a woman answers. I've obviously woken her up.

"Artie Shoreman is dying. When would you like to schedule your turn at his deathbed?"

"Artie Shoreman? Tell him he can rot in hell for all I care." This name has a red mark by her name—an almost violent X—so the code is pretty easily broken, even by someone in my drunken condition.

"Understandable," I say. "Maybe next Thursday?"

"What?"

"Do you like elevators?"

The phone goes dead.

I smile. It doesn't make sense, but I can't stop smiling. I turn to the B's. There it is: John Bessom. No red mark. A number and address and a business name: Bessom's Bedding Boutique. I run my fingers over the letters, wondering what Artie's son would be like—what our son might have been like if we'd had one. Does he look like Artie? Brush his hair off his forehead in that rough gesture like Artie? Does he own Bessom's Bedding Boutique? Or does that belong to his mother? Her name is here too—Rita Bessom. Did he offer to marry her?

It's too much. I flip past the Bessoms, to the back pages. I find another red dot—it's a large dot. Obviously Artie let his red felt-tip pen sit there for a while, let his mind wander. I pick up the phone, dial the number, look out at the night sky, the fat moon.

A machine picks up. The woman's voice is young and jaded. "This is Elspa. You know what to do."

But it strikes me then that I don't know what to do. I don't have any idea what I'm doing. I don't say anything at first. I just listen to the dull static, and then I say, "Artie Shoreman is dying. Please call to schedule a time at his deathbed." And then I pause. "Artie is dying."

Chapter Six

Forgiveness Doesn't Wear a Rolex Knockoff

While I pour my coffee—hung over and miserable—a new male nurse is arranging a tray of soft foods and a number of pills in little white paper cups the size of creamers—which remind me of the creamers I used to drink and stack while at fancy restaurants with my mother and her various husbands. I believe I did this not only because I loved the cream, but because it irritated my mother to no end. Actually, Artie's #42 is about how I'll still sometimes pop open a creamer in a restaurant and down it like a shot of tequila, which struck him as charmingly odd and uninhibited. The male nurse's hands are huge, and I marvel at how he can handle all of the dainty cups with such dexterity.

I realize that he's fixed Artie a lunch platter, which seems all wrong except that I look at the clock, which tells me it's noon. The burly nurse picks up the tray and the plates rattle—loudly—so loudly that I'm reminded how very much I drank last night. I wonder just how many of Artie's sweethearts I called. (And I realize now that I've absorbed the term *sweethearts*. Even as I hear the word echo in my head, I pronounce it with a sneer. It's a term of derision, not endearment!) Did I call a half dozen? A full dozen? More? And why did I call them? I can't remember. A dare? It seemed like a dare. Was I calling Artie's bluff? Did one of the women tell me to report to Artie that he can rot in hell?

The burly nurse glances up at me. I've been staring. I know that he's doing my job, really. I should be the one with the tray. "I'll take it to him, if that's okay," I say.

"Sure," the burly nurse says. "He knows the drill on the meds."

"Has anyone called this morning?" I ask.

He nods. "A bunch of hang-ups, actually," he says. "Maybe three?" And then he looks at a pad of paper held to the fridge by a magnet. "One woman called and said"— and here he begins an exact quote—" 'Tell Artie I'm sorry but I can't forgive him.' "

"Did she leave a name?"

"I asked her, but she said, 'Does it really matter what my name is?' And I said that I thought it did, but she just hung up on me."

"Sorry about that," I say, knowing that this is my fault, in part. I put my coffee on the tray and head upstairs, wondering what I'll tell Artie exactly. So, none of the women have volunteered for a deathbed time and one wants him to rot in hell.

When the bedroom door creaks, Artie opens his eyes. He's too weak to sit up, though. He peers at me with his quick blue eyes and smiles, but doesn't really move. "What happened to Marie?"

"She said you weren't her type."

"What? She likes the living? If she's going to have those kinds of standards. . . ."

"Women! They have such high expectations," I say with mock exasperation and more than a little ire. "Are you able to sit up?"

I put down the tray as he pushes himself up. I plump a few pillows behind his back. I pop out the tray's short legs and position it over his lap. He stares into the little paper cups, disgusted, and picks up his fork wearily.

"When were you organized enough to come up with a system of red dots?" I ask.

"I have some secretarial skills."

"Skills with secretaries is a different thing." This isn't really fair. I don't know that Artie's ever been with one of his secretaries.

But he takes it. He pushes around some applesauce on his plate. "So you looked through the book?"

I nod.

"Did you find Bessom?"

"I saw his information."

"Are you going to call?"

"Why don't you?"

"Do you think I just abandoned him?"

"I have no idea."

"She never wanted me to see the boy. Her parents didn't either. *Just send the checks,* they said. I've written pleading letters over the years, and when John turned eighteen, I sent a letter to him, telling him my side of things, but he never wrote back. He's taken up the family's standard response: no response. He's mine, but he isn't." He closes his eyes and lets his head fall back to his pillow.

"Why didn't you tell me all of this?"

"I don't know." He shakes his head. "I didn't want you to think I was like your father. One of those types. Loveless, a disappearing act. I'm not. I would have loved that boy with everything I had—if they'd have let me."

"I wouldn't have thought you were like my father," I say. "I wouldn't have put that on you."

"I didn't want to risk it. I know how much your father hurt you. I didn't want you to put me in the same bad-father category as him. That would have broken my heart."

I'm not sure what to think anymore. Artie has secret lives. He has compartments—his past, his sweethearts, his sorrows and failings. "I didn't call him but I did make some other calls."

"You did?" He raises his eyebrows.

"You don't know me as well as you think you do. Sometimes, in fact, you confuse me with other women."

He looks at me. His eyes are tired. He hasn't actually put any of the food in his mouth. "I love you. No matter what."

This doesn't seem fair. I know that I should see this declaration the way that my assistant, Lindsay, could—as pure, without any manipulation, as love, but I can't. I can't trust Artie. I walk the edges of the room. "None of them are coming. Oh, two had messages for you, but I doubt you want to hear them."

"Before you found out, you used to overflow with feelings. You were so uncontrollably alive. Do you remember that?"

I do, barely, vaguely. "Not really," I say. I feel like that person was stolen from me. Sometimes I don't miss Artie and me and our relationship as much as I miss the person I used to be. And I miss that Artie, too, the one I used to get mad at for such simple things—driving the car around with the gas warning light on, putting back the empty orange juice container, wanting to bear-hug me when I was in a foul mood. Oh, these were such minuscule annoyances. I long for them.

Artie coughs. It's a ragged cough, from somewhere deep inside him. When he's quieted, I say, "It's just you and me—in this together."

"That's what I want," he says.

And it's a reflex. I can't help myself: "Since when?"

Artie pushes his tray away from his chest, brushes his hair off his forehead. "Do you think you'll ever be able to forgive me? Your mother was here the other day and said that I should be forgiven, that I was put on the earth this way."

"My mother's advice on men is highly suspect. She doesn't have a perfect track record."

"I would forgive you," he says.

"I wouldn't want you to." I feel suddenly very tired now under the weight of all these emotions. I sit down on the side of the bed. Maybe I do want to forgive Artie, if forgiving him means that I can forget everything. I turn and look at him.

He reaches out and touches a freckle on my chest and then another and another. I know that he's looking for Elvis. This is the silent intimate language of memory between us. Nothing needs to be said. I want to tell him that he's not allowed to die, that I forbid it.

Then he becomes perfectly still. He stares at me. "I *will* forgive you."

"For what?"

"When I'm dead, you're going to regret a lot of things. And I want you to know that I forgive you."

I stand up. I'm caught off guard. I nearly say, *How gracious—the thought of Artie forgiving me!* But there's something more deeply unsettling here. Artie is planning to die. He's seeing into the future and trying to set things straight, and I know he's right. It strikes me that there are so many things that I will miss about him—not just his grand gestures, his incredible charm, but I'll even miss the things that I've always found most irritating—the way he sipped his coffee and sometimes grunted when sitting down as if it were some kind of effort; the way he fished the olives out of his martinis with his fingers and walked around while he was brushing his teeth—*the nomadic brusher,* I always called him. And I know that I will find plenty of things to regret. I may even wish I had been the bigger person.

My eyes tear up as I leave the room. I turn quickly down the hall and then feel light-headed. I steady myself with one hand on the wall, then lean against it, let my head press against the coolness.

There's a knock at the front door below. It vibrates up into the house. I can't move, though, not yet. I assume it's my mother, having already buzzed through her to-do list, here to see if I'm up and about, if I've eaten breakfast. *I'm fine,* I'll say. *Look at me! Holding up! Good as new!* I'd like to fake it for a while so that I can avoid more self-reflection—just for a little while. I jog down the stairs, faking peppy, and swing open the door.

"I'm doing fine!" I say happily.

But it isn't my mother. It's a young woman with deep purple hair, jaggedly cut in a pixie. She's heavily pierced—all the way up both ears, a dainty diamond stud in her nose, and a ring on her bottom lip that gives her an extra pout. She's wearing a sleeveless black concert T-shirt for a band I've never heard of—Balls-Out—at least I think it's a band. She has a wreath tattoo around her biceps—a muscular biceps—and she's carrying what looks to be an army-issue duffel bag.

"I'm Elspa," she says. "I'm here to take my shift."

Chapter Seven

Hope Sometimes Knocks on the Door, Walks into the House,
and Puts Down Her Duffel Bag—as if Here to Stay Awhile

ou're here to take your shift?" I ask. Oddly enough all of Elspa's piercings and the tattoo and the hair color remind me of my mother—all of that makeup to disorient the viewer. Actually, though, all the extra stuff doesn't distract me for very long. It's evident that this Elspa is very pretty—almost breathtakingly so. She has full lips and dark brown eyes with thick lashes and a small nose and great cheekbones. She isn't wearing a bit of makeup. I'm still so caught off guard by all of it—the conversation with Artie, the fact that this isn't my mother—that I'm completely baffled. I manage to say, "Did the nursing agency send you?"

I'm not guarding the door. It's wide open because I was expecting my mother to breeze in. I'm standing back, actually, almost welcoming her in. Almost. And that's all she needs. She walks past me, duffel bag and all, right into the hallway. She has a real sense of urgency. She's nervous, or more specifically, shaken. Her eyes dart around the house. "No, I'm not from the nursing agency."

"That's a relief, actually."

Elspa ignores the comment. She looks at me directly. "You called me."

"I did?"

"I came to take my turn at Artie's deathbed. That's what you said you wanted. Right?"

"Oh. Yes. And the duffel bag?" I'm a little unnerved by the duffel bag—it has a kind of I'm-here-to-stay-awhile vibe. This is one of Artie's sweethearts? She's a little younger than I imagined—twenty-six, tops?

"I drove in from Jersey as soon as I could. I had a class this morning, but left right after. I already worked out an incomplete with the professor," she says, as if this explains everything. She's too old to be an undergrad. She puts her bag down. "Where is he?"

"You can't stay here." Is this one of Artie's sweethearts during our marriage—one of his flings, dalliances? Is it possible she's old enough to have known Artie before we were married? I mean, Artie and I had been married four years when I left, and we only dated a year before we got married—a whirlwind, in retrospect. Was he dating a twenty-one-year-old before me?

"I'll just crash on the sofa. I won't be any trouble. Is he in a lot of pain?"

"Look," I tell her. "I was drunk. I was kidding. I didn't think anyone would take me seriously."

Elspa spins around. Her eyes are wide. She looks like a little kid, overly hopeful. "What?" She regains some of her jadedness. "Look. Is Artie dying or not?"

I get the sense that she has a lot riding on this visit. There's a lot at stake for her. I want to lie to her, to tell her that Artie's fine and to go home, but I can't. I think she may actually love Artie, or need him. I can't tell. "He is. He's dying."

"Then I want to help however I can. He was good to me."

"He was?"

"He saved my life." And she says this not in the way that someone talks about a lover, but a saint.

The burly male nurse walks by, up the stairs. Elspa watches him.

"Is he up there?"

I nod.

"Can I?" she asks, pointing to the stairs.

I'm stunned by her desperation. "Go ahead."

And so Elspa, this complete stranger—saved by Artie Shoreman, the saint—runs up the stairs, taking them two at a time.

Chapter Eight

Everyone Is Selling Something,
So Be Your Own Pimp

I stand in the hallway, not sure what to do now. I look up the stairs. Elspa. What does she have to say to Artie? Did I say she could sleep on the couch? I'm tired of not knowing Artie's secrets, tired of tripping into the cordoned-off areas of his life. I go to the guest bedroom, pick up the address book. I grab my keys off the lowboy and walk out the door. There's a rusty Toyota parked on the street.

I hope it will be gone by the time I get back.

My car is in the driveway. I haven't driven in six months. I climb into the front seat. It's all adjusted to Artie, and I'm glad he's not dead yet. I'm sure I would have jumped out of the car if he were dead, too unsettled the seat and mirrors all adjusted his way. But Artie's not dead, and I take my time adjusting everything to fit me. I should do this with other stuff around the house. I can think about this logically—Artie's death. I can prepare for it intellectually before it hits. I can take precautions—as I would while preparing for a new audit at work.

Bessom's Bedding Boutique is in an older part of town, one that's supposed to be turning over—going plush. Every fourth storefront is being redesigned. I find the cross street I'm looking for and turn left, pull into a parking spot. Bessom's Bedding Boutique. Since when did everything go boutique? I don't care for the alliteration. It's a pet peeve of mine, Klassy Kuts, or Kitchen Kutlery. For God's sake, spell the damn words correctly! I walk up to the shop and see my reflection in the whited windows. I'm surprised to find myself here. I look tired. My eyes are puffed, the skin under them tinged blue. My lips are chapped. My hair is unkempt. I tuck a strand behind my ears and lick my lips, and quickly look away.

I push the door open and hear the archaic chime: *bing-bong.* The place is a parking lot of beds, like an entire hotel collapsed and the tightly made beds all ended up in the basement—but a swank basement. There is even some avant-garde art, and sleek bedside tables, and the walls are one of those nouveau colors: something lime-inspired? The carpet is plush wall to wall. The beds are beautifully made-up with throw pillows galore. There are no other customers in the store, no Muzak playing. All I hear are the muted street noises behind me and the empty tocks of a retro silver sixties wall clock—the kind that looks like grade-school science projects of the solar system.

I want to steal something. This is my first instinct. I don't know why. My second instinct is no better: I want to run across the plane of beds. I picture myself running down the beds all the way to the back of the store.

And that's when I notice that there's a lump in the covers of an elegantly made four-poster near the back. With no other salespeople around, I assume this must be the straight-C-plus college student who's been left in charge.

I'm not sure whether to wake this loafer or not, but I do feel a little protective of Bessom's Bedding Boutique—for no good reason.

I walk over to the bed. "Excuse me."

It's a full-grown man—in his late twenties, early thirties. I'm surprised that he doesn't jerk himself upright and launch into some ingrained sales pitch that occupies his shallow subconscious. Instead, he opens his eyes slowly, looks at me, and then smiles lazily. He stretches and flattens down his blond hair. He's good-looking and I can easily imagine him shirtless, barefoot, wearing only pajama bottoms—someone John Bessom hired onto his sales team for his looks, and is unaware that he sleeps on the merchandise while the boss is out. I decide that when I find Bessom, I'll have to report this salesman.

"I'm looking for a mattress, um, heavy-duty, firm. You know, a good, solid, dependable mattress. Do you know where I can find John Bessom?" He looks at me, a little mussy and sexy, sleepy-eyed.

"We don't sell dependability, firmness, heavy dutiness, solidity," he says in a half-yawn.

"You do sell mattresses here, don't you?" I smile at him and cock my head. I feel like I've wandered into a word game where I don't know the rules. I like word games and I'm good at them.

"No, we don't really sell mattresses. Not exactly."

"What do you sell?" I ask.

He smiles flirtatiously. I've taken his bait. He's come out of his nap selling. It just didn't look like what I thought it would. "I sell a lot of things. I sell sleep, for one. I sell dreams."

"Sleep and dreams?" I say.

"Exactly." He hasn't gotten out of bed, just propped

his head on his hand, and now I'm convinced that Bessom has made a fantastic hire in this kid. I feel like buying a bed. And then he says, "I sell high-end premium real estate for love."

This comment stops me in my tracks. I hold up one finger. I retrace the conversation in my head. I notice that he's stopped saying "We sell" and has started saying "I sell." I look at the plate-glass window, the lettering of Bessom's Bedding Boutique spelled out in reverse. There is something so purely Artie about "high-end premium real estate for love" that I feel frozen for a moment. This guy doesn't look like Artie at all, except for maybe a tiny bit in the jawline, but he's inherited his father's flirtatious genes nonetheless. "Are you John Bessom?"

"In the flesh. How can I help you today?"

I just stare at him a bit more—still looking for Artie. I tilt my head. Part of me was expecting the boss of Bessom's Bedding Boutique and part of me, I admit it, was expecting someone more sonlike, more kiddie-pool, more summer camp, more Little League.

"Are you okay?"

"I'm fine." I glance around the store. "Well, unfortunately I only need a mattress."

"Who could live day in and day out only selling mattresses?" He sits up and swings his feet to the floor. He's wearing suede bucks. "It would be too bleak."

"Right. I get that," I say. I'm suddenly not sure what I'm here for. Am I going to tell him that his father is dying? Is that my place? If he wanted to talk to Artie, he could have years ago. I start to walk to the door.

He stands up then. "Look," he says, "wait. I'm sorry. I've had a bad week. I've had an even worse year. I get like that." He points back to the bed. "I flirt. It's a coping mechanism. I'm working on it. What I mean to say is, I'd love to sell you a mattress. I'd *prefer* to sell you something a little more abstract, but I'll settle for a mattress."

I stiffen—like I'm a little drunk, like my austerity is eroding, and I'm in my stilt-walking mode. I draw up my toughness. I wonder if my brow is knotted. Is this toughness, this austerity, going to cost me wrinkles? Botox? I have no choice at present but to be tough. That's all I have to offer. "Next time I need an abstraction, I'll know where to come," I say, and I walk out the door.

Chapter Nine

Sometimes the Stranger Says
the Thing You Need to Hear

I pull into my driveway and note that the rusty Toyota is still parked on the street. It's a jagged, lopsided parking job, to boot.

Walking into the house, I spot Elspa's duffel bag, which sits in the hallway where she dropped it. As I put my keys in the bowl on the lowboy, I feel like a stranger— a polite burglar, someone who's breaking and entering but only to rummage through the crackers, pop some bon-bons, and maybe make herself a gin and tonic.

I'm not sure what to do. I stand in the hallway. Stock-still. I peer into the living room. Everything is so hushed, so still. On the mantel, a massive flower bouquet in a grand vase is falling over itself. I walk over and pull out the little card from its plastic stake. It reads: *#58: the way you came home, you came back. The way part of you, some tiny, deep down part, might still love me?* I'm not sure what to do with this. He's right. Some part of me still loves him, of course, and sometimes it's the part that wells up and fills me to the brimming top of my soul. Maybe

I should tell him that. Maybe it's something he should know.

And that's when I hear the singing.

It's soft, high, lilting. My hands drop to my sides. I let #58 fall to the floor.

I follow the singing up the stairs. It's coming from the bedroom. I open the door. Artie's bed is empty. The sheets are thrown back, as if Artie has been healed, miraculously, and has gone to the office.

But the singing isn't coming from the bedroom. It's coming from the master bathroom. The male nurse is standing by the bathroom door. He looks a little bewildered, not sure of his role here. I nod to him. He nods back.

"I'm standing by," he says, "to help him in and out of the tub."

But this doesn't explain the singing. I walk through the bedroom to the bathroom door, which is cracked just enough for me to see Artie's back. He's sitting in the tub, and it's Elspa's voice—a beautiful voice—rising up from somewhere deep inside her. She's there, kneeling beside the tub, singing softly. I don't recognize the song. She dips a sponge in the bathwater and squeezes it out over Artie's back. There's nothing the least bit sexual going on. No eroticism. Only tenderness—like a mother taking care of a child with a high fever. This takes my breath. The moment has a simplistic beauty. A purity.

My chest is tight—a sharp pain. I feel light-headed again and walk unsteadily out of the room, down the stairs, and to the liquor cabinet in the kitchen. It's too bright, too loud, too airy. The ceilings are too high. I feel tiny. My hands work quickly. The ice clinks in the glass. It's a lonesome sound.

The phone rings. I answer it. Lindsay starts talking

full-tilt, so fast I can only make out the words—someone might get fired, Danbury? And there's a client who might drop us? One of the partners is freaking out? I can't make sense of any of it.

"It'll all work out," I tell her. "Just don't get involved emotionally. Just don't take things personally. I can't talk right now."

But she forges on about Danbury almost getting fired and the possibility of a small promotion and back to the partner again.

"I can't talk right now," I tell her. "Don't take this personally, Lindsay, but, here, let me show you how to disconnect." And I hang up the phone and stand there.

Elspa walks in and pulls a salad out of the fridge. The salad is news to me. I've never seen it before.

"You want some?" she asks. "I made plenty."

"No."

She grabs a small bowl and starts fixing her own. "He's so thin. I wasn't prepared for that."

I don't say anything.

"But he's got his mind. It's all there. Still Artie."

"Still Artie."

Elspa starts eating heartily. "You sure you don't want anything?"

"No, thanks."

She talks while chewing. "He was telling me this story about this one time—"

I hold up my hand. "I don't want to hear the story."

Elspa freezes, then continues to eat. "Okay."

It hits me then that I don't feel like a burglar—quite the opposite. I feel stolen from. "That was my moment up there."

"Excuse me?"

"Bathing him. That's what I'm supposed to do, and you stole it."

"I didn't mean to . . ."

"Forget it."

Elspa puts down her fork. She looks at me. Her brown eyes are gentle. "He cheated on you, right? That's why you hate him. How many?"

"He had lots of women before I met him, and I didn't know it but he kept two of them—souvenirs."

"He isn't good at good-byes."

"That's a nice way to put it," I say, taking a moment to consider how much I don't appreciate that reading of things. "And then he added a third. It was the third one I found out about and then the other two. When was the last time you were with him?" This is a fair question. I ask it boldly enough.

But she doesn't seem caught off guard, only matter-of-fact. "Before he met you. I started working in one of his restaurants when I was really young." She still seems young. "Gosh, it's been, like, six years since I smelled like Italian food all the time. Artie came in to spot-check. It wasn't *that* kind of relationship though. I mean, I'm not really one of his old *girlfriends* or anything. Artie was more like a father. He helped me through a hard time." She pauses, still pained by some memory there.

I'm not sure that I buy it. "More like a father?" I ask.

"It was a long time ago," she says. "I survived—because of Artie."

She's so earnest that it's hard not to believe her. She has a face that seems completely open—as if too naive to lie.

Her expression lightens. "He told me a lot of stories today about you, how you met, your wedding. It's all so beautiful. But I like the story about the bird on the porch the best."

"I remember that, vaguely."

"You saved the bird."

"It was beating around the shutters of a friend's guesthouse, not long after we met. Artie's a coward in many ways. He was afraid of birds indoors. He hates to fly, too, on planes. I opened the right window, that's all." But now I see it in my mind and everything seemed so right then, so perfect. Artie walked up behind me, wrapped his arms around me, and the bird flitted off into the trees.

"Sometimes that's all it takes, opening the right window," Elspa says.

And I like her, just then, just like that. I need someone like this—someone not afraid to enlarge the moment.

"When he was telling that story," she says, "he was so alive I forgot he was dying."

I wonder how, exactly, Artie saved her life. I imagine her in her waitress uniform, the red shirt and nametag, the checkered apron, holding her tray of drinks. I wonder why she's really come here and why she loves him so much. I walk over to the large salad bowl, pick up a cherry tomato, and eat it. It's tart and sweet in my mouth. She would think that Artie deserves to see his son before he dies, wouldn't she? She's right. Because even if Artie has done a lot of things all wrong in his life, he deserves to know his son. Isn't that an inalienable right of parenthood? And, more important, John Bessom—that mess of a young man—deserves to know his father.

"I want you to do me a favor," I say.

She looks up at me, expectantly. "You do?"

Chapter Ten

❧

Love Is as Love Does—but Sometimes It's Abstract, Blue, and Obscene

While Elspa finishes eating, I call my mother on the phone in the guest bedroom. I feel like I need to run this by someone. But as I explain my plan—which I do thoroughly, I might add—she's still confused. I start over again. "The problems are clear. I want Artie to meet his son. I want his son to meet Artie. But I want Artie to be the one to tell him that he's his father and that he's dying. That's his job, not mine. So, I was thinking, how do we get the two to meet? And I came up with this perfect plan."

"They meet through a mattress?" my mother asks weakly.

"For the hundredth time, yes! A mattress!"

"Now let me see if I get this: You don't want to be the one to talk John Bessom into anything. Why's that again?"

"Never mind that. It isn't important." I don't want to have to explain that if he hit on me anymore and then found out that I was his stepmother, that would be, well, uncomfortable.

"Okay. Never mind that," my mother says. "But you're going to get this girl who just showed up, who loves Artie because he saved her life, to talk John Bessom into delivering a mattress to the house himself?"

"Exactly."

"Well, I don't get all of the ins and outs, but it does seem like a plan. And I'm glad you're doing *something*. I think it's healthy for you to be in motion. I'll stop by in a bit and make sure everything's okay with Artie while you're gone."

"Thanks."

Shortly thereafter, on the way to Bessom's Bedding Boutique, I tell Elspa what to say. I give her a script that will play on John's need to sell things more important than mattresses. She nods along. "Got it. Right. Okay."

And then the conversation dies, and it's just the two of us in a car. She leans forward to fiddle with the radio.

"What do you do, Elspa?"

"I'm an artist."

"Ah, Artie likes artists." He liked the photographs I used to do. He'd always encouraged me to find time to stick with it. "What kind of art?"

"Sculpture."

"What do you sculpt?"

"Men, mostly. Parts of them. I let them choose."

"And Artie? Don't tell me what part he chose. Is it the part I'm thinking of?"

"He had a good sense of humor. He insisted. But it was all from my imagination. I made it abstract. And blue."

"Abstract and blue. Huh." I suddenly see a sculpture of Artie's penis, blue and misshapen. Abstract how, I wonder. All from her imagination? "I'd love to see it sometime," I tell her. It doesn't matter if it's from her imagination or not. It's intimate, and even though she's told me that she and Artie were together before Artie and I even met, and that they didn't have a sexual relationship, it still stings. The jealousy is always just below the surface now. I couldn't have sung to Artie while giving him a bath. I'm too angry for that. My anger is as deep in me right now as Elspa's song is deep in her.

"Really?" Elspa asks.

"Of course," I say.

There's a pause. I'm not sure if she knows how to read my tone. I'm not sure if I know how it *should* be read.

"It's raining." Elspa gestures toward the water-smeared windshield, beads crawling toward the roof. I don't say anything. I twist on the wipers. They squeak and bump across the glass. I'll need to get new ones.

We pull up to Bessom's just as John is locking up the front door. He's talking to a man in a dark suit, who doesn't look like he's buying a mattress. The man has an umbrella, and he looks indifferent, cool, almost British. John's got a newspaper propped over his head. It obviously isn't a pleasant conversation. John holds up his hand as if to say, *Let's put this on hold. We're gentlemen here.*

I crack open my window three inches.

The man in the dark suit says, "We need to get on this, Mr. Bessom."

"I know," John says.

The man walks off in one direction, and John starts to head off in the other. The rain has slowed a little. He shakes his newspaper. I nudge Elspa and she steps out of the passenger door of the car. I watch her cross in front.

"I need a mattress," she says.

"I've closed up already."

"It's an emergency."

"An emergency mattress? Look, my delivery truck has broken down two towns over and—"

"This mattress is for a father," Elspa says, just as I've told her. "A dying father. His son is going to come and see him before he dies and the mattress should be nice." I'm proud of her. Her high school drama teacher would be proud of her.

"Well, I'm closed up, see."

"I don't really want you to sell me a mattress. I want you to sell a dying man's peace. I want you to sell me a deathbed scene. I want you to sell me a father and son who make amends before the father dies."

John smiles at Elspa, then he looks behind her into the car at me. He recognizes me from earlier, and I can tell from his eyes that he knows I've told this young woman what kind of lines he might fall for. He waves. I fiddle with the ashtray.

"A father and son? I'm a sucker for a good deathbed scene, I guess. You'll need a pretty nice mattress for that. Top dollar."

Mercifully, the rain lets up. John has lashed the plastic-wrapped mattress to the roof, and he and Elspa hold on to it through the windows on either side of the car. The mattress is flapping.

"So, do you just sleep in your shop all day?" I ask.

"I wasn't sleeping. I was modeling."

"It looked like sleeping to me."

"I'm a very good model."

"Does the modeling sell a lot of mattresses?" Elspa asks.

"He doesn't sell mattresses. He sells sleep and dreams and sex," I add.

"Does it sell a lot of sleep and dreams and sex?" she asks.

"Not too much. This is just one of my businesses, though. I'm an entrepreneur with a wide variety of current projects."

"Current projects?" I ask.

He doesn't follow up. Instead he looks out the window, checks the challenged mattress, that real estate of sleep and dreams and sex. We continue through a tollbooth and get a skeptical look from the operator, like she's seen a few mattresses fly off car roofs. She's a little territorial, too, a look that says: *You're bringing that onto my highway?* I can ignore it though. My plan seems to be working.

We pull into the neighborhood and start the suburban wind through the dimly lit streets.

"If you don't mind me asking, who's dying?"

Before I have a chance to make something up—which is my instinct, for some reason—Elspa says, "Her husband."

"I'm sorry," John says. "I'm very sorry to hear that." There's a catch in his voice that seems to reveal he's been through some loss of his own. We all have our losses.

I turn the corner onto my street. I see the house lit up like Christmas, every light on, and an ambulance parked out front, the red lights circling. A spiked shiver runs through me. The front door is open. Light spills onto the lawn and across my mother's back where she's standing, arms crossed, staring down the driveway.

"It's too soon," I say in an urgent whisper. "Not yet. We aren't finished!"

"What is it?" John asks.

Elspa is saying, "No, no, no, no."

Just before we reach the driveway, I stop the car and jump out. The car rolls forward, bumps the curb. I knock my head ducking back inside to throw it into park. I drop the keys in the driveway and search my mother's face. She just shakes her head. "I don't know what happened! I called 911!"

I begin to breathe heavily like I'm about to hyperventilate. I stagger toward the house and stop on the porch. Elspa passes me on the run.

I turn to look at John Bessom, who stands next to the car and the mattress. He doesn't undo the straps. I feel sorry for him. He doesn't know what he's in the midst of, what he's come too late for. I'm stalled here on the porch, breathing in sharp gulps.

"And so you must be the son. I'm so sorry," my mother says to John.

I take a woozy step toward them, just another step that comes too late, but then I realize this is the way it's got to unfold. My mother looks calm now. She'll do this well. She takes his hand, puts her arm around him, maternally. John looks like a kid all of a sudden.

"They're trying to save your father," she says. "But I don't know . . ."

John is confused. He stares up at the lit bedroom window. "My father?" he asks. "Arthur Shoreman?"

"Yes," my mother says, "Artie."

Artie isn't dead yet. They're trying to save him. I run through the front door and up the stairs. Arthur Shoreman,

I hear my mind repeat. Arthur Shoreman. I hate the formality of it. The way it sounds like a name on a form, a death certificate. Not yet, I tell myself. Not yet.

I turn into the bedroom. Artie is lying on the bed, an EMT on either side speaking in code, as they do. There's machinery. Are they running an EKG in here? I can't see Artie's face.

The male nurse stands back, looking on.

Elspa is shouting, "Why don't you fucking do something?" Panic-stricken, she falls on top of the bedside table, swiping everything on it to the ground.

"Get her out of here," one of the EMTs yells.

I grab her arms, then pull her to me and out into the hallway. I hold her and rock her. She calms down and grasps onto me, weeping.

"If he dies, I'll die!" she says.

"No, you won't," I tell her.

"I won't be able to make it through this," she says.

I can't begin to comprehend that Artie might be dying already, that it may only be his body lying on the bed. I have no idea how long I hold Elspa like this, but I realize this is the first time I've really been there for someone else for a very long time.

And then I hear Artie's voice. "Hey, back off!" he shouts.

And then one of the EMTs says, "That's good to hear!"

Elspa hugs me tighter.

"He's back," I whisper.

Chapter Eleven

Sometimes It's Hard to Figure Out What Happens When Your Eyes Are Wide Open

*A*ll that follows is a little surreal.

The EMTs are still bustling around Artie, joking some now. I picture Artie's son still out on the lawn, the mattress, I assume, still strapped to the roof of the car. Elspa can't stop crying even though Artie is miraculously alive. I lean through the bedroom doorway, one arm still around her. "He's really back?" I ask the EMTs. "He's all right?"

"He was never gone, ma'am," says the one with the boxy back. "False alarm. Tension. Indigestion. His heart problems are serious, as you know, but he's doing just fine."

"Hear that?" I repeat for Elspa's sake. "False alarm. Tension. Indigestion."

Artie rolls his head toward me. His eyes are moist and he smiles nervously. "Is she gone?" he asks.

"What?" I ask. "Who?" I wonder if he's talking about Elspa. This strikes me as an odd thing to say. I wonder if he's still out of it. And then he flinches and shuts his eyes.

"False alarm?" a woman asks, in a strangely familiar voice. She's suddenly standing at my shoulder—a tall, elegant woman, in her early fifties, wearing a pale blue fitted dress and smoking a cigarette. She's pretty in a shrewd-looking way—arched eyebrows, high cheekbones. Her shoulder-length brown hair is pulled back in a silver clip at the base of her neck.

"Who are you?" I ask.

"I'm Eleanor," she says, as if this clarifies everything.

I simply stare at her, shaking my head. My ears are buzzing. Artie almost died, but now he's alive.

"*You* invited *me*," the woman explains patiently. "I thought I just wanted Artie to rot in hell, but then I decided that I wanted to see him before he does." She brushes something from her skirt. Ah, yes, I remember the voice now—the woman I called late that drunken night who had the oh-so-sweet message for Artie. Here she is. Another one of Artie's sweethearts—a lovely entrance. "Wouldn't it be wonderful if Artie were able to make peace with his past—all of it—before he died?" she adds.

"You shouldn't smoke in here," Elspa says, regaining her composure a little.

She smiles at Elspa as if she's just said something thoughtful but unimportant. "I barely ever smoke. This is an emergency cigarette. Only that." And then she turns to me. "I think my being here may have upset him," she says, with a small—delighted?—sigh.

"You think so?" Artie roars from the bed.

"Your mother had to call 911," Eleanor says calmly. "I may have upset her, too."

"Did you try to kill him or something?" I ask.

"Oh, no," the woman says with a wry smile. She raises her voice so that Artie can hear her perfectly well. "Killing Artie would elevate me to a leading role in his life. He would never pay me that kind of respect."

Eleanor, I say to myself. I kind of like her.

I tell Artie that I'll be back in a few minutes. The male nurse says that he'll stay and get Artie ready for bed. I usher Elspa and Eleanor downstairs quickly. I notice that Eleanor walks with a limp, an uneven rhythm, though she's still wearing a pair of heels. It's a deeply embedded limp, not the kind from a blister or a tender ankle.

"Why don't you sit here for a minute?" I tell Eleanor, pointing to the breakfast nook chairs. "Pour yourself a drink."

"I prefer to be sober."

"Okay then."

She sits down, elegantly, crossing her ankles.

I guide Elspa outside to the backyard by the pool. I tell her to wait here, that I'll come back for her. She's still sobbing off and on, her arms wrapped around her shoulders, her back hunched. I'm not sure she knows where she is, or whether she can hear what I'm saying.

Ignoring Eleanor for the moment, I walk swiftly back through the house with the urgency that accompanies a minor emergency—a fire in the oven or a party that's taken a bad turn. Artie must be the guest of honor, but if I'm the hostess I have to tend to my needy guests. I walk out the front door. One of the EMTs is packing up. The neighbors' house across the street is lit up. The Biddles—Jill and Brad—shift behind their bay windows, watching.

The next-door neighbor, Mr. Harshorn, is bolder. He's standing in his front yard, his arms crossed against his chest. He waves to get my attention, but I ignore him.

My mother is still standing there next to John Bessom, but neither is speaking.

When I approach them, I can tell that my mother's been crying. Her makeup has shifted to a blurry version of what it normally is, but John is stoic.

"I'm the son," he says, "in the father's deathbed scene?"

My mother looks at John and then at me with the same expression—pained sympathy. "One of the paramedics told us he's alive."

"Yes, he's alive. It was a false alarm." I'm not sure if John's angry or not. I don't know how to read him. "I wanted you and Artie to talk. He's dying to see—" I stop myself short.

"I'm very sorry about your husband," he says, shaking his head. "But I don't need to get to know Artie Shoreman."

"Okay," I say, "I understand," even though I don't.

"I'll call a cab. I'll have someone come back for the mattress tomorrow."

"I'll pay you for the mattress."

"You still want it?"

"No, but we can't return it. We've strapped it to a car. It's damaged goods. I insist on paying."

"I couldn't accept your money. Someone will come and take it away tomorrow."

"I'll call. I'll keep you updated on Artie, if you want . . ."

"I'm sure he's a good person." He shrugs, shoves one hand in his pocket, almost smiles. We stand there awkwardly for a moment. He pulls out his cell phone. "I'm going to call a cab." He hesitates. "Artie Shoreman was always good to us financially. And I'm thankful for that, but there isn't anything else between us. It wouldn't be right to . . . Well, I'm not sure what to say." He's beautifully sad. A gust of wind ruffles his shirt, his hair.

"I'm not sure what to say either," I tell him.

"I'm glad it was a false alarm," he says. "In the car, you said you weren't finished. I don't know what wasn't finished, but maybe now there's time—for you and Artie?"

I'd forgotten I'd said this. I didn't want Artie to die so soon—we still have so much to sort through. "You're right," I say. "Things are complicated between us. And there's time for you and Artie, too, to get to be together."

"I didn't know him, really, other than a name on a check, and I don't know that I need to now," he says, and he walks toward the sidewalk and flips open the phone, which lights up, a blue glow in his hands.

My mother follows me back to the porch. "Are you okay?"

"Everything's fine!" I say, but my tone is overly cavalier. I barely believe myself. I grab my mother by the elbow before we head inside. "Did you let some woman named Eleanor into the house?"

"Don't get me started on Eleanor," my mother says as if she has known the woman all her life. "She has to go."

"Really?" I say. Eleanor's take on Artie runs through my mind. I hear her say: *Wouldn't it be wonderful if Artie were able to make peace with his past—all of it—before he died?* And how there was something menacing, but ultimately true, about that.

As my mother and I head into the house, my mother says, "I'll get rid of Eleanor. Don't worry."

We walk into the kitchen and Eleanor is gone. "Well, there you go," I say. "She's found her way out."

My mother walks to the French doors that open to the pool patio and points. "Not so lucky."

There's Elspa, sitting on a lounge chair, and there, sitting across from her, is Eleanor. She's listening intently. They seem deep in conversation—about what? I can't imagine these two have much common ground. Would they discuss, for example, the blue abstract sculpture of Artie's prick? Maybe. What do I know about Eleanor anyway?

"What are we going to do?" I ask my mother, both of us staring through the glass door.

"I don't know," she says, nervously zipping up her velour sweat-suit jacket. "I think that we may end up inheriting Elspa, tattoos, piercings, and all. You should check if she's in Artie's will."

This startles me—maybe because it seems so likely.

We both step out on the stone patio. Neatly trimmed grass spreads beyond the pool, which glows from its underwater recessed lighting.

"Elspa?"

She doesn't turn around.

Eleanor waves to us. "Sit, sit," she says, with an urgent tenderness. "This is important." And then she turns to Elspa. "Go on. Tell us."

My mother and I glance at each other and then approach slowly. We sit where Eleanor told us. She's the kind of person you obey instinctively.

Elspa starts talking. "He broke down my apartment door to save me. There was a parade and the streets were blocked off. He picked me up and carried me to the emergency room, arm wrapped in a bloody towel. I remember the balloons bobbing in the sky and his breathlessness and how I could feel his heart beating in his chest more than I could feel my own. And he just kept saying, *Don't close your eyes. Don't close your eyes.*"

I don't know what to say, what to do with my hands even. I look to my mother, like I'm a child, really, and I want to know what the appropriate affect is for a situation like this. What is this situation? Consoling your husband's ex-, too-young girlfriend on the night he almost died? My mother leans forward. Her hair ruffles stiffly in the breeze. I'm jealous of her makeup for, perhaps, the first time ever. Her real emotions can be hidden somewhere underneath the complexities of color and design.

Elspa says, "I'm alive because of him. And now he's going to die. What will I do without him?" She is rubbing her left wrist. She pulls up her sleeve and shows us the fine scars. "I was completely out of it. I did a sloppy job."

Eleanor, who seemed so cold and austere before, touches her shoulder. Elspa tucks her delicate chin to her chest and squeezes her eyes shut.

Neither my mother nor I know what to say. We aren't prepared for such honesty and tenderness.

It's Eleanor who leans toward her and whispers, "Don't close your eyes."

Elspa opens her eyes slowly, raises her head, and looks at Eleanor and then my mother and me. And although her face is streaked with tears, she smiles—just with the corners of her lips.

I've found my way back to the bedroom doorway. The EMTs are gone. The male nurse has packed up for the night. I can hear him backing out of the driveway. I've left Elpsa, Eleanor, and my mother talking in the dark, outside, beside the pool.

Artie shifts in the bed and then looks up at me as if he sensed me there—or perhaps he only sensed someone. It could be any of the women in this house. I can't take it so personally, I suppose. His eyelids are heavy.

"False alarm," I say. The only light in the room is the bit thrown in from the streetlamp.

"When I suggested you call up my sweethearts, I should have told you to skip Eleanor."

"You didn't think I'd do it."

He smiles at me. "For once, I underestimated you."

"I have to say, I like Eleanor. She's . . . complicated."

"She's a royal pain in the ass."

"She's smart."

"She's here to torture me."

"Maybe that's what I like about her the most. When were you two an item?"

"An item? If you were your mother, I'd have to tell you that people don't use that term anymore."

"When did you two date?"

"I don't know. Not too long before I met you. It didn't end well."

"Why?"

"Because Eleanor is *Eleanor.*"

"And how old was Elspa when you two dated?"

"Elspa," he says with a gentle sigh. "She needed me. I didn't have a choice." I want to ask more questions, but he looks exhausted. He closes his eyes. "I want you to talk to Reyer." This is Artie's accountant. "I want him to explain things. There are things you should know."

Artie and I have always kept separate accounts. We

both came to the marriage with professions of our own. I insisted that we go halvsies on everything, and our money never mingled.

"I was going to have him talk to you after I'm gone, but I thought, this way, I could at least answer questions."

"Will there be a lot of questions? A formal inquiry? I hope not. I charge a lot of money for formal inquiries."

He doesn't respond to my auditor banter—people usually don't. "Will you talk to him?"

"I will."

"I'm tired."

"Go to sleep," I say, leaning against the door frame.

His breathing quickly becomes heavy and rhythmic. *We're not finished,* I say to myself. *We have some time, but not much.* The light from the window is falling on him. I walk over and see Eleanor heading to her car. Her uneven gait is quick. She's parked up the street a bit. After she unlocks the door, she looks up. It's dark. I know she can't see me, and yet I feel like she knows I'm here. For some odd reason, I think I might need her in some way. She stares a moment and then gets into her car and drives away.

I pull the curtains together and turn to look at Artie. The sheets are rising and falling with his breaths. I lie down on the bed, lightly, so as not to wake him—my body curled toward his body. I take in the dark outline of his face.

And then his eyes slowly open and I'm embarrassed to have been caught like this, so close to him. I sit up. He says, very softly. "It wasn't a false alarm."

"It wasn't?"

"It was a rehearsal." Artie shouldn't be dying. It's unreal—a misunderstanding, a bureaucratic mix-up—something that could be cleared up with a few phone calls. I know that I haven't done much with my role as wife, but it still seems like Artie's impending death should be run by me first. I'd like to explain to someone in the Department of Untimely Deaths that I did not sign off on this. This sounds ridiculous, I know. But this is how my mind is working at present.

"Are you afraid?" I ask.

He closes his eyes, shakes his head no. "That's putting it too mildly."

I hadn't thought he'd be so honest. I wonder if he's being worn down into some purer version of himself—like soap smoothed down until eventually it disappears. I decide to switch gears. "Trivet," I say, "for a boy, and Spatula, for a girl. I've kept collecting." This is from our old game of naming our imaginary babies as ridiculously as possible. Telling Artie that I've kept playing the game is a huge confession.

He understands. He looks at me tenderly, gracious. Our babies—the ones we'll never have. We both know that there was a small window when I could have gotten pregnant—two months that now seem like such a tiny, fragile bit of our relationship that they barely existed. And then I found out about the infidelities and I was gone—unable to deal with anything real, not the paperwork to start a divorce, not another honest conversation with Artie about betrayal. Now our babies will only be imaginary. I still think about them. I miss them. I miss that version of Artie that was going to be a daddy. This is dangerous territory—but I want to give Artie something now, after almost losing him.

"Caliper," he says. "Argyle. For either gender, really. And for one of those babies who's born looking like an old man: Curb. Good ole Curb Shoreman."

"I like Flinch for the old-man baby," I say. "My top two right now, though, are Hearth and Irony."

"Hearth Irony Shoreman," he says. "I like that." He smiles at me with so much love, with the weight of all our history together, that I'm scared, suddenly, that I've given in too much. I want things to be clear. I almost tell him that lying there like that next to him, it didn't mean that all's forgiven.

But I decide against it. Not now. He's afraid. He's maybe even terrified. I touch his cheek with the back of my hand and then stand and walk to the chair by the window. "Get some rest," I say. "Close your eyes."

Chapter Twelve

You Can't Always Eat Your Way Out of a Problem—but If You Want to Try, Begin with Chocolate

*I*t's morning. Blurry light collects at the edges of the bedroom curtains as if these simple bedroom curtains have been framed, glowingly, and taken on some holy stature. Artie is asleep, one arm draped over an extra pillow. I stand up and quickly walk out of the room. Although I know it's all wrong, I don't want to get caught having slept here all night—by Artie or my mother or Elspa. It would be too much of an admission of tenderness.

When I walk downstairs, I know immediately that my mother slept here again last night. There's the smell of bacon and eggs . . . and chocolate? She's felt the near-miss of losing Artie and now she's having a cooking seizure—as if, in some old-fashioned way, we can eat our way out of this.

As I make my way through the living room, I stop and stare at the sofa. Elspa. She isn't there. I wonder if she's gone. I'm surprised by a feeling of sadness—an ache of missing her. But then I spot her duffel bag in the corner, and on top of it, a set of my folded sheets and blankets. No, she's still here. My mother is taking care of our meals. My mother is in charge.

I walk back to the guest bedroom and get dressed— jeans, a T-shirt. I brush my teeth, wash my face. I stare at myself in the mirror. I'm wearing all this strain. My expression is pained. There's a tightness, a rigidity, in my cheeks and my neck, and yet a weary looseness around my eyes. I wonder if this is what grief will look like.

I walk into the kitchen and there she is—in all her frenzied glory. My mother. She's putting a tray of wobbly pale uncooked biscuits into the oven. Her homemade chocolate sauce is simmering on the burner, which means that this is serious, a situation that has gotten so dire that maybe only chocolate will haul us to safety. She seems to know that I'm there without even glancing in my direction.

"I've been thinking about everything," my mother says. "I know that things are going to start coming at you very quickly. And I want to protect you from as much as possible." The biscuits safely in, she sets a timer and turns to me—seeing me for the first time. "Okay. Listen to me. I've been through this. You should get most of the logistical stuff done beforehand."

I notice Bogie sprawled out on the floor. He isn't wearing one of his jockstraps and has the air of a man on vacation. "Bogie's naked," I tell her.

"I knew I was coming here and the tile floor in your kitchen is very, well, glideable."

"I guess so," I say.

"Listen," she says. "There is logistical stuff to be done beforehand. Do you hear me?"

"Logistical stuff . . ."

"Last night made me realize that there are actual things that need to be handled." She sighs and then goes on. "Some young woman from your work keeps calling. I haven't told her anything, but she's very, well . . ."

"Anxious?" I kneel down and pet Bogie. He has soft fur and tiny crooked teeth that look like they've been freshly polished.

"Yes. You should call her."

"Lindsay's always anxious."

"And your accountant called. He had a conversation with Artie yesterday and found out you were back in town. He wants to discuss details with you—sooner rather than later. He said that you could stop by whenever you want." I remember now that I've promised Artie I'd talk to Reyer, though I have no desire to do anything that remotely resembles going over the books. "There are endless details. It's best to get them done in advance. Has Artie mentioned any preferences?"

"No," I say, realizing how little Artie and I have talked about death, funerals, all of those practicalities. I don't particularly want to start talking about it now. "I don't think I could say the word *funeral* in front of him."

My mother walks over to me. She holds me by the shoulders. She knows what's ahead for me. She's buried husbands before. I know that she's trying to infuse me with her own strength. Then one of her hands cups my face for a moment. Normally—since the breakup—I wouldn't have been able to handle this kind of tenderness, but it feels good to be looked at this way.

"Where's Elspa?" I ask.

"She's still shaken. She said she was planning on spending some time with Artie this morning."

"And Eleanor? What did she say when she left? Is she coming back?"

"We're going out for coffee and getting our hair done together at four-thirty." Eleanor and my mother, side by side, at Starbucks, at the salon? This is hard to imagine. Is Eleanor a regular now? My mother walks over to the counter and pulls a paper towel off a plate of bacon. "Do you want to eat?"

I shake my head. "Thank you," I tell her.

"For what?"

I wave my hand around the kitchen, meaning everything.

"Of course. This is what mothers do."

I find Elspa sitting on a chair pulled up to the bed where Artie is sleeping. She's rubbing her bare feet on the carpet, staring out the window at the far trees—the bright sky and green treetops. She's humming softly to herself.

"Elspa?"

She turns to me and reads what must be a worried expression on my face. "Are you okay?"

She looks back to the window. "I'm fine. Just sad, I guess. I'm just trying to figure out what it's going to feel like."

I think of the razor marks on her wrist that she showed me last night by the pool. I'm not sure if I believe that she's fine. And as I watch her, I grow quietly more nervous. "I'm going to go to the accountant's office. But I could postpone it, if you want. I mean, we could have lunch?" I don't know what will happen if she feels this too deeply. I remember her saying last night that she'll die along with Artie, that she couldn't make it through this.

"No, thanks. I'd rather just stay here, if that's okay. I can help Joan. I'll be ready. In just a few more minutes. I can be of use."

"Okay," I tell her. "That would be great."

I don't think, rationally, that she would ever try to kill herself again, but I can't stop myself from taking precautions. Before I leave, I find myself going through each of the bathrooms filling a bag with razors and sleeping pill prescriptions, which I hide in the guest bedroom closet.

My mother and the male nurse, the Toddish one, are talking in the kitchen, preparing medications and Artie's breakfast. They're discussing fiber and arranging pills in little paper cups.

I walk out to my car, and the mattress is gone. Someone came and got it, just as John Bessom promised.

Chapter Thirteen

Don't Let Your Husband Have His Own Accountant

*M*unster, Feinstein, Howell, and Reyer is the typical upper-end accounting office—the ferns are real. In fact, they're such an upper-end firm that the only thing fake in the office is the receptionist, though she looks well watered and pruned. I can't remember if it is Feinstein or Howell who's having the affair with the receptionist. Munster is dead, and Bill Reyer plays by the rules, which is why Artie chose him, ironically enough. I've never been here. I only know all of these things because Artie is a storyteller. He was so good that he could make even an accounting firm intriguing.

I tell the receptionist who I am, who I'm here to see.

She says in a kindly way, "Please take a seat."

I glance at a pile of glossy magazines, the water cooler. I'm feeling antsy. I call Lindsay on my cell phone, to check in.

She answers breathlessly. "Hello?"

"Where are you?" I ask.

"Where are *you*?" She says this a little pointedly, a real edge to her voice that I don't recognize.

I ignore the tone, mainly because I'm not sure what it means. "In an accountant's office—the awful kind," I whisper. This is the kind of accounting firm that would make me insane. I know, I know—stacks of numbers are stacks of numbers to most people, but this place strikes me as tragically dull. In auditing there's always a hunt afoot. I prefer it.

"Is everything okay?" Lindsay asks, easing up a little.

"Yes. For now."

"Well then, screw you!"

"What?"

"You heard me."

This is a complete shock. Lindsay has always been so subservient, so overly agreeable. I turn around a little in my seat and lower my voice, trying to create a little privacy. "I did hear you, but I'm not sure I know what's going on."

"You hung up on me and I had to work hand in hand with Danbury, by myself, and you know how scary he is. He's a giant with giant hands and that big square head of his. He didn't get fired, but there was all this stuff with the SEC."

"And . . . how did it go?"

There's a quiet moment. Lindsay is paying for something. I hear an exchange with a clerk. "Fine," she says. "It went fine."

"Well, then, this is great, Lindsay. It all turned out fine."

"No help from you!"

"That's just it," I tell her. "You handled it without any help from me. Exactly."

"Oh," she says, her tone changing. "And that's a good thing."

"That's a good thing."

"Okay," she says. "Then unscrew you."

"That's okay, too," I tell her. "You don't have to unscrew me."

"Are you sure?"

"Yes."

"I also got this little promotion," she says.

"That's great!"

"It's just little but it kind of gives me a little more leverage, which is important while you're gone."

"It's a step up! You deserve it."

The receptionist is standing in front of me now. She says, "I'll take you back." But I think for a disoriented second that she means she's going to take me back to the past. She's going to return me to some earlier, happier time—wishful thinking. I look at her for a moment then say my good-byes to Lindsay and snap the cell phone shut.

"Follow me," she says.

My eyes bounce along with the floofy ruffle at the hem of her impossibly tight, impossibly short skirt. When we reach Bill Reyer's door, she asks me if I want coffee, but her tone is so insincere that I can't even take this simple offer seriously. "No thanks," I tell her.

She opens the door and Bill jumps up to greet me. He walks skittishly, as if spooked by the shadow of his mammoth tax-code books. He takes my hand. "It's so nice to meet you finally. Artie has always said such wonderful things about you."

"He has?"

"Of course," Reyer says, but his "of course" is too

chipper or defensively chipper or somehow off. He coughs to recover a somber tone.

Uncomfortable silence. Accountant silence.

He walks to his desk, motions for me to take a seat. The leather chairs squeak.

"Yes, and I'm sorry we've had to meet under such difficult circumstances. How's Artie doing today?" He says it like he's just read it out of the chapter on "How to Console a Grieving Widow-to-Be," from the book *How to Be a Personable Accountant*. The formality, the professionalism, is incredibly soothing. I'm in a business meeting. I sit up.

"We had a scare last night. But he's okay today," I say. "I'd like to get on with this, if that's all right."

"There are separate accounts, which makes it a little tricky, but Artie made it clear that everything should be turned over to you. The death certificate will take about nine days and then the insurance policy—"

"I don't really need the money. I make enough myself," I cut in for no good reason.

"Well, it's yours anyway. To do with as you see fit. Except . . ." He rummages through some papers. I don't like the pause, nor his acting. I can see this is the part he's dreading. He's also been seeking advice from the chapter called "How to Dole Dicey Information to Soon-to-Be Widows" but it hasn't helped him much. Now he is stalling, worrying, trying to give me the idea that he isn't so organized. Please. He's an accountant, a really good one, too. He doesn't need to be shuffling these pages. He needs to just spit it out.

"He actually took on some financial responsibilities— though they're not necessary legally his anymore."

"Payments?"

"Well, he sends a check to Rita Bessom monthly, from a specific fund, and has for thirty years. He started doing it as a very young man, really, sending what he could, and, as you know, that amount has been able to grow."

John Bessom's mother. Rita Bessom. He's been sending checks all these years? I try to picture Rita Bessom, cashing her checks, giving the money to her grown son. Or not. Maybe she keeps it all for herself. Rita Bessom. I try to imagine what she looks like, where she lives. "Bessom? Still?"

He coughs again, uncomfortably.

"Why didn't he send them to his son?"

"I think he tried once to contact his son, but the boy, John Bessom, didn't want anything from him. Well, he isn't a boy anymore. I mean I suppose he's your age by now . . ." And then Reyer realizes that he's made a faux pas. That he's suggested that Artie is old enough to be my father. And I realize that John Bessom is a man my own age. I had immediately put him in a more disarming category, that of Artie's son, and tried to keep him there—as if he goes into the back office of Bessom's Bedding Boutique to play with small green plastic army figures. This reminder from Reyer doesn't help. He recovers from his blunder quickly. "But Artie believes that support for a child doesn't end when he reaches eighteen years of age. He wanted it to be ongoing."

"Does the money reach the son?"

"The checks reach Rita. She cashes them. That's all we know."

I sit there, soaking this in. John doesn't think there's anything between him and Artie now, but was he still okay with taking the money? Has he been receiving an allowance all this time—enough to start up his own business? Or does his mother hold on to it all for herself? What kind of family is this?

"You know, Artie's estate is quite large."

"Sure," I say. "He started up a restaurant chain. Of course it's large."

"You're an auditor, aren't you?"

I nod.

"Don't you want to know all of the figures?"

"No."

"Why not? I have people come in here who want to know the numbers but don't have any real idea what it all means. You would know. Exactly. Why don't you want to?"

"Because I *am* an auditor." This response makes sense to me, but I can tell it's lost on Reyer. What I mean is that it's too much, too personal. Aren't there some doctors who don't want to know all the details of their own illness, even when it's their specialty? I want Artie to be Artie—that's enough to deal with. I don't want him to become his estate. "You have more to tell me, though, besides numbers," I say. Reyer still looks terribly uncomfortable. "What is it?"

"Artie wants you to give a lump sum to John Bessom."

"Did he say how much?"

"No, he didn't specify. He wanted you to decide how much so you could feel comfortable with it."

"He wants me to choose? So I'll be *comfortable*?" I'm not comfortable, and I don't think I can become comfortable.

The accountant coughs again. He shuffles papers. He isn't finished. "There's more?" I ask.

"One other monthly check supports an art fund. He would like these checks to continue on a monthly basis."

"An art fund?"

"The E.L.S.P.A. Do you know it?"

At first, hearing the name spelled out makes Elspa sound like a governmental agency. It takes a moment to register. Then it does. "The ELSPA," I say. "Yes, I know it." I look to the bank of windows. Is this what he was afraid he'd muddle if he had to tell me himself? Is this what he didn't have the nerve to tell me? Fine. He's been giving money to Elspa. Now that I know Elspa I could see why he'd want to do that. It's infuriating that he's kept another secret from me—how many are there?—but okay. Fine.

"Artie and his charities," I say flatly, but then my mind starts moving quickly. What does Reyer know? Probably more than he's letting on. Now I do want some specifics, some details. "Look, tell me what you know. There's more. I know that the E.L.S.P.A. isn't a registered non-profit. These payments aren't tax deductible." And then I know exactly the one question that I need an answer to: "When did these payments begin?"

"Artie said she needed to turn her life around. He wanted to provide her that opportunity and so, graciously, he opened this account. Bill Reyer looks down at his hands. He folds them together.

"When did these payments begin?"

He fiddles with some papers, but I know that he knows. "Hmmm," he says, as if this bit of the conversation has so little relevance that it's slipped his mind. "Ah, here it is. Two years ago. July." He keeps his eyes on his hands.

"The payments began two years ago? Two years ago?" Artie and I had been married when they met, when the payments began? Elspa assured me that her relationship

with Artie happened before Artie and I had gotten married. Is Elspa one of Artie's three? But, really, does it even
matter anymore, if there were three other women or four
or eighteen? Artie betrayed me, and Elspa lied to me.
"Nice," I mutter. "Very nice."

Reyer looks at me pleadingly. "I told Artie that it
would have been better to explain all of this himself," he
says. "I was hoping that in his time remaining he would
have . . ."

I lean back in my chair then quickly gather my things.
Did Artie want someone younger than I am? Did he prefer her more delicate features? Is she better in bed? I see
Elspa's face in my mind—the innocence, the sweetness.
Springbird is just a name and my imagination, but Elspa is
real, undeniably real. I think back on the sculpture—abstract and blue—from *her imagination!* "I have to go."
Something has cracked in me. I thought I had dealt with
the brunt of the betrayal, but this is a deeper pain.

"We aren't finished . . ." I hear Bill say as I stand up
and head out the door. "We haven't worked out any details, come to any conclusions."

Things are blurry, sizzling, and a hiss is rising in my
ears along with the dull thud of my footsteps down
the hall.

"Ma'am?" the receptionist calls after me. "Is something wrong?" I wave my hand like a flag of surrender.
"I'm sorry," I tell her, barely pausing. "I have to go."

Chapter Fourteen

Don't Breathe Water

I pull jaggedly into the driveway, rip the key from the ignition, and stride across the lawn. My mother's car is gone. She must have headed out to tend to some of the endless details. I unlock the door and let it swing open behind me. Maybe this is the way grief will arrive—through anger.

"Elspa!" I shout. The house is quiet except for my voice ringing through it.

There's a fresh vase of flowers on the lowboy. I despise the flowers, the vase, every manipulative impulse Artie's ever had. I look into the living room, jog to the kitchen, the dining room.

"Elspa!"

I circle back to the stairs and run up them. My mind is flashing back to the accountant's office, Reyer's folded hands, his cough. I know the looks that accountants give their clients when they're trying to avoid the truth. I'm supposed to decide how much money to give John Bessom? I'm supposed to feel fucking *comfortable*? Artie

has been supporting Rita Bessom and Elspa? Elspa lied
to me?

I turn down the hallway and barge into the bedroom.

"What?" Artie shouts out. "What's wrong?"

The nurse is in the chair by the window, hunched over
a handheld video game. He startles, but tries to pretend
he hasn't been startled.

"Why didn't you tell me?"

Artie sits back. "You talked to Reyer. I'm assuming
he didn't break it to you with the necessary finesse. He
lacks—"

"You should have told me to wait until after you were
dead," I shout. "Then killing you wouldn't be an option!
The E.L.S.P.A. Fund? I have to decide what your son is
worth?"

The nurse quickly shuts down the game and shoves it
into his backpack, trying to pack up and sneak out.

"Now that you've met her, you can see she's deserv-
ing," Artie says.

"Yes, I hear that she's quite a sculptor! We really
should support the arts in just this way!"

"Okay, okay, I see why you're mad about Elspa. But
you can see that my son, John, deserves something,
doesn't he? What kind of a bastard doesn't leave something to his own son?"

"A completely different kind of bastard, I suppose."

"I'm a very specific form of bastard," he reminds me.

I walk to his bed and lean in. My mind flashes on one
of my mother's never-cross-stitched sayings: *When dealing
with a belligerent hairstylist, you must embrace your inner
bitch.* "You know, I could smother you with a pillow in the
middle of the night and who would think I'd done it?"

"He might," Artie says, pointing to the frightened nurse zipping his backpack.

"Maybe I'll let Eleanor help. She'd appreciate that. For that matter, I wonder how many of your other goddamn girlfriends wouldn't mind taking their turn offing you!"

"I really don't think you should threaten me in front of witnesses," he says, glancing sidelong at the nurse.

"And don't buy me any more fucking flowers!" I scream.

I walk to the bathroom, where I recall Elspa drawing Artie's bath. Empty. And that's when it hits me.

"Elspa," I say. A jolt of panic shoots through me—has Elspa felt too much, is she bleeding somewhere in the house, is she already gone? For some reason, this only makes me angrier, although the anger is tinged with fear.

"What is it?" Artie asks from bed.

The nurse freezes, his backpack tucked under his arm.

I race downstairs, calling her name even more loudly than before. "Elspa! Elspa!" I turn the corner at the low-boy so wildly that I tip the vase, which thunks to the floor, cracking wide open so that the water soaks the rug and the stems are exposed. On its tipping way, it chips a lamp—a lamp that I bought, finery that my mother would have suggested that I hide. I run through the kitchen again, where my mother has stacked the chocolate-slathered biscuits. I open the French doors and clatter across the patio. I stare into the corners of the yard and then into the pool.

There at the bottom, I see a blurred shape in the deep end—the slow underwater billow of a shirt, the glistening of a wet head. Elspa. No. I take a deep breath, a running start, and dive in—fully dressed, shoes and all. The water is cold. I swim to the bottom of the deep end, my clothes heavy each time I glide forward. My strokes seem too slow, the water too thick. I worry that I will never get to the bottom.

But then, finally, Elspa is right in front of me. Her startled face, her eyes a little wild, her cheeks puffed. I wrap one arm around her ribs and yank her toward the surface. She twists in my grip as if she's trying to pull me down with her, but I tug her back sharply. Soon we are both paddling upward.

We break the surface at the same moment, each gasping. I still have Elspa by the ribs.

"What?" she says, sputtering, trying to catch her breath.

"What?" I ask, completely confused.

"What are you doing?"

I loosen my grip and she swims to the wall. "I thought I was saving your life," I tell her. Elspa is alive and well. I should feel relieved, happy, but instead the anger returns. I feel like I might choke on it.

"I was meditating," she says.

"In the deep end?" I ask, swimming to the other side of the pool. "With all of your clothes on?"

"I was sitting in the lotus position," she says, swimming to a ladder and sitting on the top rung. "Counting seconds. Being mindful. I learned it from this roommate I once had."

"At the bottom of the deep end?" I smack the surface of the water angrily. "What were you thinking? You scared the hell out of me!"

"I'm sorry," Elspa says. "You scared me, too."

I hoist myself out of the pool, my shirt and pants clinging to me. I sit on the edge, take off my soaked shoes. I don't look at Elspa. I can't. "And were you ever going to tell me the truth?"

"What truth?" Elspa asks—as if there are so many truths and untruths to choose from.

"That you had an affair with Artie while he was already married to me? That he stills pays for your life? You lied to me and just kept lying in all of those little ways—the whole waitress thing, the whole thing about never having had *that* kind of relationship with him, the sculpture from your imagination."

Elspa is quiet for a moment. Her beautiful pale wet face is still. "He's dying. I didn't think it was, I don't know, appropriate."

"Appropriate?" I shout, incredulously.

She wipes the water from her face, hugs herself. I can see one hand gripping the wreath tattoo on her upper arm.

"Look, I can handle it from here," I say. "Your turn at his deathbed is over. So you can go. Thanks for everything." I pause, something occurring to me. "One question: do you love elevators?"

"Elevators?" she asks.

"Never mind." That must have been yet another one of Artie's sweethearts. How many are there? And each of them comes with how many lies?

When Elspa stands and starts to walk to the patio doors, I look up at her. She's shaking. "Why did you marry him in the first place?" She stops and then turns. "Didn't you ever see the good in him?"

I stare at her. This is a completely unacceptable question to ask. I don't owe her an explanation of my love for Artie, and I'm about to tell her this, but then it's back—that fissure inside me, a breaking open. I find my-self thinking of Artie and me, a very particular hilarious moment, and I start to talk in a very quiet voice. "When Artie and I were on our honeymoon, it was mating season for stingrays. We were walking out in the surf, holding hands, and this guy told us the stingrays were harmless unless we stepped on one. 'Then what?' we asked each other. 'Certain death?' We walked back toward shore. I screamed first, thinking I'd brushed one with my foot, and then Artie screamed because I'd screamed. And then I screamed because Artie screamed. And then it was just funny and we kept screaming back and forth all the way to the shore, just because."

I'm gazing into the pool. I've said it all so quietly that I'm not sure if Elspa heard me. I'm not even sure she's still there. But when I look up, I see her, across the pool, her eyes brimming. She doesn't say a word.

I keep going. "Once a punk kid from the neighbor-hood tried to steal Artie's old Corvette out of the garage and Artie heard him from bed and ran naked down the street after him, swinging a golf club."

Elspa laughs. I do, too, a soft flutter in my throat.

I can't stop now. "His favorite place to think and make big plans is a junky diner called Manilla's. He speaks a great butchered French. He always messes up the words to songs but still sings them loudly. He always has trouble hanging up on telemarketers. I once caught him sort of counseling a telemarketer hawking a lower mortgage rate. The kid—a woman of course—was just out of college and deep in debt and confused about whether or not she should get engaged to a pilot. Artie was on the phone for an hour—just handing over good advice." Strange how I simply rattle these off. I suppose these are my responses to

Artie's numbered inscriptions from the flowers he kept sending me. I suppose I've been compiling a history of my own, without really knowing it, and here they all are, spilling out of me.

"When his dog Midas died, the upstairs bathroom sprung a leak right at that same time and he tore up the house looking for the leak, where it was coming from, how it was moving along beams and pooling somewhere else. But it was really about the dog. He loved that dog . . . And he wanted me to get pregnant. He wanted that desperately. He used to put his head on my stomach in bed and pretend he was designing my womb so that the baby would have a plush pad to live in for nine months. Things like: maybe if we move the sofa over here and get one of those fluffy white throw rugs . . ." I stop myself. I can hear Artie's voice so clearly in my head that I don't want to go on. I shout across the yard, "You fucking bastard!"

"I'm sorry," Elspa says.

I blink at her. "About what?"

"You loved him, and you still love him. I wasn't sure before."

I know that I'm about to start crying. I don't want to. I'm afraid that if I start, I won't be able to stop. I look up at Elspa. "Why did you try to kill yourself?" I ask.

Her eyes skitter across the tree line. She glances up at the sky, and then back to me. "I was a drug addict when I met Artie."

This confession terrifies me. And in a moment when I shouldn't be selfish at all, a very selfish thought comes to mind. Artie had an affair with a drug addict?

She quickly reads my expression and assures me. "I wasn't a needle user. I wasn't whoring for drugs. I'm not . . . sick. We were safe and he only said the sweetest things about you, these beautiful stories. He raised you up and worshipped you. He still worships you."

I'm not sure how to take this. "He has a strange way of showing it. I mean, worshipping me like an idol, sacrificing virgins? That's not the way I'd like to be worshipped."

"Honestly," she tells me, "it was different—a different kind of intimacy."

"I think we have different definitions of the term *honestly*," I say. "I still don't understand how you lied to me so convincingly."

"I'm an addict. One thing addicts know how to do well is lie," she says, a dark regret in her voice that I haven't heard before. "I'm trying to tell you the truth now, and my relationship with Artie wasn't like that. You know?"

"No, I don't know."

She says flatly, "I was very fragile most of the time. I could barely stand to be touched. I was a mess."

"Go on," I say.

"A week before I met Artie, I gave my daughter, Rose, to my mother to raise."

"You have a daughter?"

She nods.

"And, forgive me for being a little suspicious at this point, but do you want to go over the time frame of your relationship with Artie and her birth?" I ask this question though I know that Artie is at a point in his life when he's claiming his children, not denying them.

"She isn't Artie's kid. She was one year old when I met Artie and when I gave her up. Now she's three. It almost killed me to give her up. Literally. I've been clean ever since Artie saved my life."

"Why aren't you raising her now?"

"I visit as often as I can. My parents think it's too confusing for her. Who's the mommy and all of that. But I weasel my way in as often as I can." She shakes her head roughly. "My parents made it clear that I had to give her to them. They were right. I wasn't in any shape to be a mother. They've taken on that role. And it wasn't easy for them. They're older now. And I don't know. It's not my right to ask them to give up that role now. They wouldn't, anyway. They'd never trust me with her."

"But do you want to be her mother?" I ask.

"More than anything," she says.

"Your parents took up that role valiantly, but maybe they'd give her back to you if they knew how much you've changed."

"Oh, no," she says. "They never trusted me, not even before. I was never good enough, never worth anything in their eyes. I explain to them how I'm taking college classes again, but they always think that if they give me any money, it's just going to go to drugs."

"In any case," I say, "it is your right to be her mother, isn't it? I mean legally speaking. Did you sign over your rights?"

She shakes her head. "No."

"Then it is your right, not only legally, but maybe ethically, too," I tell her.

"I want to go and get her. That's what I want more than anything. But I can't."

"Maybe you would be a good mother now, Elspa. Maybe you're ready."

She's quiet a moment. "You would be a good mother," she adds, her voice hushed.

And this is it. The fissure breaks open, and the now-too-familiar anger mixes equally with grief. I curl forward.

The sobs are deep and guttural. Artie won't be a father to my child. Whatever chance we might have had to work things out makes no difference now. He is going to die.

I don't hear Elspa make her way around the pool, but suddenly she's here, at my side. She puts her arms around me. We're both soaking wet. She holds me tightly, a hug that feels more like she's the one hauling me up from the bottom of the pool now, and I can feel myself giving in to it.

I look up at the house, and there is Artie, with the male nurse standing at his side, watching us from an upper window in the office across from the bedroom. He looks confused and relieved. He seems to know that this is a private moment, that he's intruding. I see the two of them turn back into the room.

Chapter Fifteen

Sometimes After Abandoning Ourselves to Emotion, We Want to Tidy Up

I start to tidy up by cleaning the broken vase, putting the flowers into one of the old vases I keep under the kitchen sink, soaking up the water with paper towels. I don't read Artie's #59. I'm tired of sentiments that are so tight they can fit on a little card. I'm tired of Artie-isms.

But this tidying doesn't quite satisfy me.

I decide that I need an overhaul, complete reorganization.

I know when to call a meeting. I am, after all, a professional, the kind who's genuinely suited to it—soothed by charts, amused by indexes, even sometimes delighted by a well-tallied table.

I know that Eleanor, Elspa—even my mother—and I have things that need to change. We have, as we say in the business, overlapping goals. We've been pulled together because of Artie's impending death, and I'll be damned if I can't make this thing profitable—in the emotional sense—for all of us. Every good manager knows that a catastrophe can really be an opportunity, if you look at it the right way.

I also know how to prepare an agenda. I spend the afternoon and early evening creating profiles—needs, goals, capacity for each individual to withstand risk—and, based on these profiles, I make a plan for each person I've invited.

Am I being too assertive, overly structured, hyperorganized? Possibly, but after being lied to by one of my husband's sweethearts, threatening to smother my ailing husband in front of a witness, pulling a possibly suicidal woman from the bottom of a pool, and having a little breakdown, what would you expect? Surely some of the best organizational efforts are a reaction to the world's emotional catastrophes.

The meeting is a surprise to those attending. Eleanor and my mother, fresh from the salon and perked to edginess by lattes, are sitting at the dining room table. My mother has a newly configured hairstyle stiff with spray. Eleanor's hair is still pinned back, but two soft strands are curved by her jawline, looking rigidly windswept. She seems softer than before, prettier, younger. In fact, she may not quite be fifty yet. Bogie is perched on my mother's lap. His doggie jockstrap matches the pale yellow of my mother's outfit, shoes and all—a new low. Elspa is there, too, her piercings glinting under the dining room chandelier. They're all holding the agendas I've printed out.

"I've called this meeting," I say, "because we don't have much time and we need to be organized if we're all to meet our goals."

"Why are we having a meeting? Why so formal?" Eleanor says.

"Are you wearing work slacks?" my mother asks.

I am, in fact, wearing work slacks and a nice button-down, but not a matching blazer. "These are my comfort clothes," I say. I like them because I know who I am when I'm wearing them.

"Interesting," Eleanor says.

"How could there be any comfort in those clothes?" Elspa says.

"At least I don't match my dog," I say, gesturing to poor, oblivious Bogie. My mother looks stung. "I'm sorry," I tell her. "Let's not get off course." But I know that they're onto me already. I can tell that they know I'm overcompensating, and knowing that they know, I can feel my own swelling emotions—a deep sadness and anger and love and, because of that mixture, that swelling— panic. "The agenda is clear. I've marked down everyone's goals and needs and, brought together by Artie's impending death, how we individually and collectively can reach those goals." Impending death. I thought about how to say it while I was writing the agenda. It's the most clinical term I could come up with. I was afraid that if I said anything else, I wouldn't be able to take it. Impending is a nicity enough word that it doesn't seem real. I don't want to venture too close to the reality of Artie's death right now. I can't. I know how fragile I feel.

"Who's John Bessom?" Eleanor asks, pointing at his name on the agenda.

"He's Artie's son. He's not here, but he is one of the people who's been brought together with us by Artie. And, he doesn't know it yet, but he's going to get to know Artie before Artie dies because he shouldn't repeat his father's mistakes."

"And how is he going to get to know Artie?" Eleanor

asks. "Will Artie hand over his own glorious version of himself?"

"No," I say. I've already thought of this. He can't just have Artie's glorious version. "I'm going to give him my version, too. I'm planning a tour."

"A tour?" my mother says.

"Of Artie's life. The Good and the Bad Tour."

"That's a great idea," Elspa says, but she says it so gently and with such airy wisdom in her voice that I know she means it's something I need more than Artie's son. This chafes me, but I don't feel like getting into it.

"Fathers are important," I tell them. "Even if you don't really know them that well." Mine was nearly a stranger to me when he died. "John Bessom will know his father. Otherwise he won't get his inheritance."

"His inheritance?" my mother asks.

"Yes. There's money for him in Artie's will, but it's up to me how much he gets."

"Well, dear," my mother says—she has theories about the money of dead and ex-husbands, and giving it away isn't one she thinks highly of.

"So the bastard's got a son," Eleanor says, tapping her nails on the table.

"I didn't know it either, until a few days ago," I say.

"That is so Artie," Eleanor says, fury rising to her cheeks. "So many deceptions!"

"Oh, he's just a man. What can we expect?" my mother says.

"If we don't expect anything from them, then they never learn, which explains their atrophied emotional abilities," Eleanor says.

"Which brings me to Eleanor," I say.

Everyone turns her attention to the agenda.

" 'Wouldn't it be wonderful if Artie were able to make peace with his past—all of it—before he died?' That's what you said the other night. And you're right. It would do him good." At this point, there's an edge to my voice. I can hear it as clearly as anything—spite, revenge? I want Artie to learn some lessons. I want him to have to deal with his own legacy. The anger rears up again. It tightens my throat. I cough and point to the agenda. "This point of the plan is listed under Artie's needs and goals, but it would also do you good, Eleanor, wouldn't it? And so it's cross-listed under your needs and goals." It could be listed under my needs and goals, too, but I'm not ready to own up to that publicly.

"Look, I've come to terms with men," Eleanor says. "It's quite simple: I've sworn off them."

My mother gasps.

"Maybe for now you can agree to head up the charge to help Artie make peace with his past just because it's good for Artie. And, if you happen to learn something about yourself in the process, so be it," I offer.

"And how would I go about making Artie come to terms with his past?"

"I have an address book filled with all of his sweethearts. That's how I got in touch with you. I think he should have a session with as many of those women as possible to hear about just how he failed them, just how he's done them wrong."

"Well, that would be delicious, really. My pleasure."

"But what if he hasn't done them wrong?" Elspa says.

"Oh, right," I say. "You're one of the red circles."

"Red circles?" she asks.

"Each name has one of two marks: a red circle, which means that he left the woman on good, perhaps mutual terms, or a red X, which means not-so-good terms."

"And after my name?" Eleanor asks.

I give her a look like: Well, what do you think?

"A very big X," she says, with a kind of pride. "We should only invite the women Artie did wrong. Only the red X's."

"Is that fair?" Elspa asks.

"Artie has you to tell him how wonderful he is," I say. "Artie Shoreman has come to terms with all of his good points. He needs to come to terms with the other part of himself. He needs to understand betrayal." And then I put it in Elspa terms. "We learn more from our failures than from our successes."

My mother sighs and rolls her eyes. "It's a waste of time—old dog, new tricks! Men need pampering. They're the weaker sex."

Here there is a collective sigh.

"I don't know if it'll work," I say, "but it's worth a try."

Then my mother says, "I don't understand what my goal means. *Be my own person?* I am my own person, dear."

"You could be more of your own person," I say.

"How do you plan to have her achieve this goal?" Eleanor asks sternly.

"I don't know," I say. "If she could just work toward it—"

"Well, that's ridiculous!" my mother says.

"For example, you could stop big-game hunting for your sixth husband. Just ease up a little on that front . . ."

"I'm not big-game hunting!"

"Just think about it," I say.

"I'm with Eleanor! I think this meeting is stupid!"

"I didn't say that," Eleanor balks.

My mother pulls her yellow handbag off the back of the chair, straps it over her shoulder, picks up Bogie, and starts to storm out of the room. "I'm leaving," she announces—as if this isn't obvious.

"Wait," I say. "Don't go."

She pauses without looking back. I glance at Bogie's rump poking out from under her arm.

"There are two more things that I need help with," I say to her.

"You need me?" she asks warily.

"One, I'd really love for you to take over the funeral arrangements with Artie. He and I, well, I can't. We just aren't there yet."

She hesitates, for dramatic effect. "Well, I could do that," she says.

"And, two, I'd love for you to keep the neighbors away—especially the ones who seem like friends."

She turns around and smiles with her eyebrows raised. "I'm fantastic at the polite brush-off."

"Like when you first met me," Eleanor says with a sharp frankness that catches my mother off guard, but only for a moment.

"It's one of the things I do best," my mother says, returning to her seat, watery-eyed Bogie in tow.

"Thank you," I say.

I turn to Elspa. She's been quiet. She's staring at the agenda. Her own eyes are a little watery, but she's smiling broadly.

I think of what Elspa said by the pool, that she wants

her daughter back, more than anything. She wants to be a mother again, and I know how wonderful a mother she would be, because of the tender attention she's giving to me, to Artie.

"Mothers are important, too. There's no replacement." I look at my own mother, still trying to calm her down from her short-lived hissy. "Children have a right to all the love they can get their hands on."

Elspa doesn't say a word. She looks at Eleanor, at my mother, and back at me. I can tell that we've grown to rely on one another in the strange, intimate way that people can—quickly and fully, a reliance born from necessity.

"What do you mean?" my mother asks.

"I want you to get your daughter back," I say to Elspa. Once upon a time, I opened a window and let loose a bird that had been trapped there. Artie was terrified of the damn bird, which was knocking around. Elspa reminded me of this story. I want to open the right windows again. "I've worked out a plan in which you become the mother you already are."

"What does the plan include exactly?" Eleanor asks.

Elspa looks up at me, wide-eyed.

"The plan is to go to Elspa's parents' house. She needs to get her daughter back. Elspa and Rose can stay here until Elspa gets back on her feet."

"You've thought this through?" Elspa says, with jittery excitement.

"Maybe not completely. I'm sure there are holes. But I know I'll need to baby-proof the house, the pool," I tell her. Unfortunately, I've thought of this house filled with children too many times. My imaginary babies with Artie—the ones we name who will never be. I've imagined where I would set up the nursery. I've imagined the high chair in the kitchen. I've imagined the little playhouse in the yard. I know, deep down, that I'm drawn to Rose, to the idea of mother and daughter, of making that happen, if not for myself, then for Elspa.

"They won't give her up," Elspa says. The agenda is trembling in her hand. "I mean, it's not a legal arrangement. They don't have custody. But they have power. They are, well, they are my parents. They'll tell me they know what's best. And I'll buy it."

"That's why we'll go together. I'm good at presenting what's logical and rational and best for all parties involved. That's what I know how to do."

"You haven't met my parents. They don't operate on what's logical, rational, and best for all parties involved. You'll see."

"*You'll see?* Does this mean yes?"

Elspa nods. "You want to do this for me. I wouldn't say no to that. It's too important."

"And what about you, Lucy?" my mother asks.

"You're not on the agenda," Eleanor says, scanning it.

I realized this when I was making the agenda, but I was hoping no one would notice. "Something good has to come of all of us getting together," I say, thinking the way a good manager would—catastrophe as opportunity. "But it doesn't have to happen for me, necessarily. Just something good."

"There has to be something good for you," Elspa says, shaking her head. "There has to be."

Eleanor asks, "What would that look like?"

"What would that look like?" I ask.

"Yes, something good, for you. What shape would that take?"

"I don't know," I say. I consider it for a moment. "I

wouldn't mind being more like the person I was before I found out about Artie's cheating."

"What were you like?" Elspa asks.

"I wasn't so closed off."

"I think that you should try to find a way to forgive Artie," Elspa says.

"I think that would be good for your soul," my mother adds.

"To hell with forgiveness," Eleanor says.

"I guess I'll have to figure it all out," I say. "Well, I guess my plan will have to be figuring out my plan."

Chapter Sixteen

When at a Loss, It's Sometimes Advisable to Resort to Polite Bribery

s I'm getting ready to leave the house for my first mission, there's a real buzz. Eleanor has been thumbing through Artie's address book, looking at all the red Xed names. She's set up shop at the breakfast nook and is now talking to someone on her cell phone. My mother is on the land line, already in negotiation with three funeral homes. She's started writing out a list of questions for Artie. Elspa is pacing, notebook in hand, on the patio. I've given her the assignment of jotting notes on the inner workings of her parents' psyches. Who are her parents? What motivates them? What makes them tick? Their politics, religion, failures.

Artie is in the bedroom above. Is he aware of the buzz? He must be. He has to feel the energy, the new stirring of air. But he doesn't know what's coming. He doesn't know what Eleanor has in store.

Lindsay's calls have come to punctuate the days like hearing the same pop song over and over on the radio. I never know when they might happen, but when they do, I know I've been expecting them. On the way to Bessom's Bedding Boutique, she rings me. I feel myself floating away from the concerns of work that used to consume me. I'm shocked at how easily I talk Lindsay through things. "Yeah, that will take care of itself," I hear myself saying. "Don't worry so much about that one." I sound like a stranger—my voice even sounds detached, as if I'm not speaking at all; it's really someone behind me, or just off to the side. Work used to consume me, but now, faced with Artie dying, it's a little scary, actually, how little it all fazes me.

"How are you doing?" she asks.

"I have a plan," I say.

"You make great plans," she says. "I miss your plans."

"Well, I don't know about this one. It's a little wobbly. It deals with a lot of variables—like the human heart."

"Oh," she says. "Well. The human heart! What can you do?"

"Exactly."

After Lindsay and I finish up, I try to reach John on the way in. No one has been answering the phone. I call three times from the highway. The ringer lapses over to the machine—John's voice saying, "You've reached Bessom's Bedding Boutique. We are temporarily closed. We hope to resume store hours in the near future to serve your needs. Please leave a message."

The first time I hang up, wondering what's gone wrong. I remember the banker type talking to him in front of the shop when Elspa and I came for the mattress and wonder if John's business has gone belly-up. The second time, I listen to his voice carefully. It sounds a little rougher than I remember, a little more worn down—and then I hang up. The third time, I'm sure I hear a catch in his throat halfway through. The catch is moving, in a way, even though I'm not sure what it signifies, and I leave a message. "I'd like to come by, to talk, about Artie . . . I hope you don't mind. It's just that . . . Well, hopefully I'll talk to you in person." I leave my phone number and then I pause a moment, wondering just how dithering I must sound. "I'm going to say good-bye now before I say anything else." But I don't say good-bye. I just hang up, which is what I meant.

The sign on the door of Bessom's Bedding Boutique reads Closed, but when I push, the door swings open so quickly that I feel like I've been pulled inside. There is no bell. Is it turned off? Broken? The beds, all decked out in their comforters and layers of pillows, look big, fluffy, bright.

This is part of the plan—something good has to come of Artie's impending death, something good for each of these people who've been thrown together. But now that I'm standing here among the beds and staring at the office door in the back of the showroom, I feel completely unsure.

The door is open just a crack. As I walk up to it, I can hear someone inside—a rustling of papers. I feel awkward, and I should. I'm trespassing. I raise my hand to knock but I'm afraid I'll startle him. It dawns on me that I should have at least waited for him to return my call. He needs more warning.

I pull out my cell phone and select the number. His phone starts to ring. He ignores it. The message kicks in— his voice echoing in the small office—the words: ". . . Temporarily closed . . . Please leave a message."

"It's me, Lucy." I can hear my own voice now from inside his office. "I'm here. I mean, I am really right here."

I turn away from the door then back again. "I mean I'm on the other side of your office door. I didn't want to scare you."

There's a moment of silence as, I guess, this announcement settles in.

"What are you, the big bad wolf? I've had bigger badder wolves at my door," he calls out jokingly. "What do you want?"

I talk halfway into the phone and halfway into the crack in the door. "To talk."

"You can put the phone down," he says.

I flip it shut.

"And you can open the door."

I do. The door creaks. He looks up from his desk, smiling a little, that crooked grin—and a gentleness around his eyes. His shirt collar is unbuttoned and askew, revealing one of his collarbones.

"You can come in," he says. I step inside. I've given up on the hope of little green plastic army men. John is Artie's son, but he's no kid. But what I'm not prepared for is the fact that it's obvious he lives here. There's a minifridge humming in the corner, a fruit bowl with two green apples and a bruised banana in the middle of the paper piles on his desk, and towels stacked on the filing cabinet. The closet door is open, revealing shirts and pants on hangers, and a tidy grid of shoes below.

"How are you doing?" he asks.

"I've been better." I try to sound light, but I don't pull it off. "I'm sorry about how things turned out the other night. That's not the way I had it planned."

"No, I'm sorry," he says. "I mean, he's your husband and I can't imagine how you must feel, knowing . . ."

I shake my head. "It's okay. I'm not good with the whole death thing. I suppose I'll have a bunch of sympathy cards with lilies on them at home soon enough." There's a lull. He's not sure how to proceed. Neither am I. "I'm here on business, in a way." I look around the small office. "How is business?"

"Not exactly going swimmingly." The phone starts to ring.

"It isn't me, I swear," I say.

He picks up the cordless receiver, without answering, and looks at the incoming caller's name. He hits a talk button once and then again, hanging up. "Wolves at the door," he says. His eyes look tired, his face a little slack. He shrugs a little, a bounce in his collarbone. "That's an accurate description of how business is going, actually. Why do you ask?"

I don't quite know how to put all of this. I fiddle with my phone, opening it, closing it. I talk about money at work all the time. It's never this personally messy. It's never attached to the weight of my own emotions. I decide to fake it, at least for a moment, to revert to my professional self. I square my shoulders. "Artie has a will, and you're in it."

This takes him by surprise. He's intrigued. He flips through a small stack of papers without really looking at them. He leans forward. He's about to say something. He even raises his finger. But then he shakes his head. He pushes the papers around on his desk again. "I don't want any of his money."

"I don't know that it's up to you."

"Who is it up to then?"

I was wondering when we'd get to this part. So soon?

I can no longer hold the professional pose of Lucy-as-auditor. I walk to a small chair and sit down. In fact, I slump. I glance up at him and then away. "Me. Artie wants me to decide what portion of his money will go to you."

"You?"

There's an awkward silence. "It wasn't my choice."

He stands up, as if overcome with a sudden restlessness. He's taller than I remember him, taller and leaner, more handsome, too, and I'd thought he was pretty damn handsome before. "Look, you've heard me say this before and I'll say it again . . ."

"I know—there's nothing between you and Artie now." I'm tired of this take. "Maybe you think of yourself as some immaculate conception, but your mother doesn't have any problems taking Artie's money."

"What's that supposed to mean?"

"As far as Artie knows, he has never stopped supporting you. Your mother's been cashing monthly checks all your life."

"She has?" He's stunned. Angry, too. He stares at the papers on his desk—overdue invoices, debt collection notices. He leans on them with both of his fists clenched. And then he starts to laugh. He shakes his head.

"What's so funny?"

"Rita Bessom," he says. "I've been giving her monthly checks, too. That's my mother!"

"Her checks from Artie are ending," I tell him. "That's up to me, too."

"It's about time," he says, and then he sits down again. "Listen, I don't want any part of it. Let's just move on. I, for one, have a lot going on here. I'm in over my head and . . ."

I'm here for a reason and it really doesn't have anything to do with Rita Bessom, or even that much about money. "Don't you want to know something about your father? Aren't you curious?"

He rubs his forehead. "I understand where you're coming from, but it's not exactly like that . . ."

I want him to love some part of Artie Shoreman, and I want him to know some of Artie's failings, too. I want him to understand his father. "I didn't get much of a chance with my father," I say. "He left when I was young and then he died before I was old enough to have a real relationship with him. I have stories about him—good and bad—and they help. What I'm saying is that this is important. I don't want you to miss out on getting to know Artie, even if just a little bit. This is your only shot at that. If you don't do it, you might end up regretting it."

He stares at me like I'm some exotic bird that's come into his office to squawk. I can tell he isn't quite sure what to say. He tilts his head to one side. We stare at each other for a moment—a long moment. It makes me blush, but I refuse to glance away.

"Look," he says, and I know that he's going to try to go back to his old stance.

I interrupt. "Let me get to the point. I want to make you a proposition."

"You're propositioning me? It's not every day a woman walks in to proposition me."

I ignore the comment. "Artie wants to leave you some money. He left the amount up to me. You can use that money to help your business or give it to blind children or strippers. I don't care. All I'm asking is that, in return, you meet the man and try to get to know him a little. I want you to hear his stories—from his own mouth—and, just so you don't get a lopsided impression, I'll be giving my version, too. A short guided tour of his life."

"A guided tour of Artie Shoreman's life?"

"Yes."

"Complete with a PowerPoint presentation? And you would be the guide?" he asks.

"It may not be state of the art, but I'll be the guide. I'll do my best." I cross my arms and then uncross them. I can't remember the last time I've felt this unnerved.

The phone starts to ring again. He ignores it.

"And then you'll decide how much money to give me?" He squints at me, then leans back in his chair. "Are you bribing me?"

I let my eyes wander around the room—the ceiling, the microwave that I missed earlier, the green carpeting. That's when I notice he's barefoot. The tan feet, the frayed cuffs of his jeans—I feel like I'm gazing at something intimate. I look up at him, and only barely recall the question. Am I bribing him to know his father? "Yes," I tell him. "If that's what you want to call it."

He smiles again and I'm staring at him—looking for some remnant of Artie. I can only see the thinnest fraction of some vague relation. But there's some other beauty there—something more serious, more sincere. "Fair enough. I'll do it. I'm in," he says. "Resorting to bribery. You're quite a mobster."

Without thinking, the words fly out of my mouth: "Next time I might have to rough you up." And as soon as I say the words, they're on reverb in my head: *Next time I might have to rough you up?* I think about trying to take them back, stammering out some: *I didn't mean that the way it sounded*—but I decide that will only make things worse. I want to tell him that I'm not attracted to him, that I would never say anything like this to Artie's son. What kind of a creep would say something like that?

John is clearly enjoying this. He's trying to rein in a smile. "I'll keep that in mind," he says.

I simply back out of the office, shut the door, and jog to the exit. One chorus going through my head: *Next time I might have to rough you up. Next time I might have to rough you up?*

Chapter Seventeen

The Past Is Best Relived in Half-Hour Time Slots

When I get home, it's evening. Dusk is collecting at the edges of the yard. A few ragged fireflies are blinking and batting up into the trees.

I find Eleanor and my mother sitting at the kitchen table, drinking coffee. Eleanor proudly shows me her chart—I'm not the only one with organizational compulsions. The chart is a plan for the next three days, organized into half-hour time slots with built-in breaks for meals and rest. Half of the time slots are already filled in with women's names.

"How did you get them to commit?" I ask, pulling up a chair.

"Well, it wasn't that hard. I just modified your method. I called sober before midnight. Oh, and I appealed to their vanity."

"Fair enough," I say. "My method may have had some flaws."

"Any luck with Bessom?" my mother asks.

I nod. I'm still jangled from the meeting. It dawned on

me during the car ride home that in addition to saying I'd rough him up, I also used the word *proposition,* which in retrospect, seems much worse. I'm not sure whether I'm overthinking my responses because I'm nervous about messing up Artie's chance to meet his son or because I find myself so inexplicably attracted to his un-Artie looks, his way of looking at me, talking to me. "He's in," I say. "I think he needs the money."

"Well, I left time slots open for his visits as well," Eleanor says, pointing to the chart. (Did I mention it's color-coded?) Bessom's visits are marked in dark blue.

"Where's Elspa?" I ask.

"She's lying down in the guest room," Eleanor says. "Writing about her parents, and, well, it's harder to do than she thought."

This worries me. I hope that Elspa can do it, that she won't give up on this. It's too important.

"Elspa isn't as lucky as you are in the parental department," my mother says, without any irony, and pats my hand.

I ignore this little self-congratulatory moment. She shouldn't be encouraged.

"And Artie?" Eleanor says excitedly, with one fist held up near her heart. "When are we going to inform him of our plan? I've filled in time slots starting tomorrow morning."

I put both hands on the table and push myself up. "How about now?" Why not now? I already have nervous energy to burn, and there's something inside me that wants to punish Artie. Is that becoming a habitual desire? I'm aware of how very much I want to see his expression when he hears the plan.

"Now?" my mother says.

"Sounds good to me," Eleanor says, gripping her chart.

"I still would like to state, for the record, that I don't think this is a good idea," my mother says.

"There is no record," I say. "It's just us, making this up as we go."

"But still," my mother says. "Artie, well, poor Artie . . ."

"He asked for this, don't forget. He told me to call up his old sweethearts. This was, in part, his idea!"

"You know how I feel about men," my mother says. "I just feel like they are . . ."

"Delicate creatures?" I ask.

"I prefer the term *weak*," Eleanor says. "Delicate implies that it's our responsibility to handle them with care."

"Boys will be boys," my mother says, shaking her head. "There's no changing them."

"This is the problem," I say. "I mean, once we started excusing their behavior with that phrase 'boys will be boys,' men had no reason to change, to grow, to become something new. Women have continued to evolve, because we've had to. Elasticity is the female's strongest evolutionary trait—it's why we survive. There was never anything expected of men once someone invented the phrase 'boys will be boys.' They could all just be themselves—and their repertoires shrank to burps and groping."

"And lying and cheating," Eleanor adds.

My mother takes this in. "You're saying that this is a step for mankind?"

I think about that. "Yes," I say, "for mankind."

And then a voice pipes up behind me. "For Artie, too," Elspa says, walking into the kitchen. "Digging up your past is hard, but it's important."

I'm relieved to see Elspa. She's been working hard. She hasn't given up. She should be with us for this. "Okay, then," I say.

The four of us stand in a loose semicircle around Artie's bed. He's asleep, but even in sleep his breath sounds a little labored.

"Let him rest," my mother says, holding Bogie and nervously patting his head.

"He's tired," I say. It surprises me how much he's aged. "Let's go. We can do this tomorrow."

We start to head out the door, but then Artie's eyes blink open and move from one of us to the next. He lifts himself to his elbows. "Have I died and gone to heaven or do you all always watch over me in my sleep?"

"He's unbearably cocky," Eleanor mutters.

"Ah, well, this is not heaven evidently—unless you're crashing," he says to Eleanor. "I thought you were leaving."

"I was asked to stay, brought in on a special assignment."

"Oh, really," he says. "To murder me? Don't go to the trouble. Didn't you hear? I'm dying."

"No," Eleanor says, "there's no real murder plot. This is more of a send-off of sorts."

He turns to me. "Lucy, what's she talking about?"

"We have a plan. It's the one you wanted from the beginning and Eleanor is overseeing it," I tell him, with some strange false cheer in my voice.

"Just for the record, Artie," my mother says, rubbing Bogie's ears, "I was not in favor of anything of this sort. I—"

But I glare at her sharply and she zips it quick.

"We think you need to sort through your past," Elspa says. "We think that it could be cleansing."

"Cleansing?" Artie repeats.

"Your sweethearts," I explain. "Eleanor has set up visits with them. It turns out that people take things more seriously when they aren't called up by a drunk woman in the middle of the night."

"Really?" Artie says, sitting up in bed, thinking all this over. I wonder if this is all he has to say. No squirming? He isn't anxious or unnerved by the idea. He seems . . . pleased with himself. In fact, he's overly pleased with himself. I'm more than a little disgusted. "Well, that's nice of them. I mean, they don't have to, but I suppose, well, I suppose they want to."

"You're actually looking forward to this," I say, a bit surprised.

Artie recovers. "No, no, I'm not looking forward. That's not right. It's just, well . . . it *is* flattering . . ."

Eleanor is fuming. "Perfect then. We'll start tomorrow."

"Who's coming tomorrow?" Artie asks, still way too eager, a boyish grin on his face.

"You see," my mother says, pointing at Artie like he's evidence on display in a court of law. "I told you. Old dog. New tricks. He can't be changed! Men are delicate creatures!"

"Old dog?" Artie says, insulted. He looks to Bogie for support. "Don't listen to her," he says. "She's just intimidated by our masculinity."

"You know what I mean," my mother says. "It's an expression."

"I'm going home," Eleanor says to the rest of us.

"Don't go," Elspa says.

"*I'm* the old dog?" Artie says, jokingly.

"You'd better be nice," my mother hisses at Artie. "I'm in charge of your funeral. I may just decide to bury you Liberace-style. Imagine, arriving in heaven in a purple velvet suit!"

"Or like poor Bogie there, oh so sad Marquis de Sade of the dog world? In an elegant jockstrap? Don't be cruel," Artie says. "It's unbecoming."

"Stay with us, Eleanor," my mother says, glaring at Artie now. "Artie may never change. But it may be worthwhile to try to make him."

"Please stay, Eleanor," Elspa says.

But Eleanor doesn't relent. "Good night."

"C'mon, give me a hint," Artie says. "Who's coming?"

"Good night," Eleanor says, limp-marching to the door. Her limp doesn't seem like a weakness, but a force that propels her forward, as if her injured leg gives her more momentum. "We'll see if you're still all smiles when this is over, Artie Shoreman. We shall see." And she slams the door.

"She always was uptight like that," Artie says.

I'm fuming now, too, however. This was supposed to feel good. This was supposed to help me even the score. What if these women are coming to adore him? What if they aren't going to teach him any lessons? What then? I realize all at once that this entire plan is built on assumptions and that I could be completely wrong. "Your son is coming, too," I say to Artie. "But I had to bribe him. You'll have to explain yourself to him." I say this with a hateful tone.

This part of the plan *does* startle Artie—the news and maybe my tone as well. He looks nervous suddenly. "John?"

"I found his name in your book, in the B's, just like you said. Bessom."

"I'll have to take a bath in the morning. This will require a shave, too." He's feeling the hairs on his neck, talking to himself more than to the three of us. "Are you sure?" he asks, and his face goes soft. His eyes are wet, shimmering, and for the first time in a long time, he reminds me of the man I first fell in love with—love struck, anxious, almost shy—and this makes me ache for him. I miss that uncomplicated version of Artie with a sharp desperation that catches me off guard.

"John Bessom," he says, "after all of these years. My son."

Chapter Eighteen

Occasionally, in Life, Myths Become Real— Be Thankful for It

I remember a boyfriend I once had, Jimmy Prather, who mythologized his exes. There was the glamorous one who left him to go to Hollywood, the archfeminist who went into politics, the insane one who made him run naked through the snow to prove his undying love for her—she went on to some ministardom right at the dawn of reality TV. There was no competing with these myths, and, worse, I could feel him mythologizing me when I was standing right there, flesh and blood, in front of him. We didn't last long. I wonder if Artie's sweethearts will be mythic. Will I be able to endure a parade of them, one after the other? After they've all gone, will I discover a psychic pattern that I fit into? Will I see myself in them?

I'm thinking about all this in the middle of the night—still not asleep. To distract myself, I turn to my own parade of sweethearts—which, by the way, is not a good idea if your aim is sleep. I open a floodgate. Jimmy Prather is only

the beginning. I shuffle through some high school boys—
a few athletes, a drummer in a bad garage band—and
college—one guy who, after the breakup, went through a
bit of a stalker phase, a lazy business major I later heard
turned into a junkie, and a guy I was desperate about who
went into the foreign service. And then the string of bad
decisions before Artie—coworkers, a few guys met in bars,
two bogus proposals, a let's-move-in-together that lasted a
record three weeks.

I've been no prize. I mean, if I were told I'd have to
confront a parade of my own sweethearts, I might have re-
acted like Artie first did—delighted to be able to see them
all again—a little segment of *This Is Your Life.* But what if
one or two (or more) had some real axes to grind? The
reason the let's-move-in-together only lasted three weeks?
I cheated on him. I know betrayal from the inside out.
Sure, I wasn't married. I hadn't taken a vow. Artie's sins
are much worse, but still, my record isn't pristine.

And then I find myself thinking of Artie—our simple
Sunday morning routine of newspapers and bagels, our
first-warm-day-of-spring celebration when we'd take off
from work and get drunk in the afternoon, the time he
took me fishing and I caught an enormous trout.

Around 5 a.m. I fall asleep with the remnants of a
guilty conscience and dream about being trapped under-
ground with a newspaper, bagels, and an angry raccoon
that's wearing my watch.

I wake up late and, still a little bleary, I shrug on jeans and
a T-shirt and walk into the kitchen to find Eleanor running
things with a little too much brusque professionalism, clipboard in hand. While I'm having breakfast—made by my

mother, who's still hovering in the kitchen—I hear the doorbell ring. Eleanor cries out, "I've got it," and rushes to the door. I can hear her ushering a woman into the living room, telling her to make herself comfortable. And then, to my astonishment, I hear her rattle off a number of questions. "Do you have any weapons? Poisons? Explosives?" I hear the woman faltering, but responding with indignant no after indignant no. And then Eleanor says that someone (I'm assuming Eleanor) will be right with her. Throughout it all, she maintains a forced gentleness in her voice, the kind reserved for gynecology office help and therapists' secretaries.

While I replay the images that flashed through my mind the night before—the raccoon, the parade of my exes in comparison to Artie's (now, in this version, some of them are armed)—my mother tells me that she's canceled the nurse for the day and that Elspa is upstairs, helping Artie get ready. My mother is scrubbing the pan she fried my eggs in. I can't eat the eggs. I just push them around on my plate. It's too early to feel my first pang of jealousy—Elspa taking care of Artie again—so I stop myself. *Let her get him ready for his dates,* I say to myself. But then I picture Artie slapping cologne on his cheeks, and this makes my neck itch.

Eleanor reappears long enough to open her cell phone, but then the doorbell rings again, and she's charging off with the clipboard. When she returns to collect a tray of coffee and Styrofoam cups and creamers and sugar packets, she says, "Our ten-thirty came early and our nine-thirty wants to be bumped." I stare at Eleanor. She picks up on it immediately. "My husband was an orthodontist. I used to run the office. This is what I do," she clarifies.

My mother and I both nod.

"And have you worked for the airlines? Security?" I ask. She's confused. "No," she says.

"I think the rundown of questions about being armed is, well, a little over the top. It has an impending strip-search vibe."

"Are you going to start confiscating their toothpaste and nail clippers?" my mother asks, enjoying this.

"I was just being precautious," Eleanor says. "God knows we've all wanted to kill him at one point or another, so . . ."

"I think we can omit the list of questions," I tell her. "You know, let's just run the risk."

"Fine by me," she says. Her cell phone rings and she quickly abandons the tray to answer.

And now everything sinks in. Two of my husband's sweethearts are sitting in my living room, waiting to visit with him, and I'm the one who brought them here—to teach him some sort of lesson before he dies? What's the etiquette? Do I introduce myself? Do I bring them the coffee tray, offer bonbons, a stick of gum?

In any case, I have to see them with my own eyes. I'm compelled to try to understand why they've decided to come and what they might have to say to Artie. And, of course, there's the unsettled matter of the pattern of sweethearts that I may or may not fit into.

The two women are sitting on the sofa, side by side, backlit by the bay window. One, an intimidatingly leggy brunette, is thumbing through a copy of *People,* as if this truly were a waiting room. Did she bring it? Has Eleanor provided magazines as a courtesy? I feel like there should be a fish tank and a little check-in area with a sliding glass window.

I can't approach them. I zip on by, up the stairs. I'll check in on Artie instead.

First off, I can smell him from the top of the stairs. Aftershave, cologne—his favorite, a muscled scent that has a hint of the great outdoors and a tennis pro. I brace myself. He's going to be all done up, and I know it. And, in fact, when I step into the room, I see it's worse than I imagined. He's propped up in bed, all the pillows at his back. His dark, shaggy hair is purposefully mussed with plenty of product. He's looking out the window, where I'm pretty sure he can only see the tops of trees. He looks wistful. Actually, maybe it's worse than that: he's practicing looking wistful.

"Is that a smoking jacket?" I ask.

He doesn't look at me. Maybe he's a little embarrassed. "It's a robe. I don't want to sit here in my pajamas."

"It looks like a smoking jacket," I tell him, and it does. It's black and shiny—maybe even velvety. Where did he get such a thing? "You could just get dressed."

"Too much effort," he says, as if he hasn't gone to tons of effort.

I realize now that Artie is nervous. He's sitting up here like a teenager who's primping before a prom, and, of course, he's accentuating his newest attribute—namely the heroic drama of a man facing death. "It's too much effort for someone who's dying, you mean? You have to look the part, right?"

"I *am* dying," he says, a little defensively. "I'm not making it up."

For a brief second, I want to believe that he is lying, that he's made up all this business about dying just so he can have a moment like this—the smoking jacket, the sweethearts. I'm wrong, of course. Artie is vain. Maybe that is his greatest weakness, his need for adoration. Did I not give him enough adoration? Could any one person have given him enough? The desire to slap him rises up inside me so quickly I'm shocked by it. "And so you want to enjoy the role, right?"

"I'm a crowd pleaser," he says, now looking at me. "I give 'em what they want. Plus, you know, not everyone gets to play this role. A person can get hit by a bus. The end. No real death scenes at all."

"I'd lose the smoking jacket," I tell him. "You look a little desperate in it—like my mother in that gold dress with all the cleavage."

"It's not a smoking jacket," he says. "It's a robe!"

"Whatever you say."

I walk out of the room and down the stairs. I'm offended that Artie wants to see all these women. I hadn't expected him to be so eager. Couldn't he have at least faked some disinterest for my sake? It isn't so much that these women may do exactly the opposite of what I'm hoping for—that they might come here and ruin everything by giving him even more adoration. The real problem is that, even now, I feel like I'm still not completely enough for Artie. His heart still isn't wholly mine.

However, the fact that Artie is nervous makes me more confident. I want retribution, a good dose of revenge. I want Artie to own up, once and for all, to the lousy way he's treated women, accept responsibility for his actions. I pause at the bottom of the stairs and then cross the hall quickly and step into my own living room, in jeans and a T-shirt, without any makeup, with my hand poised for shaking. I say, "Hi, I'm Artie's wife."

The leggy brunette drops the magazine to her lap and

stares at me blankly. The other woman is small, with a blond bob and wispy bangs. She'd been gazing toward the stairs, and I've startled her. "Oh," she says, her hand on her chest. "I didn't expect to see you."

No one meets my half-hearted attempt to shake so I shove my hand into my back pocket.

"Artie's married?" the leggy brunette says, completely shocked.

"Didn't you know that?" the blonde asks.

"How did you know that?" I ask.

"Oh," the blonde says. "The woman on the phone mentioned it."

The brunette shakes her head, and then looks me up and down. "So, then, he finally *settled* down." I don't like the way she's stressed the word *settled,* and there is an implicit *for you* that I don't care for. Suddenly I regret not dressing up, not wearing full makeup and heels. My mother would have pulled out the big guns for such an occasion. And maybe she's right. My lack of dressing up was supposed to be a statement of my confidence, as in I don't need to dress up to compete with all of you. That competition is long over and, unless you forgot, I won. But instead, I feel unpolished, vulnerable, settled for. Did Artie choose me from all these women because I represented something safe, but all the while he desired something more dangerous?

"It's nice to meet you," the blonde says, trying to make up for the awkwardness. "I'm just so sorry. I mean under these circumstances." Her eyes well up, and I'm worried about her. Is she going to give Artie hell or is she going to go in there and mourn?

"Under these circumstances?" the brunette says.

"Artie's lucky to have made it this far. Lucky he didn't get shot in bed with someone else's wife." She glances at me. "No offense," she says, but I'm not sure whether she's saying this because I'm Artie's wife or just because I'm a wife in general. "When did you and Artie get married?" she asks.

"When did you and Artie date?" I counter.

"A decade ago," she says. "But he still pisses me off."

"Artie can have that effect," the blonde says, and then adds, "I mean I'm sure he's a great husband. He was just a lousy boyfriend. I mean, if you're not his favorite."

"What's your name?" I ask the blonde.

"Spring Melanowski," she says.

"Spring?" I repeat. As in *Springbird*? I want to ask.

"I was born in April," she says. And then her eyes go teary again. "I just don't want to be surprised if he looks very, well, different," she says. "If he's too sickly. I mean, does he look, you know, like he's . . ." This display of emotions makes me think that Artie is a fresh wound. How fresh?

"Artie's a showman," I say. "I'm sure he'll perk up for you." And then because there's a slack moment in the conversation, I add, "You know Artie!"

This is a grave mistake.

The blonde nods her head nervously. And the brunette smiles at me in a way that means *I sure do.* And suddenly my chest is swarming with jealousy and more than a little embarrassment. These two women do know Artie. They know him each in their own private, intimate ways. They know him in ways I never could. All these women I now know who have pieces of Artie . . . And this Spring Melanowski's piece could have led to the destruction of my marriage. Once upon a time, I'd at least had the illusion that he was mine, wholly, but now I can't pretend.

The blonde is crying again, and this irritates the leggy brunette and, more important, me. "Look, honey, I know why I'm here," she says, and then asks the blonde, accusatorially, "Do you?"

It's a tense moment, and I wonder if the blonde is going to fall apart. Why is she here? All of these women have X's by their names. They all ended on bad terms with Artie. The blonde takes a tissue from her pocketbook. She blows her nose and flips her bangs from her eyes. The brunette and I are both waiting for her answer. Will she answer? The blonde glances at me and then at the brunette. Her voice becomes steely. "I sure as hell do know why I'm here," she says.

I didn't realize it until this moment, but I've been hunched toward the two seated women, and now I kind of rear back. I'm unsteady and, overcompensating for tipping backward, I take a step forward, banging my shin into the coffee table, where I've placed the tray. There's a clatter of spoons. I bend over, steadying myself on the table. "Fucking shit," I say.

In this moment, I realize what I've done. I've gathered the wolves. I'm sending them in to seize Artie, one by one. Does he deserve this? I look at Spring(bird?). Yes. He does. Both of these woman are self-possessed in their own ways. Artie wronged them. They deserved better. I deserved better. I wonder if I'm just sending in these women to do my own dirty work. And why don't I want to face Artie? Am I afraid I'd lose heart, cave in? But what will this fear cost me? It's possible this parade of sweethearts is as much for my sake as it is for his. Maybe I set this up, on some level, in hopes that the hurt of seeing all these women will make it easier to let him go.

"Are you okay?" the blonde asks.

"That's going to be a bruise," the brunette says.

"I'm fine," I say. "Thank you for coming. Help your-selves to some coffee."

I'm not sure how to exit gracefully. I'm not sure what I'm supposed to do next. But I don't have to ponder too long. I'm saved by a knock at the door. I've got a jump on Eleanor. I excuse myself, rushing to the door, but stop just shy of putting my hand on the knob. I feel nauseated be-cause I don't want to meet another sweetheart, another woman hauling in her *People* magazine and her own se-cret version of Artie into my living room.

But I have to answer the door. I'm standing here. What else can I do?

I open it, staring at first at the stoop, willing myself to look up.

Then I hear a man's voice. "I made it," the voice says. And there stands John Bessom. He's running a hand through his blond hair, patting it down on top, and then he tucks in the back of his shirt, and suddenly he does seem incredibly young, boyishly nervous.

"You made it," I say, filled with relief.

He glances around. "I know," he says, leaning for-ward. "I just mentioned that."

I'm disoriented. His shirt is so blue. The day is cool, the yard so green. There's a whole world out here.

"Are you going to invite me in?" he asks.

"No," I say.

And he's taken aback for a moment.

"Artie's schedule is filled." I look back over my shoulder. "Thanks again," I say to the brunette, "for coming." And then to the blond Ms. Melanowski, I say, "See you later, *Springbird.*"

Her head snaps toward me with the shocked expression of recognition—an unmistakable gesture of: *How did you know that?*

I turn to John. "Let's get out of here."

Chapter Nineteen

Where Should a Tour Begin? In the Heart

*J*ohn is driving. He has the window down. The car is gusty with warm air. I told him to head into downtown Philly, so we're zipping along Route 30. Almost everything I have to say about Artie can be found downtown—his childhood on the Southside, the hotel where he first worked as a bellhop, U Penn, where he likes to say he went to school (he confessed to me early on that he really only took a few night classes there—one in art history, another in public speaking), and the places where we met and had our first date. I'm enjoying the ride, sitting back with my head on the headrest.

"I should start talking, shouldn't I?" I say. "I mean, I'm a tour guide. I should be saying, *On your left, you'll see . . . and on your right, keep an eye out for . . .* Well, there are a lot of things I don't know about Artie—that's what I realize now." I think about the leggy brunette's smirk, the blonde's nervous nodding.

"Stick to what you know, then."

"Okay. We met at a wake, actually, in an Irish bar called, cleverly enough, The Irish Pub."

"Really?" John says. "That's a little morbid."

"A man named O'Connor had died. Artie had known him from when he was a kid, and I knew his daughter from work. The wake was beautiful. People were laughing and crying and drinking and giving grand speeches. Artie told a story, a great story about the man losing his daughter's bunny somehow and how he and Artie spent one drunken afternoon and evening trying to catch it. Artie was so full of zing. Turn here.

"I was the one who approached him. I was loaded. I gave him my card. I told him that I wanted to book him for my wake. I said, 'You give a great eulogy.' He said he was expensive, but he'd be willing to give me a deal. Turn here. It should be right around the corner."

John pulls up across the street from the bar. It's typical, humble. It doesn't have a plaque out front that reads Lucy and Artie First Met Here.

"Do you want to go in?" John asks.

"It's an Irish bar. No. You get the picture."

"I've always thought that eulogies come too late," John says. "People should get eulogies while they're still alive. It should be mandatory."

I think about this a minute. "No casket. No lines . . ."

"No embalming fluid," he adds.

"No funeral director with an assembly-line delivery."

"That can all come after. But everyone should hear the eulogies. Just the good stuff."

"You're right, I guess."

"Did they catch it?" John asks.

"Catch what?"

"The bunny."

"Oh, the bunny. Yes, they caught the bunny, and they were both so relieved and drunk that they cried. Both of them together, two grown men and this little white bunny, they just cried."

"I like that story." John pulls up to a red light. He looks in both directions. "Where to?"

Where to?

My first date with Artie: the heart.

The Walk-through Heart is exactly the way I remember it—two stories tall, enormous, red and purple plastic, etched with major arteries and veins—except bigger, fatter. Has it swelled up? We stand in line with kids and their parents. The kids are shouting, muffled inside the heart, but loud and bleating once out of it. They pull on their parents' hands, usually circling back to the line to start over.

"Artie had been to the Franklin Institute on a field trip when he was a kid, but the heart was shut down—undergoing surgery, their teacher said."

"Has the heart been here that long?"

"Since the fifties. It was supposed to be a temporary exhibit and was first made of, like, papier-mâché. But it was so popular that they kept remodeling it. That's when Artie's class came through, during some remodeling. They could see it, but couldn't go inside. That's why he brought me here on our first date." I remember he told me the story right here, waiting in this line. The kids were loud, but he stood right behind me, whispering into my ear. "Artie knew his parents wouldn't bring him back when it was opened. He knew this would be his only shot, so he let his class go on without him, lingered, tying his shoe, and then darted into the roped-off area."

"Did he go inside the heart?"

"No. I asked that, too. He was too scared. I think he just wanted to touch it, to see if it was beating. He placed his hands on it, and then pressed his ear up to it, like a doctor. But it wasn't a real heart."

It's our turn to step inside. We walk up the narrow stairs that form the main artery leading to the heart. We hear sound effects. It's beating, pounding blood. The twisting corridors are dark. Artie kissed me in here—our first kiss. I don't tell John this detail. I think of Artie touching my cheek, turning my face toward him. The pause. The kiss. But even this memory is filled with doubt now. Did he really break away from his childhood field trip to see if the heart was real? And if it did happen, how many women did Artie seduce in this heart, maybe even in the same chamber? Has my little Springbird Melanowski been here? I realize this is precisely the kind of thing I have to tell John. He doesn't know the truth about Artie, and I'm here to present it. But I can't really. Not here. Not now.

A herd of particularly rowdy kids all wearing the same blue school shirts are pushing their way around me in the right ventricle. The space is too small, too confined, for all these people. I'm ready to go. Why linger? I look back, but John isn't there. I push forward then, following the flow through the chambers and then, finally, out.

I look around again, but John's nowhere to be seen. I'm a little worried. I wonder if I've lost Artie's son. I remind myself he's a grown man—not a five-year-old.

I get back in the line, which moves swiftly this time. And when I get inside I say his name, quietly at first, but then a little louder. Again, I find myself at the spot where

Artie first kissed me—the place I always thought of as *our* first kiss. How many women have I shared this with? How is it that once someone is dishonest, everything about him is shadowed in doubt? Is the heart beating louder? Or is that my own heart, pounding in my ears?

"John!" I shout. "John Bessom!" I wish I knew his middle name. If I did, I'd use the whole damn thing.

I steady myself with one hand on the plastic interior and make my way against the flow of traffic, exiting one chamber and entering another. I'm a little breathless, standing there, searching the crowd, and then I find him and I'm flooded with relief or joy. It surprises me how strong it is. It's as if I thought for a moment that he was really lost, that we'd never see each other again.

He's down on one knee inside the heart next to a kid who's crying, his face glossed in snot. It's a little boy in a white shirt, dotted with mustard. "She'll come back," John's saying. "She said to just stay put if you got lost. So let's just stay put. This is a very big heart. It must have belonged to a very big person. Don't you think?" He looks so sure of himself with this messy lost kid, and there's something about a person who can relate to kids, isn't there? Something about a person who can see a kid as a human being, who can, almost immediately, remember what it was like to live in that world. His voice doesn't have any of that fake singsong sweetness. He's just talking, and tending to the boy, distracting him so he calms down. The boy is staring up at the heart. He's stopped crying for a moment. And I realize this is what I want for myself—to be found, to be tended to. Maybe it's what we all want. Is there much more we can ask for?

"John Bessom," I say, as if I'm saying his name for the first time.

He looks up. "We got lost," he says. "But, see," he says to the kid, "I got found by my person. You'll get found by yours."

And then the kid shouts, "Mommy!" and, for a moment, I think he's throwing himself at me. I even brace myself, but then he shoots past. A woman with her hair pulled back in a mussed ponytail catches him. He hugs her thighs. "Okay," she's saying, "it's okay now. It's okay."

John looks up at me. I can tell by his expression that my face has come apart in some way. He's a little worried, but then he smiles and reaches out his hand. "You want to hold my hand this time so I don't get lost again?"

I want to say, *Yes, yes, that's all I want right now. That's all.* I take his hand, and he leads me out of the heart.

John drops me at home, and I walk into an impromptu debriefing. Elspa, Eleanor, and my mother are all there, eating baked pita and brie, drinking wine from some glasses that Artie and I got for our wedding. Bogie has been left at home, I'm guessing.

"Three were divorcées, two widows, one single," Eleanor says, consulting more charts. "There was a very emotional attorney, a soft-spoken ex-stripper who's learning sign language, a top-heavy Russian teacher . . ."

"Does Artie speak Russian?" Elspa asks me, always looking for Artie's upside. "I didn't know that!"

I manage, "Um, I once heard him say the word *cigarietta,* which he claimed was Russian . . ."

"The Russian was a smoker," my mother says disapprovingly, and not without a hint of fear that—if I could pinpoint it—would lead me to believe she regrets having let a Communist into my house. "She spent most of the time on the front stoop, stubbing out cigarettes in a planter."

"Was he wearing that smoking jacket through all of this?" I ask.

"Smoking jacket?" Eleanor says. "No. Just his pajamas."

"Does Artie have a smoking jacket?" my mother asks, a little impressed.

"What's a smoking jacket?" Elspa says.

"It's a jacket you smoke in," my mother tries to explain.

"Well, I liked the stripper," Elspa says. "She's doing a residency in a deaf school to see if she likes it."

"And the crier. I liked her very much," my mother says. "She stayed for some tea."

"Spring Melanowski?" I ask.

"Melanowski?" Eleanor says, checking the notes on her clipboard. "Strange woman. She left before it was her turn. She mumbled something about missing another appointment."

"Really?" I say. "Good." I want to know about Artie's women and I don't. I feel like I did as a child watching a horror flick, covering my eyes, but looking through the slats of my fingers. Don't I want to know which ones he dumped, which ones dumped him? Don't I want to know details—the why and the how and the what went wrong? No. Not really. I thought I'd have more stomach for it, but I don't. All the women make me feel a little queasy. I want them to be less attractive than I am, more fragile and bitter, so I can afford the luxury of disdain, but I know, too, that this is a club that I belong to—Artie's women— so I don't want them to be too unattractive, fragile, and bitter.

"I think we shouldn't get too involved with the *individuals*. It's a cumulative effect we're after here," Eleanor says. "Let's keep our eyes on the prize. The long haul. What's really important . . ."

"Wait," I say. "Just wait a second. What about Artie? What about our prize? Does he seem repentant?"

"He's sleeping," Elspa says.

"Does he look like . . . Did he mention . . ." I'm not sure what kind of question I'm trying to ask.

"Look," Eleanor says. "This is day one. These women— even the ones who leave cigarettes in the planters, maybe especially them—they will all have an effect. I have faith in jilted women, in general."

My mother is concerned about me. Her face has bunched up, and it's one of those strange moments when you see yourself in your mother's face. It just passes through quickly, a ghost of yourself within someone else. "Lucy, tell us, how was your day with Artie's son?"

"I've scheduled him to meet with Artie tomorrow morning for half an hour," Eleanor reports, perfunctorily.

"That will make Artie happy," Elspa says, making up for the detachment in Eleanor's voice.

"Elspa has done some work on her parents," Eleanor reports to me.

"It's not easy," Elspa says.

"Tomorrow, you and Lucy will go over it," my mother says to Elspa, having forgotten her question about John Bessom. "She'll get it all just right."

"The appointments begin with Artie's son in the a.m. and then there's a woman driving in from Bethesda . . ." Eleanor forges on.

The conversation has revved up again, and I'm tired. There are too many voices. I mumble that I'm heading to bed and walk out of the room.

My mother follows me though, catching me in the hall. "Are you okay?" she asks. "Is it too much? If it's too much, we can call everything off."

"All of this . . . life is too much," I say. "Artie's dying is too much. Can you call that off?"

She smiles sadly and shakes her head.

"I'm going upstairs to watch Artie breathe," I say. I want to know that his lungs are still pushing air.

She nods and watches me walk up the stairs.

Artie's room still smells faintly of cologne. I sit in an armchair, pull my knees to my chest. I don't know who else has taken a seat here today or what those women had to say to him or what he had to say to them. I could shove him awake and tell him that I ran into Springbird, and grill him about the brunette, but I decide not to think about that now.

His face is relaxed. He's breathing softly. The smoking jacket is nowhere in sight. I think about one of his notes to me—one of the ones shoved in my bedside table. I don't remember which number it was. It read: *the way your soft lips sometimes touch and puff while you sleep.* I don't remember watching Artie sleep when we were together, but he'd watched me. He has a depth of attention that comes with his love that is keen and sharp. Does he really love me? Could he love me and still have cheated on me? At the very least, I feel like he owes me more love to make up for his betrayal. He owes me.

And then I think of John Bessom in the car outside of the bar. Everyone should hear their own eulogies—but the notes, aren't they a kind of love song? And aren't the best eulogies a kind of love song? And what in the world will I say about Artie when the time comes?

Chapter Twenty

Don't Mistake Your Lover for a Savior

Every day is different, but still they begin to blur. Each of us finds a strange rhythm. There are often women in the living room, drinking coffee from the serving tray that Eleanor has supplied—and some homemade cookies my mother hasn't been able to restrain herself from baking; she can't resist an audience.

And, my, what an audience she has!

Artie's sweethearts have no pattern—no discernible pattern, at least. They run the gamut. Some are bimboesque and boisterous. Some are refined and elegant. There's shyness, breeziness, boldness. They wear cardigans and comfortable shoes. They wear belly shirts and high-heel slingbacks.

If you look at it in terms of the cookies alone, I can put it this way: some nibble the cookies politely. Some refuse and complain about a diet. More than one has eaten as many as they can, wrapping a few extras in a napkin and stuffing them in a pocketbook.

Bogie delights in them. Even ball-less, he waddles around the room, begging for cookie bits, licking bare legs, soliciting affection. Once he humped a handbag that was long and cylindrical in shape—not unlike a female dachshund.

And I'm relieved that Springbird came early and left. Now I don't have to search for her, though, I must say, I'm tempted to ask every one of the sweethearts how they feel about elevators.

There are a few I will never forget.

MRS. DUTTON

She is elderly. I mean really ancient. Her hair is creamy, her hands are knotted, and her lace-up shoes have thick rubber soles. But beneath the arthritic ointment, there's a hint of dangerous perfume.

I ask her a few questions. "So, how do you know Artie?"

"I was his high school algebra teacher," she says, introducing herself in a schoolteacherly way: "My name is Mrs. Dutton." I expect her to stand up and write it in large swirling letters on a chalkboard.

"Ah," I say. "Did you know him well?"

She smiles, patiently, and nods.

"Did you keep up with him over the years?"

"Not so much," she says. "My husband didn't care for him."

I assume the husband may be the reason why Mrs. Dutton's name has an X by it. Husbands can sometimes put a real strain on a romance. "I see," I say.

"I don't think you quite do," she says. "But that's okay." She pats my knee and gives me a wink.

MARZIE HOLDING THE MOTORCYCLE HELMET

Shortly after Mrs. Dutton leaves, a lesbian arrives. My mother is the one to answer the door, and she walks into the kitchen and whispers to Eleanor and me, "The next woman to see Artie is, well, she's a little *butch*. She's carrying a *motorcycle helmet*. Her man's shirt doesn't have any *sleeves*." My mother is so distressed, she has to wash her hands and sit down for a while.

I volunteer to bring out the cookies.

The woman is very friendly. Her name is Marzie. She's ridden in from Jersey. Artie hasn't seen her in a while. "I'm looking forward to surprising him," she tells me.

"Well, he's probably seen your name on the list," I tell her. "He's expecting you, I'm sure."

"I don't think he's really expecting *me,* though," she says with a laugh. "When I was dating Artie, I didn't know who I was. But he made me see the light."

"Artie helped you figure out who you really are?" I asked. "Do you mind me asking how, exactly, he did that?"

"How can I put this?" Marzie says, helping herself to cookies. "He set himself up as the ultimate man, you know what I mean?"

I nod. Artie charms himself sometimes.

"And when he really didn't do it for me, well, I figured that if the ultimate man isn't doing it for me, maybe men in general won't. Ever."

"Or maybe he overplayed his hand?" I say. "I mean, ultimate? Who's the ultimate?"

"It's all self-advertising, I guess. But that's all I had to go on. And he did nothing for me—you know, in bed. Nothing! At all!" Marzie reports all of this very happily. "So, I figured a few things out."

"If you don't mind," I tell Marzie, "I'd really like you to share all of that with Artie. I mean, it's really important for him to know, you know, how he did nothing for you, in bed . . . all of that." This is such a beautiful turn of events that I can barely contain myself. Artie has to hear about his sexual failings, how he turned a woman not only away from himself, but from all men. I couldn't have dreamed up a better scenario.

"Okay," she says. "My pleasure! I owe him, you know."

"Well, now's the time to really pay him back!"

JUNIOR

Later that same afternoon, a woman about my age shows up at the door. She looks like she's left a nine-to-five office job a little early. I introduce myself as Artie's wife. She grabs my hand and says, "I'm so sorry." But I'm not sure if she's sorry that Artie's dying or that I'm his wife or for being his lover.

"Take a seat," I tell her. "Have a cookie." I direct her to the living room, where another woman is already waiting, filing her nails. This woman is closer to Artie's age, maybe even a few years older.

When the apologetic nine-to-fiver steps into the living room and sees the older woman, she stops dead. "What in the hell are *you* doing here?"

The older woman stands, letting her pocketbook fall from her lap to the floor. "Oh, honey," she says. "Let me just explain."

"No!" the nine-to-fiver screams. "No, no, no! This is just so like you! I thought all of this was Artie's fault, but I guess not! Why have you always been so jealous of me! Why can't you just live your own life! Like a normal mother!"

I stand there, completely frozen to the spot.

The nine-to-fiver turns around swiftly and slams out the front door.

The older woman bends down to collect the things that have fallen out of her pocketbook. "What can I say?" She looks up at me and takes a seat. "She always was a very dramatic child." She shakes her head wearily. "And," she adds, "it really is mostly Artie's fault."

I'm not so sure, this time around.

THE NUN

Eleanor enjoys taking a position at the bottom of the stairs listening to the louder, more heated conversations. Sometimes she disappears upstairs and is stationed, less subtly, in the hallway. She jots things down from time to time, but I'm not sure what exactly. More than once I've heard her mutter curse words aimed at Artie.

Occasionally a woman will start yelling up there, her voice ringing throughout the house. There was a redhead who was so passionate that we all gathered.

She shouted, "I was a nun when I met you!"

Artie replied, "You were playing a nun in a dog-and-pony version of *The Sound of Music*. That's not the same thing!"

There was a steely silence, and then the woman said, "How *dare* you. That was an Actors' Equity production."

WOMAN BEARING CASSEROLE DISH

Eleanor is the one to invite her in. I'm in the kitchen, not paying any attention. I don't even look up from some spreadsheets that Lindsay faxed to the house. But later I hear the part of the story that I wasn't present for. It went like this.

The visitor is rosy yet wearing just the right amount of concern on her face for the occasion of an impending death. She hands Eleanor the foil-wrapped lasagna.

"I went easy on the spices. I didn't know what kind of effect they'd have, you know." She glances at the women gathered in the living room, flipping through magazines.

"Well, this is unnecessary," Eleanor says.

"It's the least I could do," the woman says. "I was feeling quite useless."

"Okay, then. What's your name?"

"Jamie Petrie. I live up the street."

"Artie," Eleanor says, under her breath. "Well, I guess I wouldn't put anything past him at this point."

"Excuse me?" the woman says.

"I don't remember your name on the list," Eleanor says.

"What list?"

"Why don't you take a seat?"

"Is Lucy here? I'd like to see her."

Eleanor stares at the woman. "Lucy," she says. "We'll see. Just take a seat."

The woman moves toward Eleanor. "Who are all of these women?" she whispers.

"Artie's other sweethearts. You think you were the only one?"

"The only one?" The woman stiffens. "I'm a Party Candle representative!" she says, as if this explains everything.

"Wait one moment, please," Eleanor says, then she walks into the kitchen. She says to me, "Someone's trying to weasel her way in with a lasagna and no appointment. She also seems to want to talk to you."

"To me?" I say.

"Yes."

"I don't want to talk to any of them. Too much information. You know?"

"Well, this one may be of interest. She says she's a neighbor. A candle representative? What in the hell is that?"

I pause. My first thought is that I despise Artie Shoreman. A true and vivid hatred rises up inside me. Did he have an affair with one of our neighbors? My second thought is: a neighbor? No. Artie confessed to everything. He confessed to too much. A neighbor with a casserole? A candle representative?

"Oh no!" I say. "What did you tell her? No, no, no." I walk quickly to the living room and there is Jamie Petrie, my neighbor. The consummate Party Candle representative, she has taken this moment to hand out her business card to all the women in the living room. I've never liked Jamie Petrie, I can honestly say. She's overbearing. She brims too much with joy over things like her new line of autumnal scents—everything from amaretto to apple cider! Every time I see her she asks me to call her with *any of my scented-candle needs!* I've never had a scented-candle need.

"Please call me if you ever want to set up a party!" she's telling the women, who are staring at her in complete confusion.

"Jamie!" I say. "So good to see you! Thank you so much for coming by!"

"My pleasure," she says. "I was so worried. Here," she says, pulling a little white box with a purple ribbon out of her handbag. "It's lavender-scented. Great for healing."

"Thank you."

"Well, that's proof that there's a scented candle for *every* occasion!"

"Even death," I say.

"That's right!" She ignores the awkwardness and seizes the chance to make a sales pitch. She glances around the room of prospective clients. "I'm so glad that I chose this moment to show up. I always enjoy the opportunity to get together with women. It's important that we take time for each other and ourselves!"

"So true," I say. "Cookie?"

DENIAL, BARGAINING, AND, FINALLY, ELEANOR'S TAKE ON ALL OF THIS

Another woman walks down the stairs and makes her way gracefully to the front door. She stops short and then turns to the other women. "He denied cheating on me. Can you believe it? He said he just didn't remember it that way." She stares at the women. "Good luck to all of you." And she leaves.

Another woman, later that day, reports on the way out that Artie had tried to barter. " 'What would it take for you to forget what an asshole I was? What would I have to do?' The woman grabs Eleanor's elbow. "I loved it," she says. " 'There's nothing you can do,' I said. And that was that."

Eleanor seems to relish this bit of information. She jots furiously on her clipboard and ushers the woman out. On her way back through the hallway, I stop her. "What are you writing down?" I ask.

"Not much," she says prudishly.

"You keep your clipboard pretty close to your chest," I say. "But it's only fair to share your information. What's all the scribbling?"

"Little insights, I suppose."

"Like what?"

She thinks for a moment, as if trying to decide whether or not to let me in. "Okay," she relents. "Artie is moving through the seven stages of grief."

"He is? Toward accepting his death?"

She looks at me wide-eyed, as if scandalized by my naivete. "Toward accepting his infidelity! Toward accepting the bastard he is!"

"Oh. I thought maybe he was accepting his own death."

"Well, that may be happening, too. But I can't chart that. What I do know is that he has denied cheating on that one woman, then he tried to bargain his way around it. He's been angry—you know, with that actress especially. Eventually he'll despair, and then accept."

"Do we want him to accept himself?" I don't want Artie to embrace his cheating self. That's for sure.

"Not the way he is," she says. "But accept what he's done, to become someone new."

"And you're charting all of this?" I ask, skeptical. How can you chart the inner workings of Artie's conscience?

She looks at her clipboard then presses it against her chest. "Yes," she says. "I am."

Chapter Twenty-one

ॐ

Eavesdropping Is an Undervalued Life Skill

John Bessom has become a permanent fixture. He's still a little nervous in the house. There's something left over from his childhood, I guess, some desire to please his father. He flattens his shirt as if he's worried it's wrinkled. He puts his hands in his pockets, but in a way that makes you think he's just trying to look more at ease. When he sits down, waiting for one of the sweethearts to finish up, he jiggles his knees. It's touching, actually, poignant. After all these years, he's still invested, and despite all his arguments to the contrary, there is still something between Artie and him—something unfinished, something he wants and is now trying to sort out.

He and Artie hole up in the bedroom to talk each afternoon. But the first time he showed up for an appointment with Artie, I was stuck on the phone with Lindsay. She still calls, but is no longer panicked. She asks for advice. The small promotion and the nice jump in pay have given her confidence. She throws out offhanded, ballsy ideas. She doesn't sound like she's always in the middle of a full sprint.

I could hear John in the hallway. He was talking to Eleanor, who has maintained her professional facade and keeps everything moving with incredible punctuality. Lindsay was prattling a little.

"You're a pro," I said, trying to cut her short. "You've got it down." I could hear John and Eleanor on the stairs, and I needed to get off the phone. I had to eavesdrop; that's the awful truth.

But Lindsay was up on the SEC rulings and was briefing me, like a pro.

I was impressed. "That's great," I told her. "Can you write all of that out? I'll have to break it down for our clients."

Finally, I got off the phone, quickly passed a woman in the living room wrapping cookies in a napkin, and tiptoed upstairs. There I found Eleanor dusting a top ledge of the door frame across the hall from the bedroom and Elspa, who wasn't even faking a reason to be there, sitting cross-legged next to the door. My mother was out that morning, talking to a funeral director—she doesn't bother me with these difficult details. If she weren't otherwise engaged, she would have been there, too. Eleanor and Elspa looked at me, caught.

I shook my head and whispered, "Too many of us. It's too obvious. Go on downstairs. I'll report back."

They were both obviously disappointed. Elspa picked herself up off the floor and slumped down the hall. Eleanor handed me her clipboard, pencil clamped to it. "Take notes," she said.

Once they were gone, I put my ear to the door. I'd already missed a good bit, which I blame on Lindsay. Their voices were soft, muffled, interrupted by laughter. It took me a few moments to start to understand the words.

"She lives out west now," John said.

"With a cowboy?" Artie asked.

"A rich cowboy."

"So it wasn't a bad childhood, was it?"

"I had a paper route and a dog. Sometimes she cut the crust off my sandwiches. She taught me to curse effectively and some minor-league forgery."

"Life skills," Artie said.

"That's what it was like, more or less—affection, a lot of noise."

"I learned to curse from my mother, too," Artie said. "So we have that in common."

There was a lull, and then Artie said, "I wanted to be there all along. Did she tell you that? I wanted to be a part of your life, but she wouldn't have it."

I wondered if John would tell him what he'd told me, that old line about how there was nothing between him and Artie now. It seemed like something John had told himself to survive, a strange mantra that I couldn't understand. I closed my eyes, held my breath, knowing that Artie needed to hear something else, a promise of some sort.

"But did you really *try*?" John asked.

"She told me that you hated me. She told me that I'd only mess things up and confuse you."

"I was plenty confused," John said. "It doesn't matter now anyway."

"I was there, though, anyway."

"What?" John asked.

"I saw you in that play about the princess on all of those mattresses."

"In eighth grade?"

"And I saw a lot of your ball games. That one you lost in extra innings because of that bobble by the shortstop. That tournament."

"You were there?"

"And at graduation, too. I was watching from the edges of things—last row of the bleachers, back of the gym. Your mother saw me once, I think, but she didn't confront me. She just let me sit there." More secrets from Artie—but these seem humble and sweet.

"Well, I wanted you to be a part of my life," John said. "So we have that in common, too." It struck me as one of the most tender things I'd ever heard. I didn't know if it was true or not, but it sounded true.

That was all I needed to hear. I realized I hadn't quite trusted John to be gentle with Artie, but now I did. They'd had a relationship all these years even though John didn't know it. He seemed to understand that this meeting was monumental for Artie. Now I knew there was a lot at stake for John, too. Maybe he didn't quite believe his own mantra that there was nothing between him and Artie now. Maybe he'd told Artie the truth. In any case, I suddenly felt guilty. This was their relationship to invent. I slipped away, giving them their privacy.

One of the problems with eavesdropping is that you can't unhear what you've heard. So I find myself wanting to ask John questions about his childhood. I want to know if he was angry at Artie all those years. I want to know more about his mother and to talk to him about that edge in his voice. I want to know if something's changed now that he's heard Artie was there, skirting around the boundaries of his childhood. Has he been forced to reimagine every-thing? What does that feel like? I wonder, if I'd found out something like this about my own father, how would it change me now? I'm a little jealous of John, that he's got-ten the chance to see his father differently. I'll never have that chance.

But we don't talk about any of these things while we're on what John calls "the Tour d'Artie." We take drives around Philly together. Now that Artie has told John some things about his childhood, John asks that we make certain stops. We've driven by Artie's childhood home, some of his schools, and one day we end up at the hotel where he worked as a bellhop. The hotel is still intact, sur-viving with some old-world charm, some gold plating, heavy ornate rotating doors, and an overdressed doorman on hand.

"It was a taste of the rich life," I tell John. "He worked this job so that he could be around the wealthy, get a feel for their lives. Well, more than that. He wanted to learn their gestures, their accents, the way they'd fold their tips and slip them into his hand. He was supposed to be saving his money for college, but he spent it on tennis lessons and golf. The rich sports.

"And it paid off," John says, his broad hand jiggling the gearshift.

"Yep," I say.

"This is where he met my mother, you know."

This is the first time John's ever revealed anything from his side. "No, I didn't know that."

"I thought you did."

"What was she like back then?" I ask.

"I don't know. Like she is now but younger, maybe a little less wily, but I doubt it. She was learning to fake things, too." John rattles the gearshift into neutral. "Did you like that about Artie?"

"What?" I ask.

"That he was rich." John looks at me directly. His eyebrows sometimes give the impression that he's wounded. They pinch up in the middle, slanting down sadly.

"No," I say. "In all honesty, I liked that he came from nothing. The money made things harder, in a way."

"In what way?" he asks.

I'm not sure. I haven't ever put words to it. I guess the money separated us. I didn't want him to think I was glomming on to it. I made plenty myself. So it became an area in which we went our own ways. It allowed Artie his freedom, too, and that turned out to be more than he could handle. If we'd had joint accounts, wouldn't I have noticed the expenditures on his sweethearts? Hotel rooms? Dinners at restaurants I'd never been to? But all this is sidestepping the issue. It's not getting at the heart of the matter. "I guess this is where he learned to fake being rich. He learned the art of faking." I can feel my eyes fill with tears. I look out the window. I want to tell John that this could be the origin of Artie's betrayal. If he hadn't learned to fake being rich, could he have faked our marriage so well, his vows?

"Oh," John says. And I can tell he's starting to catch on that there's a lot riding below the surface between Artie and me. "You know what we need?"

"What?" I ask, pressing the tears from my eyes.

"A cheesesteak distraction. An ancient invention, the cheesesteak holds great powers. Incas used it as a form of anesthesia for laboring women. Buddha used it as a focus for meditation. It's what Egyptians ate while designing the pyramids. What do you think?"

"Two blocks up on the left. A great place. They let you order extra grease."

"So it's a holy place," he says, putting the car in drive.

"A shrine, really, to grease."

"Complete with a patron saint of extra grease?"

"Of course," I say, noticing that when he says something funny, he jiggles one of his knees like a restless schoolboy.

"Saint Al?" he says.

"Did you go to Catholic school or something?"

"It was a great place to meet Catholic girls."

For a quick moment, while he turns the wheel, hand-over-hand, I imagine what it would be like to have been one of those Catholic girls—real or not. I imagine what it would be like to kiss him in a cramped backseat or in the blustery wind of a high school football game. I wonder what he was like back then. Was he too tall, too skinny, all arms and legs? Did he have perfect hair? Wear a jean jacket? I know this is wrong. I shouldn't let myself think this way. What kind of person would think this way about her husband's estranged son? What would Freud say?

John pulls up in front of the sub shop. "The holy land," he says. "Do we have to go to confession first?"

And what would I confess? I don't want to dwell on it. "Let's skip confession, assume guilt, say our three Hail Marys later," I say.

Chapter Twenty-two

Should We Feel Oh-So-Sorry for the Generation of Confused Men?

I spend part of each afternoon with Elspa. We've been trying to create a plan to get Rose back. I've come to think of Elspa as articulate, full of wise perceptions that catch me off guard. But when it comes to her parents, she shuts down. She hems and haws. She's vague. She talks in clichés about tough love.

She sits on the bed in the guest room, fiddling with the zipper on her sweatshirt or the spiral of her notebook, and I pace, asking questions as gently as I can, but get nowhere.

I know that her parents live in Baltimore. She describes them in harsh terms—her mother was "gruff and distant," her father was "mostly just not around." She's also given me abbreviated descriptions of crack houses and her drug connections. She's written a lot in her journal, but she doesn't want me to read it. "I'm a terrible writer. It's all so clumsy. I'd be embarrassed." But she also refuses to paraphrase it.

The afternoon that ends up being our last spent with me as social worker/therapist goes like this.

"You told me before that you never signed anything. What's the custody arrangement?"

"It's all informal. There weren't ever any lawyers. Lawyers would only make my parents uncomfortable."

"That's good," I tell her. "No lawyers—that's a good thing." And then I pause. "But it would also help if I knew them a little better before we ask for your daughter back."

She nods, but says nothing.

"Don't you have any specific memories? Any at all? What's wrong with you?" I snap. I've been so full of memories these days in my role as tour guide that I just can't imagine how she can't find one—just one—to offer me. Until now I've always thought I was pretty good at drawing things out of people, but Elspa refuses to be drawn out.

She's silent as she stares out the window for a minute, maybe two, and when she turns back to me, she's crying. And I know that she has memories, of course. She's choking on them, drowning in them. I sit down next to her.

"Let's just go," I tell her. "You can call them and tell them you want to come for a visit. Maybe the ride down will make you able to help me help you. We'll do one of those road trip things. Can you call them up?"

She nods.

"And we'll just have to do our best," I say.

She nods.

"Okay then," I say. "We have a plan. It's not much of a plan, but it exists." I stand up and cross the room. My hand is on the knob when she stops me.

"Wait," she says.

"What is it?"

"Is it okay if we do this soon? I mean, sooner rather than later. I can't hold off. It's too much. What if it doesn't work? I have to know . . ."

"Okay," I say. "Okay. Call your folks. See when we can come."

She sighs, wipes her eyes with her forefingers and her nose with the back of her hand. "I will. I think I'm ready." She looks at me. "I'm ready."

When I walk out of the room, I head to the dim kitchen. I don't turn on a light. *Am I ready?* I ask myself. *Am I ready for any of this?* I feel like I'm in over my head. I need something sweet and comforting. I open the fridge and stare inside. Am I going to help Elspa get her daughter back? Who is Elspa? Have I been taking my husband's son on a tour of his father's life because I want him to know the man before he dies? Or am I doing it for myself now? Wasn't I just fantasizing about him in a jean jacket at a high school football game?

The fridge offers only a few light yogurts. They won't do the trick. I open the freezer and pull out the heavy artillery—triple-chocolate Häagen-Dazs. I put two pints down on the counter.

I turn around and there's my mother, sitting in the almost-dark, a bowl of ice cream in front of her.

"You, too?" she asks. Her makeup has sagged a bit and makes her look older than she is.

"Yep. Nothing's easy right now."

"It's like that sometimes," she says, delicately eating her ice cream. She has always been a dainty eater, never overloading a spoon, always pursing her lips. "Life comes at you in waves. How's Elspa?"

"She's ready. I think," I tell her vaguely. I start spooning up the ice cream—a few scoops of each. "Did you teach me this?"

"I taught you everything."

"Some things I chose not to learn, though."

"Really? You think?"

"I don't think. I know," I tell her.

"We're not so different."

I sit down across from her and sigh. "Let's not have this discussion."

"Well," she says. "There is one marked difference."

"What's that?"

"You're more generous than I am."

"I don't think so. I mean, you would have forgiven Artie already. That's a form of generosity, one I can't quite muster."

"Yes, but here's the secret. I would have forgiven Artie because it's easier."

"Easier? You're crazy."

"Easier in the long run," she says. "A kind of giving in to it all. Also, I have a huge advantage over you. I was born in *my* era where we expected men to be weak, to cheat. We expected that we would have to forgive them for this. We're lucky that way."

"That doesn't seem very lucky."

"You women today," my mother says. "You have high expectations. You want a partner—an equal. My generation, well, we knew that men could never be our equals. In the ways it matters most, we're stronger. Go to any nursing home. Who's there? Women. Almost always women. Why?"

"Well, war, for one."

"War, okay, I'll give you war. But, frankly, it's women because women know how to survive. It's what we do. We have more inner strength, and all those years that men thought they were superior, it wasn't true. It was something we allowed them to believe, because they're weak. And then women's lib came along—and don't get me wrong, I love women's lib—but they messed up the whole charade."

"It was a bad charade," I tell her.

"It had its bad sides, I know. And, Artie, well, he's the generation between us. That confused generation of men for whom nothing they'd learned in their childhood applied anymore. They suddenly had to acquire skills they'd never practiced. Listening. Intuition. Tenderness. Patience with shopping, an interest in home decor. Sad to see them caught in the crosshairs, isn't it?"

"I don't feel sorry for them."

"What I'm saying is simple. We didn't expect much of men, so it was easier when they failed us. And it was easier to forgive them."

"But they don't really deserve to be forgiven. Not always. Not my father."

"Your father," she says, raising her spoon in the air as if poised to make a crucial point. "He was who he was. Who couldn't forgive him for that?"

"I haven't," I tell her. "I still blame him for leaving us."

She pauses then. She leans toward me. "Make sure," she says, "make very sure that you're blaming the right man for the right crime."

"What does that mean?"

"You know what it means."

"No, I don't."

"Guilt is nontransferable. You can't make one man pay for the accumulated crimes of another," she says, scraping her bowl to get the swirls of triple-chocolate. "I hear they do that in China, but this is America."

"In China?"

"Yes, China." She picks up her bowl, walks to the sink. "In China, a son inherits his father's crimes. It's true! And it's another reason why I like being an American. Everyone gets a fair shake," she says, rinsing her bowl. "You should take some lessons from my generation. And try not to confuse fathers and sons." She stops in the doorway. "I'm heading home for the night." She claps her hands and from one of the corners of the room, Bogie comes skidding toward her. Lifting him up, she points to the light switch. "You want this on?"

I'm stuck on the phrase "try not to confuse fathers and sons." Is she trying to tell me something? That's another thing about her generation of women—they say things without saying them. They speak inside their words. There's a language hidden in their language. Does she wonder what my afternoons with John Bessom are like? Is she suspicious? My mother has always been suspicious of men and women being alone together. Maybe this, too, is generational. "No," I tell her. "Leave the light off. I don't mind being in the dark a little.

"See, neither do I. We *are* so much alike!"

Chapter Twenty-three

If There Is a Generation of Confused Men, Is There a
Generation of Confused Women? Are You Part of It?

A few days later, I take John to the spot where Artie proposed on the Schuylkill River. It's the natural progression of the Tour d'Artie, but I feel a little uneasy. I'm still haunted by my mother's comment, "try not to confuse fathers and sons," but even more so by the comment that crimes are nontransferable. What did she mean by that one? I could ask her, of course, but I'm not up for another one of her conversations, and I'm not convinced that she would work as her own translator.

John and I watch the crew shells pacing back and forth, the rhythmic dip and sway of their oars. It's windy and warm. There's a swift breeze off the water.

I'm supposed to be relating the story of the proposal. I seem somewhat stuck, though, and I'm afraid my silence is becoming too dramatic. "I'm not sure where to start," I confess.

"What time of year was it?" he asks.

"Winter," I tell him. "The edges of the river were crusted with ice."

He can tell this is coming out a little strained. He says, "We don't have to do this right now, you know."

"Who do you think is the stronger sex—emotionally—men or women?"

"Women," he says without hesitation.

"Are you just saying that because you know you should?"

"No," he says, looking at me squarely in the eye.

I'm thinking how easy it was for my mother's generation to claim that men were stronger than women. "Are you being condescending?"

"Are these trick questions?" he asks narrowing his eyes. "How am I supposed to answer?"

"Are you part of the Generation of Confused Men?" I ask with a nervous fluttery gesture of my hands.

"Isn't every generation of men confused? Isn't that our trademark?" he says, cocking his head to one side. He's winning this argument by seemingly disarming it.

"You're just doing that thing again," I tell him.

"What thing?" he asks.

"Where you're telling me what you think I want to hear or, worse, what you think I *need* to hear."

He pauses as if searching his motives. "I really didn't know that there was such a thing as the Generation of Confused Men. Was it written up in *The New York Times Magazine* or something?"

"My mother made it up."

"Oh, right. Okay then." He clears his throat. "I may be part of the Generation of Confused Men," he says sincerely. "I am confused, most of the time, and I find that women don't help clarify things. Is that a straight enough answer?"

I nod. "It wasn't a fair question."

"But, hey, look, your mother should write up an article for *The New York Times Magazine*. She's got a catchphrase. That's all you need these days."

"I'll let her know." I turn away from the river and look at John. "We're here. This is a spot on the Tour d'Artie. Ask me another question."

"Not about who's stronger, men or women? Not a Battle of the Sexes stumper?"

"No, not one of those."

"Okay," he says. He shoves his hands into his pockets and looks down at his feet, then back at me. "Was Artie's proposal rehearsed or spontaneous?"

I know this should all be very emotional for me in terms of Artie and our past. And it is, but not in the way I expected. Somehow telling John all about Artie is a relief, something I've come to rely on. On the one hand, it seems important to John. He takes everything in. He listens to all the details of his father's life. He stares at me with rapt attention, and I feel like he is getting to know his father, that some of what I say is burrowing into his heart and taking root. And, on the other hand, I feel like I'm handing it over to someone—not like handing over a burden of memory, though after each visit I feel lighter. It's more like having someone to share this with.

"He seemed spontaneous, but Artie rehearsed important things. He climbed up from his bleak childhood by acquiring a certain smoothness. Sometimes I could see through the veneer. Sometimes I couldn't."

"When the time comes," John says, "I don't want to profess my lifelong love for someone in a calculated way. I want to be overwhelmed, compelled." He looks out over the Schuylkill, the wind rippling his shirt.

"You're right. No veneer is best. Just the truth. Artie's veneer got him in trouble, actually. He knew how to fake a moment so he did, again and again, and those moments added up to a life of petty crimes."

John looks at me, confused.

"Small crimes against the heart." I shrug. "I don't know—maybe they even ended up accumulating into some kind of felony."

"What do you mean?" John asks, but I pretend I didn't hear him and head back to the car.

We head to Artie's favorite diner, Manilla's—a run-down place in St. David. We sit in a corner booth. "Artie liked this place. It's where he came to think," I tell John.

At first he's confused. "He had all of that money and he would come here to think?"

"This is the type of place where he felt comfortable," I explain.

We order all things diner—greasy, sugary, creamy. Our fingers and lips take on a shine.

While dipping my fries in a chocolate shake, I say, "Tell me something about your life."

"I grew up the way boys do—Boy Scouts, losing at Little League, people who refused to tip me on my paper route. Not much by way of ideal role models, all information about women and love and sex dredged up from all the wrong sources. My life was typical."

I realize now how cagey he's been about his own life—past and present. There have been any number of moments when it should just naturally pop up, but now that I think about it, his life stories never have. Instead of telling a story of his own, he asks a question about Artie, about me, about Artie and me together.

I try again. Maybe he's just being modest? "Tell me a story of your own childhood."

"Like what?"

"Something," I say, "anything."

He thinks a moment. "A story from my childhood. Anything. Something. Okay . . . Well, I have this one story about a man named Jed." And he recites the lyrics to the theme song from *The Beverly Hillbillies.* I flash on Granny, Jed, Jethro, Elly May and that poor uptight banker and his austere secretary, and I wonder about the story that John's not telling me.

"I know," I say, and then I hum the part in the opening credits where they're rolling along in their old truck full of junk under all the palm trees.

"So you already know this story?" he asks, faking astonishment.

"It sounds vaguely familiar. Did you once take a three-hour tour on a tiny ship called the *Minnow*?"

"Yes, actually, and you should know that I didn't fall for Ginger. Mary Ann was the real catch all along."

"I think you can divide men into two categories—those who fall for Ginger and those who fall for Mary Ann."

"And those who fall for the Skipper," he adds. "That's a very specific type."

"True," I say. "Good point." I'm disappointed that John won't go quid pro quo. But I tell myself what matters is that he's going to stick to the plan. He's here to learn about his father's life. Why should I expect him to reveal anything about himself? That's not part of the deal. I don't press.

And how can I blame him really? I still find myself skipping over the most intimate details—like that first kiss in the Walk-through Heart. I'm not sure why. Does it feel like a betrayal to reveal too much? Or worse, I worry that I don't want John to see how soft I still am, how tender, toward Artie. And why is that? Because I'm not ready to show that softness, because I'm afraid I'll never be able to toughen up again? Or is it because I don't want John to know how much I still love Artie, and one of my greatest fears, that I'll never get over Artie? I know it's okay to think John is handsome, even charming. He is. It's a simple fact. But aren't I flirting with him (maybe in some instinctive way that's beyond my control) when I don't reveal how deep my love for Artie runs—flirting by omission?

And I also know I haven't been telling him the truth about Artie—the whole truth. He knows about Artie's betrayal by now—he's seen the Parade of Sweethearts—but he doesn't know my own story. This is a sin of omission, too.

I decide to get it over with, to come clean. I blurt, "Artie cheated on me. I left him. And then when I found out that he was so sick, I was still on the road. I'd been away for six months.

John doesn't hesitate. "I noticed that you seem set up in the guest bedroom," he says. "I figured something had happened."

"It makes things complicated," I say.

He stops, puts his elbows on the table, and leans forward, closer to me than I expect. "Human beings are complicated," he says softly, as if he's confessing to his own faults. His eyes have the beginnings of these beautiful creases, and he seems bigger at this close range—more muscular. And again I imagine him before things got so complicated. I imagine him in a jean jacket, just a high school kid, and I imagine myself then, too. What if we'd crossed paths? What if we'd known each other way back then? What would we have thought of each other? I lean back in the booth, distancing myself. I'm frustrated, frustrated that I've seen him in my mind like this again—like I've given in to some weakness.

"I think you should know this about him," I say. "You haven't settled down yet. You're, what? Thirty? And clearly you could have found someone by now and made a commitment. I mean, there have to have been women . . ." I'm stammering a bit. All of this is coming out harsher than I mean it to, but I don't stop. "I mean, you strike me as a charmer, like Artie a little in that way, and if—"

"And if what? If the nut doesn't fall far from the tree . . . What are you getting at? Maybe I just haven't found the right person. This goes under what category of the Tour d'Artie exactly?" He's annoyed.

"It's just that I want you to know his faults."

"So I don't repeat them."

I nod.

"Because I *strike you as a charmer* . . ."

I don't want to agree, but I've just said these exact words and I nod again, reluctantly. Actually, I see John as someone who might fudge receipts or shuffle funds with a little light kiting, as we auditors put it—he's not an outright thief; I don't think he'd have the stomach for it. But he's capable of fraud—of the easily rationalized variety—nonetheless.

"I'm not anything like Artie Shoreman," he says. "I mean, I don't think you know me well enough to make that kind of leap." I've insulted him. I'm sure of it. We sit there in silence for a few minutes. He takes a few more bites of a BLT and then pushes it to the side. "Do you want to talk about what's going on now? With Artie?"

"What?"

"We've stuck to the past. We've stayed true to the Tour d'Artie. But, well, what I'm saying is that things are hard for you now. If you want to talk about that, it's okay. We can veer away from the official tour. You can take off your official badge. You know, stop pointing out the monuments for a little while."

"I don't have an official badge," I say, deflecting.

"Okay," he says. "That's fine, too. We can stick to the plan." He looks around the diner and then sighs and looks at me—really looks at me. He looks at me as if he's trying to memorize my face, here, in this diner, in this moment. I have no idea what I must look like. Confused, I suppose. Is there also a Generation of Confused Women? Am I part of it?

"I know why Artie liked this place," he says, and then he picks up a napkin and dabs something off my cheek— ketchup? Milkshake? How long has it been there? "This diner is art. It just doesn't know it."

"That's the best kind of art," I say.

And he nods.

Chapter Twenty-four

Are All Men Bastards?

t's become a habit that I find myself sitting in the armchair next to Artie's bed watching him sleep every night. And tonight is no different. I walk up the stairs in the quiet house once again.

I wish I could come here during the day, like any other nicely dressed ex-sweetheart, to praise him or to scream at him. But I'm as afraid of my own anger as I am the sudden turns of love I have for Artie (and the sudden turns of weakness I have for John). It all makes me feel wildly out of control. But when Artie's sleeping, I can feel whatever I want. I can just let it wash over me. I don't have to *decide* how I feel. I don't have to *decide* what gentleness or anger Artie deserves at any one moment. I don't have to *decide* anything.

But on this night, after my day with John Bessom, my realization that I belong to the Generation of Confused Women, I stand over Artie, lying in bed, and he looks completely different. Two oxygen tubes now hang over his ears like a fake Santa mask, and two feeders are fitted under his nose. The tubes are connected to an oxygen tank on wheels purring in the corner. His head is turned toward the door, but it looks gray, slack. I want to save him from this new turn, this weakening of the body. I stumble and catch myself on the side of the bed.

He wakes up, turns, and finds me in the dark so quickly that I wonder if he knew, in his sleep, that I was there.

"You're here," he says.

And then there's a voice behind me. "Oh, Lucy, you're here!" It's Elspa. She's sitting in the armchair.

"What happened?"

"It was awful," Elspa says, looking worn out. She stands up and grabs my arm with a shaky hand.

"It wasn't awful," Artie says. "It was fine."

"Your mother left messages on your cell phone and a note on the door," Elspa says. "Did you see the note?"

I shake my head. "What happened? What went wrong?" I want to add: *while I was gone, while I left you alone.*

"This has been a long time coming," Artie says. "No surprise. All part of the process."

The process, I repeat, under my breath. The truth is that Artie will die of congestive heart failure, in the end. He has an acute heart infection caused by the Coxsackie virus. I hate these details and have tried to avoid all cold clinical medical-speak, but I know that his heart has been compromised. The heart no longer contracts as it should, and so fluids build up. They make their way to his lungs, and eventually his heart will flood his chest, his lungs, and he'll no longer be able to breathe—despite the oxygen. He's taking morphine for the pain in his chest, but this is a losing proposition. It will make him feel less pain, but it will weaken him, too. Either he will die of a stroke in the night or he will drown inside his own body. This is the truth that I cannot bear.

"It's like being Michael Jackson, with his obsession for pure air, but minus the talent and his other perversions," Artie says.

"That's not funny," I say. "Nothing's funny."

"Or like an oxygen bar." He smiles. "Pretend we're in a bar."

I nod. "A bar." I look up at Elspa.

"I'll let you two have some time together."

"Is he stable now? Is everything okay?"

"He's fine now," she says. "The nurse is downstairs, too. He has a buzzer set up." She points to a knob with a red button clipped to the pillow.

"Thanks, Elspa," I say.

She smiles and walks out of the room.

"Why don't you come up and visit me during the day?" Artie asks. "We should talk more."

I sit down in the armchair, trying to act less startled. "You're a busy man. There's always a waiting room full of visitors."

"Only because you made it this way," he says. "Are you trying to avoid me?" His tone is all Artie. There's no real weakness in his voice.

I try to play my role, too. "I think so," I say.

There's a pause.

"I hear you're going to help Elspa get Rosie back. That's a very nice thing you're doing for her."

"Did she tell you?"

"She visits me—while I'm *awake*."

I don't respond.

"She's fragile," he adds. "I hope it works."

"She's tougher than you think."

The room is quiet, but it feels a little haunted by the sweethearts who've come and gone throughout the day. "What do they say to you in here?" I ask, pulling my knees to my chest.

"It's strange," he says.

"How?"

"There is this one thing that comes up over and over. It wears different hats, but it's kind of the same thing each time." He thinks for a moment. "What do they call it? Variations on a theme?"

"What's the theme?"

"Well, if they don't completely hate me, the theme is that I tried to save them, to cure them, of something. Some heartache. And that despite my betraying them, I helped them. Their lives were better for having known me even if I made them worse for a while in the process."

"And if they hate you?"

"Well, they say I tried to fix them or change them and that I made a promise to them, and the promise is what would make their lives better. The promises made them feel, well, safe, for example. And when I failed them or betrayed them, they ended up with two problems instead of one, or I made the one problem worse. It's always complicated."

"You made the problem worse how?"

"You know."

"Worse how? I don't know."

"Well, I didn't exactly help anyone get over their belief that no man can be trusted. There was a variation on that theme: all men are bastards. If you taped all the women, you could play it as a chorus."

I stand up before I even know it. "And is that what

you thought when you married me? That there was something wrong with me? That I could be some project for you—a lifelong one? That you could save me?"

The room goes completely silent, aside from the oxygen tank. I don't move and neither does he. I can barely see his face in the dim light. "No," he says, his voice cracking as if he's shouting, but he's speaking in barely a whisper. "I thought that maybe you could be the one to save me."

I'm not sure what to say to this. It breaks my heart, but hardens it, too. I never signed up to save Artie Shoreman from himself. He never told me he needed saving. It seems unfair to throw this at me now—after the fact. "How could I save you when you were making a mockery of our marriage? Haven't you given me good cause to really believe that all men are bastards?"

"I have. I know. I'm sorry . . . I just want to—"

I raise up one hand. "Stop," I say. "Don't." I sink into the armchair, cover my face with my hands, and take a moment to regain my composure.

"When are you going to get Elspa's daughter? Soon, I hear."

"I can't go away now." I sit up.

"You have to."

"No, I don't. I wasn't here when you needed me. I'm supposed to be here."

"I know you better than you think," he whispers.

"What do you mean?"

"I know how your brain works. From a bad situation, you want to make something good. You want to make something that will last. That's why you want to help Elspa. Am I right?" He pauses only a moment. "Don't tell me. I know I'm right. It's that thing inside of you that got my son here." He smiles. "I'm right. I know I am."

"Elspa has waited this long. She can wait a little longer," I tell him, refusing to give him credit for reading me so closely. I wonder what else he knows about me. Does he know things that I don't?

But then his voice goes rigid. "No," he says, almost as if he's afraid of something. "No."

"What? No what?"

He lets his face tilt toward me. "It means too much to her. It means too much to you. Your way is the right way. Make something good from something bad. Turn the thing with the ending into the thing that will last."

"Okay," I tell him. He looks like he might cry.

"Promise me," he says.

"I promise."

"Go and get some real sleep," he says.

"I don't think I should . . ."

"I'm a man on my deathbed. That carries some weight. Go. Get some sleep. You're weary."

I am weary. I stand up unsteadily and move to the door.

"Next time you come in at night, wake me up," he says. "First thing . . . please."

"I'll try to."

"Thanks for bringing me my son," he says. "I'll never be able to repay you for that."

And, once again, there is an enormous shift. Artie is indebted to me? Artie *is* indebted to me. I can't bear to say *You're welcome.* I'm afraid I'll start to cry and that once I start, I won't be able to stop. I slip out of the room, down the hall, down the stairs. I pause for a moment in the hallway, but suddenly it doesn't feel like my hallway. It doesn't feel like my house. I grab my car keys and walk out the front door. I turn and see the note that my mother has written me, taped to the door. I don't read it. I don't take it down. I walk quickly to my car. The night is cool. By the time I've pulled out of the driveway, I am crying, and I was right, I can't seem to stop.

Chapter Twenty-five

The Ability to Pretend Is a Life Skill

I'm standing at the front door of Bessom's Bedding Boutique. I can see John through the plate glass storefront windows—the jutting angle of his shoulders as he sleeps in one of the showroom beds. I knock on the door, watch him rustle, sit up, rub his head. When he sees me there on the other side of the door, he rears for a moment. I've frightened him. But then it registers that it's me. He stands up quickly and rushes down the aisle, works the series of locks, and opens the door.

"You scared me. I thought you were a polite burglar," he says, but then quickly he sees that my face is red and wet with tears. "What is it?" he asks. "What's wrong?"

"We've got this all wrong," I say in jagged breaths. "He's dying. He's dying *now.*"

John reaches out and holds me—my arms are folded to my chest. He doesn't say anything. He smells like fresh sheets and sleep. He leads me into the store and sits me down on a bunk-bed display with a baseball motif.

"I can tell you about the past as much as you want, but

it doesn't matter," I say. "It doesn't matter because he's dying now, and when he's gone, it'll all be gone. I don't want it to all be gone."

He still has his arm around me. He rocks me a little, just a soft sway. "Tell me anyway," he says. "Tell me about the past."

I look up at him. "But it doesn't matter."

"But what if it does?"

I take a deep breath and blow it out toward the ceiling.

"Tell me one more thing."

I think for a moment. I see Artie in his tux, beaming at me from the altar. "Our wedding," I say.

"That's right," John says. "You never told me about your wedding."

"Artie started crying first and that got me going, but then I started to laugh, while crying, and he did, too." I take another breath. "And it became contagious until the whole church was filled with people laughing and crying. It was strange," I tell him, "to feel like laughing and crying all at the same time."

"It sounds like real life. Funny and tragic at the same time," John says. "Real sadness has to also include joy. Doesn't it? Someone famous said something like that once, the idea that there can't be sadness about an ending without having known real happiness along the way."

He's caught me off guard. I look up at him. He has a strong profile, but soft eyes, thick lashes.

"It's going to be okay, Lucy." He holds on to me tightly and it feels so good to be held with that kind of gentle strength. I realize how long it's been since I've had a man's arm wrapped around me like this. He kisses me on the forehead, and then his face is right there, right next to my face, still wet with tears. And I don't know how or why, but I lean in and kiss him softly on the mouth. It isn't a long kiss. It isn't heated or rapturous. But he has a wonderful mouth, and he doesn't shy away from the kiss. And although this kiss could almost pass for a peck—the kind you'd give a hostess at a cocktail party—it lingers just enough to become something else. And, I should say that it doesn't seem wrong—not in the moment, not within the kiss itself.

But then I pull away. I open my eyes and I'm calm. I know it won't last. I know I will have to deal with the consequences of this moment—the guilt that will surely follow—but right now I'm serene.

"We have to pretend we didn't kiss," I say.

"I don't like pretending."

I stand up. "But you will, for me. I need to pretend right now."

"Okay," he says. "I'll pretend, but it won't be easy."

"It wasn't a real kiss," I say, and it's almost true.

"What kiss?" John says, true to his word.

"Right," I say. "I'm going home."

"Are you okay to drive?"

"I'm fine." And I am. In fact, I'm strangely serene. I turn and walk to the door. I know that I'll go home and take my spot in the armchair, watching over Artie while he sleeps, that I might cry again, or I might not. Real sadness has to also include joy. It's all part of the bargain.

Before I head out, I ask John, "Did you wear a jean jacket in high school?"

"Yes, I did," he says. "All the time. Stonewashed denim."

"I thought so," I say. "I thought you did."

Chapter Twenty-six

At Some Point Each of Us Is Someone Else's Bad Guy

The kiss plays out in my mind like a reel of film caught in a loop, but with all its physicality. I can feel his lips on my mouth, and each time, heat starts in my chest and flares up into my cheeks. I can be washing the dishes at the sink, brushing my teeth, getting mail out of the mailbox, and then suddenly for no reason apparent to anyone but me, I'm blushing. And then there is the blush of—Artie's son? His very own son? And that's a different kind of heat in my chest, a different kind of flush. Can I look at this any other way but as punishing Artie—even if he doesn't know, even if he never knows? When I'm with Artie—even when he's asleep and I'm puttering around refolding blankets—I feel like a traitor. But I'm a traitor in the traitor's den, and so I rationalize quickly. I pretend Artie's found out and he's furious, but I just tell him in a calm (exhausted) voice, "I know how you feel."

The guilt is only part of it, of course. More pointedly, there's plenty of confusion. What did the kiss mean? Didn't it exist in a moment of kindness and sadness? Does it have to be wrapped up in all the stuff that comes with a kiss? Was it a real kiss or not? Basically, I isolate the kiss in my head, and I put it in a corner of my brain, and try to treat it like it's only a dustpan.

I make a few excuses on the phone with John in the morning attempting to avoid the Tour d'Artie. I find myself piling them on, each one less convincing than the one before. The third excuse has to do with shopping for shoes. John calls me out on it. "You're making things up. You're stalling," he says. "Are you quitting the Tour d'Artie?"

Doesn't he feel guilty? Do men lack the guilt gene? "Why do you always call him Artie?" I ask. "When are you going to call him your father?"

"You're not answering the question," John says. "You're tap-dancing."

"You're not answering *my* questions," I say. "*You're* tap-dancing." We're both tap-dancing.

"It's okay if you're quitting the tour. I just want you to know and I want you to know that I know."

"Okay," I tell him. "I know and now I know that you know."

"Okay."

"Okay, okay."

He's been coming over in the afternoons to spend time with Artie, and this afternoon is no different. I think that I've run errands long enough to avoid him, but when I walk into the house overloaded with grocery bags, I nearly walk right into his chest.

"You're here," I say.

"You missed dinner. Your mother invited me to stay." He grabs one of the bags. "Let me take this." He takes another and another until my hands are empty. I can see into the kitchen, which is bustling with women—Elspa, Eleanor, my mother.

I grab his arm. "I haven't really been avoiding you," I whisper. "I mean, I'm happy to see you. I've just been . . ."

"Avoiding me," he says. "It's okay. I get it. There's a lot going on."

He walks into the kitchen and I follow him. The women are wrapping up bowls of leftovers, doing dishes, talking all at once. He and the grocery bags are absorbed into the scene. I find myself standing in the doorway, watching all these people move around the kitchen with a certain ease—Elspa, Eleanor, my mother, John. And I should include Bogie in all this. He's found a quiet corner and flattened out on the floor, sound asleep. I don't know when the ease took over, but here it is. And even with John, since he's called me out on my excuses— twice now—I feel a certain ease, too—as much as possible with the dustpan kiss lurking in the corner of my brain.

I decide to join them. I get a wineglass out of the cupboard and pour myself a glass from the bottle that's already been uncorked.

Eleanor wants to discuss how Artie's demeanor is changing. "Do you think it's really working?" she says. "These women are sending him a message, aren't they? He's been a serial cheater. How much longer can he deny it?"

John asks, "What's your story with Artie, again? I don't know if I know it."

She waves him off. "I was just another woman to Artie. That's it. Nothing more to it."

The doctor was here earlier, reporting a slow downward spiral. My mother is still in a small dither, having spoken to the doctor, having at one point reached out and touched his hand—for no apparent reason. She is using her leftover frenetic energy to tend to us. Seeing John pull a glass from the dishwasher, she moves in and starts unloading it. "I think the doctor has a wonderful bedside manner. He's very calming."

All this business—the tending, the infatuation with the doctor—is not part of the plan I have for my mother. "You're supposed to be trying to *be your own person.* Remember?"

"Speak English, dear," she says to me. "No one knows what you're talking about when you say things like that."

"I do," Elspa says.

My mother sighs. "It's generational."

Elspa turns to John. "You tucked Artie in tonight. Was that strange? To tuck your father into bed?"

He isn't startled by the question. He says, "It was strange. I thought of him tucking me into bed many times as a kid. Imagined it."

"Interesting how things turn around in life," my mother says, and then she glances at me. "The child can become the parent at some point when you aren't paying attention."

"And the lover can become the enemy," Eleanor adds, almost under her breath.

"I'm still confused," John says, having poured himself a little Scotch, and sitting down. "When did you and Artie date?" he asks Eleanor. "Was it decades ago? Was it more recent?"

"Well, it wasn't like the situation with Elspa," she says, meaning, I suppose, that she wasn't one of the other women while Artie and I were married. It hits me that I've never even considered Eleanor as one of the women Artie cheated on me with—which isn't really fair, in a strange way. Is it because she doesn't strike me as a cheat or because she's older or, maybe even because of her leg, which is an awful thing to think? "No offense, Elspa, Lucy."

"None taken!" Elspa says, and she wholeheartedly means it. She's eating a bowl of ice cream, perched on a stool by the kitchen island, sitting cross-legged.

"None taken," I say, with a little less pep.

I walk up to my mother by the sink, deciding to get a bowl of ice cream myself. "Don't play dumb with me," I whisper, meaning *be your own person.* "You know exactly what I mean."

She looks at me a little startled and then she smiles and shrugs. "Me no speak your language!" She quacks one hand at me.

John says to Eleanor, "Have you gone in and had your heart-to-heart with Artie like the other women?"

"I wouldn't give him the satisfaction," she says gruffly, crossing her arms.

"If you did, though, what would you say?"

Everyone has stopped what they're doing. I'm holding my ice cream bowl and the Häagen-Dazs container. We've all turned to look at Eleanor. It dawns on me that I don't know the answer to any of John's questions—maybe because I never found Eleanor to be a real threat to me, which is an awful thing to even half admit to myself, but true nonetheless. Artie so clearly dislikes her. But now I wonder why she is so invested. When did her orthodontist husband die? How does she know Artie well enough to hate him so much? Honestly, I've admired her hatred of him. It's always struck me as so pure and honest—where mine is so complicated, like an enormous elaborate hedge maze.

Eleanor doesn't say anything for a moment. She glances at each of us, defensively, as if she's been accused of something. And then she says, "I was the woman—the widow—who Artie dumped when he met Lucy." She looks at me and then quickly away. She takes a seat at the breakfast nook. "So now you know."

It's quiet a moment. I'm not sure what to say. I had no idea Artie had been seeing someone when he met me. I had no idea that he'd dumped someone for me. "Eleanor," I say, "I'm so sorry."

"Sorry," John mumbles. "I didn't mean to . . ." He glances at me apologetically, and I think he may be saying sorry to me as much as to Eleanor. But just this small moment, our eyes catching, is unsettling. The kiss is there. It's stubborn. But right alongside it, there's the image of Eleanor and Artie—a couple—and oddly enough, I can see it clearly. All that fire they have for each other, now anger—once upon a time it was something else.

"It's okay," Eleanor says. "I don't blame you." She's wiping down the counter with a dish towel, and once again, I don't know who's apologizing to whom. She doesn't blame John Bessom for bringing it up? Or she doesn't blame me for stealing Artie away? "It was a long time ago. I should be over it."

"It must have been serious," my mother says, and I wish she hadn't.

"We'd talked about getting married," Eleanor says. "He called me his spitfire. He said that I was good for him. Someone his own age, who could understand him." She shrugs. "But then he changed his mind."

I'm stunned. I feel awful. It's not my fault. I know that. But, still, I'm the thief, the young thing Artie tossed her aside for. I shake my head. "Eleanor," I say again. It's all I can manage.

And then Elspa says, "This is all so good."

We turn in unison and stare at her like she's crazy.

"I mean, we're all bound together, some way or another. Like a real family. I've always wanted a family like this." And then she adds, as if this is an unexpected bonus, "And in all screwed up ways, too." She looks at us earnestly. "I think maybe each of us has wanted a real family for a long time—Artie, too."

She's right—each of us in our own way. We all have to agree. The room is quiet—a strained silence.

"I want you all to come with me and Lucy," Elspa says. "To help me get Rose back. My daughter. I want you all to come. So my family can see that I have a family."

"Are you sure?" I ask, a little panic in my voice.

Elspa says, "I know Artie can't come. But I want everyone else to. It would help give me courage. Will you all come?"

Eleanor says, "Yes, of course. I'll have to shuffle some of Artie's sweethearts, but Artie's sweethearts are used to being shuffled."

"I don't know about that. I mean, you have everything so scheduled," I say. She ignores me.

John says, "Are you sure you mean me, too?" He shoots me a sideward glance.

Elspa nods. "Yes, of course!"

"Wait," I say.

My mother smiles. "You need me, dear. Of course I'll come." She walks over to Elspa and squeezes her shoulders. "I wouldn't have it any other way."

"This might be overwhelming for you though. All of

us? Are you sure that's what you want?" I ask Elspa, hoping she'll change her mind.

"Yes," she says. She takes a spoonful of ice cream and shoves it in her mouth, smiling. "I feel much better now. Much better."

Chapter Twenty-seven

One Can Only Plan So Much. Eventually, One Must Do

*B*ut I do not feel much better. My state of mind is troubled, maybe the most troubled it's been since this whole thing began, and I can't envision this family-style road trip helping in any way. It doesn't matter how I feel, however. Elspa, infused with this new strange confidence that I don't fully comprehend, calls her parents and gets all of us invited to their weekly family Sunday brunch in Baltimore.

I walk into the kitchen early that Sunday morning only two days later, carrying my overnight bag. Hopefully we'll only spend one night—and how will that work? Will I share a room with all the ladies? Or only my mother—and Bogie, whom she's insisted on bringing along? Will we all fit into the car? That fear pops up when my mother emerges from the bathroom wearing an enormous hat, as if she's off to the horse races, and when I spot Eleanor, who's sipping coffee in the breakfast nook with an enormous suitcase and an oversized handbag sitting at her feet.

John walks into the kitchen and pours himself a cup of coffee.

"So, ladies," he says. "We're about ready?"

My mother rearranges her hat. "Of course we are."

Then Elspa enters. She's wearing what she always wears—jeans and a black T-shirt, tattoos showing. The lip ring is even a little bigger and eyeliner darker—as if she dressed up for the special occasion. I look at John. He looks at me and back at Elspa. My mother sighs and Eleanor coughs—code for *we have a problem.* No one mentioned anything to her about sprucing up for the trip to reclaim her daughter, but obviously it was something that was understood—by everyone except Elspa.

"What?" Elspa says.

I say, "We'll just be a minute."

"What?" Elspa says to me.

"You have to look the part." I take her by the hand and lead her to the spare bedroom.

Once inside, I pull out some clean-cut business casual clothes. A button-down, a cardigan, khakis.

"Khakis? Isn't that a little cruel?" Elspa asks.

"What's wrong with khakis?"

"She'll know. My mother. There's no fooling her."

I wipe off some of the eyeliner, brush down her spiky hair, give her a pair of rectangular sunglasses. I tell her to take out the lip ring. She huffs but follows orders and puts it in her pocket.

I stand back to look at my creation. "Not bad."

Elspa looks at herself in the mirror. She isn't impressed. "I look constipated."

"You look dependable. That's what we're going for here."

Moments later, we're back in the kitchen, standing in front of John, Eleanor, and my mother. But there's no moment of transformation and awe, which I realize I was expecting. My mother and Eleanor are appeased, but John's a little confused. He's staring at Elspa when he asks, "Where's Elspa?"

"She's in there," I say. "We're going to be late if we don't hurry up."

We head to the front door—Eleanor struggling with her overstuffed bags.

"I think she got eaten by the Gap," John says.

"Not funny," I say.

"Don't I look constipated?" Elspa asks.

We all move to the car quickly. Elspa takes her spot in the middle backseat, slumping a bit, but ready to go. Somehow Bogie has landed on her lap, wearing a green jockstrap today with crocheted trim on the back. Petting Bogie gives Elspa something to do. John hoists our bags into the trunk of my car. When I admitted that I had no sense of direction, he offered to drive and I've already thrown him my set of keys.

Eleanor and my mother are discussing who will take the front passenger's seat, a heated discussion that, in my mother's passive-aggressive style, never makes mention of the seating arrangements, but includes my mother elaborating on some bladder discomfort.

I'm the only one who's stalled in the yard. I'm the only one who hasn't said good-bye to Artie. I know that he wants me to go, that he's made me promise, but still I found I couldn't bear saying good-bye in person.

One of the nurses will be with him around the clock,

just in case. (And, frankly, he never liked to be alone—no surprise there.) I look up at the house and see the nurse through the window in Artie's room. I know I should have stuck my head into his bedroom to say a quick see-you-later, but I couldn't. Every time I see him, I feel like I can barely breathe. But I have to talk to him before I go. I flip open my cell phone and call the house number.

The nurse answers. "The Shoreman residence."

"I want to speak to Artie. It's me. Lucy."

"Have you even left yet?" The nurse appears at the window, looks at me, and then waves.

I wave back. "Can you put Artie on?"

I hear the nurse explaining who it is.

Artie picks up. "You couldn't leave without saying good-bye."

"Don't die in the next two days," I tell him.

"I won't. Cross my failing heart." He's at the window now, one hand drawing back the curtain. It's been so long since I've seen him out of bed. "I'm too much of an awful person to die at this point."

"Too awful?"

Have you been around lately? Have you noticed the outpouring of hate for me?"

"Did you dump Eleanor when you started seeing me?"

"I fell in love with you completely!" he says a little defensively. "That was actually a good move. I mean, it would have been worse to continue to see her, wouldn't it?"

I feel protective of Eleanor—even though I was the other woman in this case. I hate that he hurt her. I hate that his capacity to hurt her was part of his capacity to hurt me. "Let's go back to how awful you feel. I prefer that."

"Well, it's true. But I don't want to talk about it," he says. There's a long pause. "I feel pretty worthless."

I think of Eleanor's clipboard—the charting of Artie's seven stages of grief for his infidelities. "Are you feeling despair?"

The phone line is quiet. I watch Artie in the window. He covers his eyes with one hand. Is he crying? I wonder. And then there's an unmistakable sob. "I'm despairing," he says. "I'm not good at despair. It goes against my nature."

I can't look at him. I turn around and stare at the neighbor's well-trimmed hedgerow. "I think that may be good."

He clears his throat. "I know, I know," he says. "I think you may be right."

"And maybe it's better this way."

"What way?"

"Talking on the phone. I haven't done very well dealing with all of this in person. Maybe this way would work. We need to talk."

"I'll do it any way you want."

"I'll call you."

"That sounds good."

It strikes me that I'm leaving Artie again. It's different this time, but still I can't deny the fact of it and that it feels good, in a strange way, to be leaving, as if it's imprinted on my genes, the desire to leave. It is, of course. "Maybe I'm my father," I say.

"I don't think I would have married your father," Artie says. He's used to my occasionally abrupt changes in conversation.

"I'm leaving again." Maybe Artie isn't so much the Freudian version of my father, but I am. Maybe my subconscious didn't dupe me at all. "I'm leaving like my father."

"No," Artie says. "Not like your father. Because you're going to come back. Right?" There's a vulnerability in his voice that I've heard a few times since I've been home. It's new, having snuck in with the sickness.

"That's right," I tell him. "I'm coming back. Soon."

He pauses. "I love you."

"I don't know why I still love you. I guess I'm an absurdist on some level," I say, and I don't wait for a response. I'm shocked that I said that much. I snap the phone shut and walk to the car, get in, slam the door. Eleanor, my mother, and John follow suit, shutting the remaining three doors.

"Are you ready?" John asks.

For a moment, I'm disoriented. "For what?" I ask.

"To go," he says.

"We don't have to do this," Elspa says quietly. Perhaps she's having second thoughts.

"Let's go," I say. "We *need* to go."

Chapter Twenty-eight

Bribery Can Run in the Family

The trip from the outskirts of Philly to Baltimore should take two hours at the very most, but we hit traffic. Without the whir of tires, it seems like the air in the car has gone dead. John flips on the air-conditioning. I watch him surreptitiously. Does he think about the kiss? Has he wondered what it meant? Has he tried to reduce it to a dustpan in the corner of his brain?

He's the one to break the silence. "The car is full of Artie-ologists," John says. "You all should give me a crash course."

Eleanor grunts, but doesn't oppose the idea. She's won the front seat, a testament to her will and masterful ability to haggle in my mother's native tongue—the language of passive aggression. I'm sitting in the backseat with Elspa and my mother, who's been sulking.

Trying to keep things light, I put it this way—a challenge. "Okay," I say. "Let's see who can tell the best Artie story. John can judge."

"Okay," Elspa says.

"Turn up the air," my mother says, pulling off her hat and fanning her dolled-up face with it.

I go first, telling a story of Artie's great-great-great-grandfather, who came to this country as a prisoner, stole barrels of liquor, got caught, and didn't like his other option: getting hanged in England. "You come from thieving stock," I tell John.

"Thank God my mother's side is made up of Puritans," he says sarcastically.

"What is your mother like?" my mother asks, leaning forward between the seats.

"She's a character," John says with a sigh of resignation.

"What about the dog that bit him in the ass when he was a kid?" Elspa says. "Do you know that one?" she asks me.

"I do," I say. I should be over it by now, that Artie told Elspa stories, that they were close, even that they slept together. The only reason Artie would tell that story would be because of the scar. It's certain Elspa and I have both uttered the question, "How'd you get that scar?" I'm not over it, and Elspa can sense it. She catches herself. "You tell that one," she defers.

"No, it's your turn."

"That's it really. He was bit on the ass, and the dog was a terrier. It wouldn't let go. Artie spun around in circles, the dog swinging around behind him. He still has a fear of dogs because of it."

"I come from dog-spinning thieves," John says. "I'm taking mental notes."

"Eleanor?" I say, a little afraid of what story she might tell, but wanting to hear it, too. "Do you have a story?"

"Nothing anyone wants to hear," she says, fiddling with the silver clip holding back her hair.

"He needs to know the good and the bad," I say.

She pauses. "He took me dancing."

We all pause a moment. That isn't much of a story—good or bad. I look over at her, hoping there's more.

She says, "I don't dance. I've never danced." We're still waiting for more. She unfastens the silver clip as if it's been pinching her and rubs the back of her neck and goes on. "My leg, you know. I was born this way. So there weren't ever any ballet lessons. I sat through all my homecoming dances and proms. I should have danced, of course, but my mother had simply ruled it out. It never occurred to me. Artie took me dancing." She is staring out the window. Her hair is loose and full, cupping her face. "It was terrific."

"That's a beautiful story," Elspa says, and I'm glad she does, because I can't speak. The story is so simple but moving that my throat is cinched tight.

"But the beauty of it," Eleanor says, "well, that's how a beautiful moment comes to pain you later." She stiffens, draws herself up straight. "It's your turn, Joan," she says to my mother.

My mother says, without any real emotion, "I tried to bribe Artie not to marry Lucy."

"What?" I shout, swiveling sharply in my seat.

John, who's been inching along, slams on the brakes—a reaction to the news or my outburst or some actual driving issue; it's impossible to say. We all jerk forward and back again.

"Sorry, my fault," John says.

"He didn't take the bribe," my mother says, as if she's just announced delightful news.

"I can't imagine Artie taking a bribe for anything," Elspa says.

"Actually, I was married to someone very well off at the time," my mother explains, "and it was a very generous bribe as bribes go." We're all staring at her, even John, who's looking at her through the rearview mirror. My mother adds a little defensively, "This is a nice-Artie story," she says. "What are you all looking at?"

"It may go into the nice-Artie-story category, technically, but it isn't a nice-mother story," I explain, trying to be patient.

"Well," my mother says angrily, "I'm just trying to play the game. I didn't know there were such intricate rules!"

And then Eleanor starts laughing—just lightly at first—mumbling, " '. . . a very generous bribe as bribes go.' " She then becomes hysterical, her upper body shaking uncontrollably. Elspa laughs next, then John. And now my mother is smiling, like she's told a joke that people are finally getting. My mother tried to bribe Artie—*a very generous bribe, as bribes go.* Finally I'm laughing, too. The whole car is loud, rattling with laughter.

Once we're on the other side of the Delaware Memorial Bridge, traffic lightens and we're making up some lost time. This is the moment my mother announces that she has to use the bathroom. We stop at a gas station off the highway. My mother takes out her cell phone as she swishes quickly to the restrooms, carrying Bogie. "I'll just call to check in with the nurse. Make sure all's well."

Before I can tell her that I'll call, she's already started dialing. And I feel like it's for the best. I've promised Artie a real conversation. As my mother and Eleanor head off to the restrooms, I load up on all things road-trip out of habit—tubes of chips, Lucky Stripe gum, Gatorade—and when I walk back toward the car, John is manning the pump. He's sweaty and squinting. He's put on a Red Sox baseball cap that's pulled down low on his head. I look for some bit of Artie in his posture, his face, his gaze, but I only see him, one hand in his pocket, his slightly wrinkled pants, his soft way of taking the world in. His nose is a little crooked, but that only seems to make him seem more genuine.

Elspa appears beside me. She says, "He isn't Artie, you know."

I'm surprised by the comment even though there isn't a mean edge to it, and I'm trying to figure out where it's coming from. "I know," I say, a little defensively.

"You can't make him into Artie."

"I wasn't planning to. Why would you even say that?"

"No reason," Elspa says. "I've been thinking. Artie has been a father figure for me in some ways, but maybe for both of us."

"He was a bad father figure for me. Like I needed to get betrayed by my real father and then again by a father figure of my own choosing." This is the first time I've put words to this feeling—exactly one of the reasons why Artie's betrayal hurts so much and so familiarly. "My father opted for another family. Like the board game Life—he just picked up his little blue plastic self and put it in another plastic car." I'm trying to sound joke-y, but there's still some emotion in my voice, some anger underneath that surprises me. I stop myself a moment. Elspa scares me sometimes—the way she can open things up so wide.

"What did Joan do?" Elspa asks.

"She replaced him with another little blue plastic figure and then another and then another. I'm not going to repeat her mistakes."

She looks at John, wiping down the windshield with a squeegee. "Artie was a good father figure for me. John's more like—he has the wonder of a little kid, I think."

"Is that good or bad?" I ask.

"Both, I guess. Our good sides are just the flip side of our bad sides. Like you."

"Like me?" I ask.

"You were sensitive. You felt too much. That was your strength and your weakness. You loved the bird."

"What bird?" I say, irritated.

"The one you opened the window for. You loved the bird and you loved Artie for being afraid of the bird. That made him real."

"What are Artie's flip sides?"

"He loves too much. He doesn't know how not to." She walks on to the car and gets in the backseat. I'm still standing there, confounded. For some reason I want to remind her that Artie's still alive, and I'm still his wife. But this would only come across like something I'm trying to convince myself of, not her.

Eleanor and my mother waltz past me, the wind flapping Bogie's ears.

"Artie's doing fine," my mother reports.

"Are you coming?" Eleanor asks.

"What's wrong?" my mother asks me.

"Nothing," I say. I don't know whether to be angry with Elspa or not.

John is finishing up at the pump. We're all gathering around the car, but don't want to pile in yet because Elspa is in the backseat, the door open, talking on her cell phone to her parents. "Right. It'll be nice," she says. "I don't know. A little. It's important. We'll be at the Radisson. I'll call when we get close." She's hunched into the phone and then she sits back. She can't get comfortable. "Yes, like I already told you, they're clean and sober." She looks up at me and rolls her eyes, but then smiles at me softly. Her eyes get a little teary. Her voice is different on the phone talking to her family, though. Smaller, more unsure and childlike. "They're good people. The best I've ever been friends with." She says this loudly enough so that all of us can hear it. Of course none of us mention the good people stuff, but when she hangs up, there's a new camaraderie. All the windows are cracked a bit. Bogie is on my mother's lap, nosing the crack. There's a breeze whipping around, ruffling our hair. These may be the best people I've ever been friends with, too—and it dawns on me that maybe I'm the best version of myself I've been in a while. And I want it to last.

Chapter Twenty-nine

The Hives of Suburbia Are a Dangerous Place—Beware the Killer WASPs

o get to Elspa's parents' house, she directs us through a bleak section of Baltimore. Many of the row houses are boarded up with No Trespassing signs stapled to doors. The stoops are gray. A few children run up the sidewalk and disappear down a narrow passageway between two houses. Three young men have collected in front of a corner liquor store. An angry-looking old woman is standing just off the edge of the curb, searching in the pockets of her housedress for something.

My mother reaches up and locks her door. John and Eleanor do, too, but Elspa is leaning through the bucket seats to take it all in.

"I used to spend a lot of time in this part of town," Elspa says, suddenly agitated. "Slow down."

Eleanor moves her handbag from the foot well to her lap—instinctively, I think. My mother is using her hat to shade her face from view as if she's a celebrity.

As we approach a boarded-up, burned-out hull of a

house on our right, Elspa leans close to the window and watches it pass as if it were a monument of some sort. She seems far away.

"Do your parents know what you're coming to ask them?" Eleanor asks, quite practically.

"About Rose? No. They'll assume the worst. That I'm coming for drug money."

"We'll be there with you, dear. I hope that we'll help," my mother says.

"She's right," I say. "Maybe you could offer a generous bribe, as bribes go."

Elspa nods. "Let's keep going."

The sections of Baltimore change more quickly than those in most big cities. Poor neighborhoods butted up against million-dollar homes, sometimes only divided by an intersection.

Elspa keeps directing. "Right here. Left at the next light. Not too far now."

We head into a secluded development. My mother comments on the handsomeness of someone's landscaping. Eleanor agrees, as if they're suddenly on a home and garden tour.

"That's it. There," Elspa says. She's pointing across the street to a really grand home—white with a huge, green lawn. Lush and expensive. Two Volvos sit in the driveway. A minivan is parked along the curb near a Saab convertible.

"Is there a party or something?" John asks.

"Sunday brunch with the whole family," Elspa says. "I hope you like crab crepes."

"Who doesn't like crab crepes?" my mother says. "Bogie loves crab crepes!" She pats his bony head.

"They turn my stomach," Elspa says.

John pulls up and parks behind the Saab. I'm not sure what to say so I don't say a word. We all climb out of the car and rearrange ourselves, pressing out wrinkles, straightening waistbands—all of us except Elspa, however.

I bend down and look inside. Elspa takes a deep breath. She puts her hand on the passenger door's handle. She opens the door, puts one foot on the ground, and stares up at the house.

"They're just people. Just folks," John says.

"With exquisite taste," I hear my mother murmur, which is no help.

I grab Elspa by her lapels, brush off the cardigan, push the sunglasses up the bridge of her nose. "This is my secret. I perfected it after I left Artie. Here it is: you have to cut yourself off emotionally. Just a little. Just temporarily. To get through this. If you don't need them, they're more likely to think they need you." And then I punch Elspa's upper arm.

"Ouch," Elspa says.

"Wrong answer," I say. I punch her again.

She winces.

"Not good enough," I tell her. "You aren't supposed to react." I punch her again.

"That really hurts," she says. She rubs her arm.

"Um," John says, "how about you stop doing that?"

"Okay, forget it," I say. "Do the best you can."

We all walk to the front door. Elspa pushes the glasses up on top of her head, which spikes her hair back up a little. John reaches forward and rings the bell. "They're just folks," he says.

A tall, sporty woman with a gray bob answers the door—Elspa's mother. She looks at the five of us—giving a particularly hard glare to Bogie in his festive outfit. Her eyes fall back to her daughter. "The crepes have gone cold, the tonic flat. Come in, though. Come in." But before she moves back so we can come in, she looks at her daughter. She takes her by the arms. She glances again at the rest of us. "So," she says to Elspa, nodding toward me, "you borrowed her clothes. That was thoughtful." She ushers us in. "Who are your friends here? Introduce me."

"This is Lucy and John and Eleanor and Joan. This is my mother, Gail."

"Welcome," she says, waving us down the hall. "The crepes have gone cold, the tonic's flat!"

"I like a cold crepe, myself," John says.

The kitchen is a state-of-the-art affair with chrome appliances that belong in a high-end restaurant. There's an enormous and elderly St. Bernard asleep in the corner. It's a certain kind of wealthy person's dog of choice and it lays there like an expensive bearskin rug. I recall one of Artie's favorite quotes from my mother: *a pet dog should never be larger than a handbag.*

Gail starts pouring tall drinks. Elspa and I look out the window. I can see her brother and sister and their families gathered out on the back lawn. There's a man who I figure, by his age, is her father, sitting in an Adirondack chair. There's a gazebo in a back corner. Flowers hem the yard. Kids chase each other. And one, in the middle of it all, is a little three-year-old girl. I watch Elspa watch her. Rose is beautiful. She makes me ache in that way beautiful children do. I've wanted one of my own for so long. But I'm also aching for Elspa. Her eyes are so hungry for the child.

Gail hands everyone plates with crepes and garnishes. "Here you go. With my apologies. Well, now, I guess I'm apologizing for *your* tardiness. That doesn't make sense."

"There was terrible traffic," my mother says. "And I require rest stops, you know how it is."

Gail doesn't want to share this little moment of commonality with my mother. She smiles politely. "Let's head outside."

We follow her to the backyard and a young man jogs over. He gives Elspa a big hug. She hugs him back tightly. "You look great!" he says, and then turns to the rest of us. "Do I already have to say sorry for something Gail has said? Here's a blanket apology."

"Thanks, Billy," she says, then introduces us to her brother. But she's keeping an eye on her Rose, who's even more beautiful closer up. She's bright-eyed and expensively dressed in a flowered pantsuit. "She's doing great," Billy says. "She already has a good sense of irony, a real feel for injustice. Like her mother."

I tell Elspa how beautiful her daughter is. Everyone agrees.

"She really is. Imagine, you made that," John says.

Elspa smiles. "Not in an outfit like this."

Later, in the gazebo, I'm idling by the edges. Elspa is playing with Rose, scooping her up when she falls down on top of a soccer ball. My mother is off walking along the side gardens, taking mental notes, no doubt. She's let Bogie down and he's sniffing the grass.

Nearby, John is talking to Elspa's father, Rudy, a golfish man wearing a smart lime polo shirt. "So, what do you do, John?"

"Sales. I'm an entrepreneur."

"Huh. Elspa's last boyfriend was an entrepreneur. So, she's picked another pusher. I almost pulled the trigger on the last one's punk-ass." I'm a little surprised by the term *punk-ass*. If John is, he doesn't show it. But Rudy explains, "We've learned the terminology."

"I'm not her boyfriend. I own a mattress and bedding supply store."

"Mhmm. Mhmm," Rudy says. "I see."

I walk back inside to the kitchen. There's no one here, which I'm very happy about. I start putting dishes in the sink. Gail appears, carrying more dishes. She takes this moment alone with me to give it to me straight. "I'm just telling you that your efforts will be better rewarded if applied elsewhere. We've had Rose for a year and a half and we should have taken her at birth." She nods through the window at Elspa and Rose. "Oh, most babies get to learn how to hold their heads up straight, but Rose had the pleasure of kicking heroin."

"Elspa's a different person now."

"She almost burned to death in a crack house. Seven months pregnant."

We can hear Elspa and the other family members in the backyard. There's some cheering. Someone must have scored a goal. I leave Gail at the sink where she scrubs.

Soon enough the Sunday brunch winds down. The other families are leaving. Billy gives Elspa a hug, a warm and sad one. He picks up his son. His wife just waves.

Gail turns to my mother. "So, did you make that outfit for your dog yourself? It's quite, quite . . . unique."

"Actually," my mother says, "I did." I cringe as she begins to report on Bogie's affliction of overendowment—including a few loud whispers of the word *penis*. I step away, pretending to be distracted by the tall trees.

John shows up at my elbow. I'm surprised to find him so close suddenly. He smells nice—a cocktail and a little something cinnamon. He says, in a hushed voice, "Do you want to tell me something?"

"Tell you something?"

"I feel like you have something to say that you aren't saying, and I just wanted to give you a chance to say it, if you wanted to. But if you don't want to . . ."

"Or if I have nothing to tell you . . ."

"Right, exactly, then that's fine."

"Fine."

"Fine you have something to tell me? Or fine you don't want to? Or fine you have nothing to tell me?"

I'm completely befuddled. "Yes."

"Yes, what?"

"I don't know what."

"We could try this as a conversation," he says. "I say something. You say something. Like that. Back and forth."

"The kiss is a dustpan," I whisper to him. "It's nothing more than that now. It doesn't mean anything to me, really. I'm fine with it. Are you?"

"A dustpan?"

"Yes," I say.

He doesn't really respond. He's just looking at me, baffled.

"This is a conversation. I say something. You say something."

"A *dustpan*?" he says again.

"Back and forth. A conversation," I say.

"Okay, well, the kiss isn't supposed to exist at all. That was the agreement. I promised."

"But do you think of this thing that doesn't exist?"

"Yes," he says, and I know that I want him to think of it. I want him to have tried to sort it out—like I have. But as soon as I realize that I'm happy that he thinks of it, I know that I shouldn't be happy. I shouldn't have even wanted to know.

"Okay, then," I say. "That's what I wanted to know."

"Let me add here, while the nonexistent kiss kind of almost exists, that I don't think of it as a dustpan."

"Okay," I say. "I tried that but I don't think it worked anyway." And I turn back to my mother who is still yammering on about Bogie and his burden.

Gail looks confused. Her face has begun to pucker sourly, and then, luckily, Rose totters over to a cake plate she can't reach and shouts, "Mommy! Mommy!"

Elspa gets up to help her. But Gail is there, a whir of motion. Rose is, in fact, calling for Gail.

Elspa says, "I can get it."

Gail scoops Rose up. "It's her nap time."

Rose pitches her head back. "I don't want a nap!"

"I'll take her up," Elspa says.

"The routine is best," Gail says, and walks away with the child.

Elspa is disappointed, shaken. She tries to keep her composure. "I guess we should go now, too," Elspa says.

Rudy walks ahead to escort us through the house to the front door.

As we walk through the well-appointed house, I lean in. "Secure a second meeting to talk—at a neutral location."

I hear John whisper to Elspa, "You can do this."

Elspa glances at both of us nervously, nods.

Through the house, through the front door, standing on the lawn, Elspa's father is saying good-bye, shaking hands. He says to Elspa, "Are you coming by tomorrow? We'd love to see you."

"I want to talk to you two about something."

"You know we can't give you money anymore and you know full well we've been to classes on how to handle addicted children. Damn, they were a humiliation for your mother."

"I don't want money. That's not what I want to talk about." She starts to back away. I shake my head, willing her to stick with it. She stops and stares up at the house. She crosses her arms and squeezes them tightly. I can see from here that she's touching the spot where I punched her, steeling herself. "Let's meet at a restaurant instead. And I want to be with Rose tomorrow."

He glances up the stairs behind him—where Gail is putting Rose down for a nap. "Okay, I think we can do that."

"I want to, just, take her to the park or the zoo—something like that."

"We haven't really tried that before. Are you sure? By yourself?"

"Maybe with my friends, too."

"A short trip to the zoo?"

"I've been clean for a long time. I'm taking my daughter to the zoo. I'm allowed to do that."

He nods. "Okay." He steps toward her. It's not clear why, exactly, but it might be that he wants to give her a hug.

She turns and walks quickly to the car.

Once we're all inside, there's this moment when we're still holding our breath.

John says, "That is a hive of some vicious killer WASPs."

"With exquisite taste," my mother repeats.

I say, "But we have a second meeting in a different location."

"You were amazing!" Eleanor says. "Truly tough as nails." And this, coming from Eleanor, seems like the highest of compliments.

"I was?" Elspa says.

"You were," Eleanor says.

Chapter Thirty

We Are the Stories We Tell
and the Stories We Don't Tell

While standing at the front desk of the Radisson in downtown Baltimore—a swanky lobby, complete with lion statues—we can't quite decide how to divvy up the rooms. To the grave irritation of the front desk manager, a young woman in heavy makeup—someone my mother would say looks "highly polished"—we run through scenarios while standing at the desk.

"Mother and daughter," my mother says. She's agitated, shifty-eyed. This is not a pet-friendly hotel. Bogie is in the car and will have to be smuggled in. She's talking while casing the joint.

"But I want to help Elspa prep for this so maybe . . ." I explain.

"I'll take my own room, if that would help," Eleanor says.

"Don't be silly," my mother says, looking dewy with nervous perspiration.

"I'm going to get my own room," John says.

"You shouldn't have to pay though," I say. I'm not sure how this should work, but it seems like I've gotten him into this mess and I know he doesn't have a lot of money at present.

"No, no," he says.

It ends up that Elspa and I take one room. Eleanor and my mother take another, and John gets his own. After a few more moments of dithering over which credit cards to put things on—John will not allow me to pay—we ride up in the elevator.

And, as soon as it gives its first little jerk and starts to ascend, Eleanor says, "I've always liked elevators. Even when I was a little girl."

I turn and glare at her. She's the one who Artie confused me with in one of his little numbered love notes shoved onto some plastic fork in some gargantuan display of flowers.

"What?" she says, looking at me.

"Nothing," I tell her. It's over with now. It shouldn't matter, and yet I can't help it. I'm annoyed by the little reminder of Artie's infidelity.

We all get out on the same floor—which my mother insisted on for safety—and head in our various directions.

As soon as Elspa and I are in our room, settled in, I start to write a script for her on Radisson stationery, listing tips on the art of persuasion. She's lying on one of the queen-size beds, staring at the ceiling with her hands folded on her chest.

"Listen, you have to remember that you've given up no legal rights here. The child is yours. Of course we don't want to resort to this kind of language. We have to sell them on the idea of you as a mother. Are you listening?"

"I'm praying."

"I didn't know you were religious."

"I'm not." Elspa's eyes are shut tight. Her hands are clenched. "Maybe I'll leave you alone. Maybe I'll get something to eat with the others." I stand and grab my pocketbook. "Do you want to come?"

She shakes her head no.

"Do you want me to bring something back?"

She says, "A salad."

I knock on Eleanor and my mother's door. There's no answer. I wonder where they've gone. I move on down to John's door, maybe he'll know. I knock. There's a soft shuffling. The door opens. John's standing there, messy and sleepy. He's shirtless, wearing loose-fitting jeans he's obviously just hitched up.

"Were you sleeping?"

"Not really," he says, trying to sound perky.

"Napping or modeling?"

"Funny."

"I knocked on my mom's door to see if they wanted to have dinner, but there wasn't an answer."

"They already left. They asked me, but didn't want to disturb you and Elspa. I'm hungry enough now, though."

"Oh," I say, realizing that I haven't asked him to dinner but may as well have. "I was just going to get something, anything, really. We can do room service."

"No, no," he says. "Just give me a minute. Let's go out. Eat something worthwhile. Come on in. I'll just put on a shirt."

I step inside and let the door shut behind me. There he is, putting on a T-shirt and then buttoning up a shirt. It shouldn't be awkward. He's getting dressed not undressed. But, still, we're in a hotel room together. There's clothing involved. I start to chatter idly. "Well, I guess it's just us then. Elspa is praying," I say. "She wants us to pick up a salad."

"I didn't know she was religious," he says, putting his wallet in his pocket.

"She isn't."

We're sitting in a seafood restaurant, dried nets and oars and fishing poles decorating the upper reaches of the walls. We're looking at stiff menus. The waiter walks up. In lieu of a tablecloth, there's thick paper. The waiter pulls out his pen.

He says, "I'm Jim, your waiter." He bends toward the table and writes J-I-M in big letters.

John puts his hand out and Jim, naturally, hands over the pen. "I'm John." He writes his name in front of his place and hands the pen to me.

"I guess I'm Lucy then," I say, writing my name down, too. I hand the pen back to the waiter, who's a little befuddled.

"What can I get for you all tonight?"

We order the specials, some wine. And we find ourselves sitting there, primly, a little awkward.

"Do you have a pen?" John asks.

"Sure." I rummage through my pocketbook and pull one out. "What for?"

"I'm going to tell you a story from my childhood."

"Really? No more Jethro and Granny?"

"No. I'll narrate and draw."

"I didn't know you were an artist."

"I was the best drawer in my third-grade class. But I lost interest after being snubbed by the New York City art scene."

"They can be so fickle."

He's drawing now, a little figure, a woman with a large dome of hair. "I blame my third-grade teacher. Mrs. McMurray didn't push my career the way she should have," he says.

"Is that Mrs. McMurray?" I ask, pointing at the drawing.

"No," he says. "That's Rita Bessom. That's my mother."

"She had large hair."

"She believes in large hair. I think it's where she hides her valuables. She still has large hair—though it's a bit airier. This is her young hair though. She was just a kid when she had me." He's drawing a picture of a man now.

"Is this a love story?"

"Not really. My mother's not the love type, really. One of her valuables might have been her heart, which she's kept hidden in her enormous hair.

"That's a disturbing image."

"It just came to me," he says. "I'm an edgy artist."

"And this is the young Artie Shoreman?" I ask, taking a sip of the wine that's arrived.

"No," he says. "This is Richard Dent."

"Who's Richard Dent?" I ask.

He's drawing another man now on the other side of Richard Dent. This one has epaulettes and a suitcase. "And this is Artie Shoreman, dressed as a bellhop."

"Ah," I say. "I see." But I don't. "Who's Richard Dent?"

He gives Dent a duffel bag and an army hat. "He's a soldier."

"What kind of soldier?" I ask.

Jim, the waiter, arrives with our salads. "Do you want fresh ground pepper?"

John says, "No." He looks up and is staring at me intently.

I shake my head.

The waiter disappears.

I ask the question again, because it seems like we're frozen in this moment. "What kind of soldier is Richard Dent?" I ask again. "Army? Navy? Coast Guard?"

"The kind that dies," John says. "No matter if someone's in love with him back home or not." He adds a puff of stomach to the drawing of his mother. He crosses out Richard Dent. "He's the fathering kind of soldier who then dies." He circles his mother and then Artie and then ties the two circles together.

Suddenly I get it. "Is Richard Dent your father?" I ask. "Is that what you're saying?"

John nods. "Yes."

"Not Artie Shoreman," I say.

"Not Artie Shoreman."

"Did your mother lie to Artie? To get him to support the child? I mean, *you*?"

"Yes. Oldest trick in the book."

"Is this why you never called Artie your father?" I push my chair out from behind me and stand up, feeling numb in my legs. My cloth napkin falls to the floor. "This is a scam? Using Artie as a workhorse, lying to him all those years, and now . . . and now you're trying to cash in again . . . first your mother and now you?"

"No," he says. "Not me. Never me."

But I've turned away, and I'm running, shakily. I feel sick. I don't know if John's following me or not. I can't look back. I skirt around tables, past the confused hostess, and, there, right by the Please Wait to Be Seated sign, John grabs my elbow.

"Lucy," he says. "Wait."

And in one swift motion I slap John across the face. I've never slapped anyone before in my life, and I'm shocked by the sound of it, the sting of it. My hand is ringing. My eyes are blurry with tears. His hand falls away from my arm, and I run out into the night.

Chapter Thirty-one

The Difference Between Breaking Down and
Breaking Open Is Sometimes So Slight It's Imperceptible

I'm standing in front of my hotel room. I
don't want to barge in on Elspa with all this
fury and messiness. I try to straighten my-
self up. I pull out an oval compact. My skin is blotchy, my
makeup smeared. I wipe off wet mascara with a tissue
from my pocketbook, which only makes things worse. I
work at my eyes a little more. My hand is shaking—the
hand that I slapped John with. Although I know it's
wrong, I wish I'd slapped more people in my life. I think
of my father's face as he waltzes out on us the month after
my birthday. I think of Artie, sitting on the edge of the
bed, wrapped in a towel, confessing to more than I
wanted to know. I imagine slapping them, the electric jolt,
the ringing sting.

How could John Bessom have lied to me all this time?
How could he have lied to Artie? To Eleanor and my
mother? To Elspa?

Elspa. I remind myself that this trip isn't about me

right now. It's certainly not about Artie being duped when he was a kid working as a bellhop and cheated out of all that money for decades. This is about Elspa and Rose now, completely. That has to be my sole focus.

I slide the credit-card key into the slot. The door clicks, the green light flashes. I walk in and the door closes behind me.

Elspa isn't on the bed. She isn't in the bathroom.

"Elspa?" I call out uselessly.

Her duffel bag is still beside the bed, but she's gone.

There's a knock at the door. "Elspa?" I jog to answer it, but before I get there John's voice rises up on the other side.

"Lucy, it's John. Will you let me explain?" He's breathless, too.

I pause for a moment. I don't want to hear an explanation, but Elspa is gone and I know, deep in my stomach, that something's wrong. I might need John's help.

I open the door. One of his cheeks is red. There's a scratch that's bled a little near his eye, from one of my nails. I don't feel guilty in the least. For a brief moment, he looks relieved that I've opened the door at all, but it doesn't last.

"Elspa is missing," I say.

"What do you mean?"

"She isn't here!"

I push past him to my mother's hotel room, four doors down the hall. I knock. Eleanor appears and then my mother, holding a wet, yellowed flattened bunch of toilet paper. "Bogie peed," she says, by way of explanation. "It's a new place. He was disoriented. Poor baby."

"Is Elspa with you?" I ask.

"No," they say in unison.

"Maybe she went to get ice," my mother says.

And then both women, at the same moment, notice John and his red cheek and the scratch under his eye.

My mother charges forward. "What happened to you?" she asks, all in a dither.

Eleanor glances at me suspiciously. I still can't muster any guilt.

"I walked into a door," he says, waving my mother away. "I'm fine." He turns to me. "I handed you the car keys in the lobby," he says. "Are they in your room?"

I turn back and run to my room. The keys are gone. "Elspa is gone," I say.

My mother and Eleanor are ready to go. The pee-pee paper has been disposed of. Bogie's been left. They have their pocketbooks. We all rush to the elevator.

My mother says that she and Eleanor will stay in the lobby, waiting. "Someone should always stay put in these situations."

"I'll get the concierge to call a cab," I say, though I have no idea where to say we're going.

"I'll check the parking lot for the car," John says. "Just to be sure."

We all rush from the elevator. John stops at the edge of the hotel awning. He can see from there that the car is gone and reports this with a shake of his head. The good news is there's a cab right there, letting out a couple who look like they've been to a wedding.

John talks to the cabbie. Eleanor and my mother are standing outside the entranceway of the hotel in front of the automatic sliding glass doors, setting them off.

"Do you think we should call someone?" my mother asks.

"Who would we call?" John says.

"Where are you going to go?" Eleanor asks. "It's a big city."

"We should have faith in her," my mother adds. "I'm sure she'll make good decisions!"

John and I get in the backseat of the cab. He tells the driver to head toward Charles Village, which is the area of town near the burned-out building. The cab picks up speed, merges into traffic.

John tries to catch my eyes. "I didn't know how to tell you, and if you'll let me explain you'll see why."

"Not now," I say. "I can't deal with any of that now." What is there to say? He's been faking being Artie's son for his entire life, and he's been lying to Elspa, my mother, Eleanor, and me so that he can cash in. I don't want to hear that. I learned from Artie's confessions that you shouldn't ask too many questions. Betrayal is betrayal. You don't want details. "In fact, when we find Elspa, you can just go home."

"Go home?"

"There's no money. You aren't Artie's son. That's it."

"This has nothing to do with money," he says.

"You know what you can do that would actually help me?"

"No."

"When I wake up tomorrow morning, it would be very nice if you weren't here," I tell him.

"Is that my only option?"

I nod. "For the time being, I want to focus on Elspa. You're a distraction, that's all. Can you do me that favor and just leave?"

He sighs, leans back in the seat with his hands on his knees. "Okay, if that's the only option," he says.

"Thanks."

John sits forward in his seat and explains to the cabbie where to go. "Just loop around here," he says.

"I don't pick up hookers on drugs," the cabbie says matter-of-factly.

"No, we're looking for someone who's lost."

Lost? She isn't lost. She isn't a child. Has she left us? Abandoned the whole thing? Abandoned her daughter again, in this new way, by giving up?

We circle several blocks in silence. My eyes dart from one car to the next, one dim figure to the next, and then John says, "Isn't that your car?"

It is. We watch it turn around a corner, back toward the major road that leads to the highway. I can see the outline of Elspa's spiked hair. John tells the cabbie to follow her. We wind along all the way back to the hotel. She pulls into the parking lot.

Once the cabbie has stopped the car, I jump out, but then stop short. What am I going to say? Am I angry at her? Am I just relieved? As she makes her way toward the hotel entranceway, Eleanor and my mother, who were on guard, are there, too.

Elspa hands me the keys. "I'm sorry I borrowed your car without asking," she says, as if this is the only thing to apologize for. She walks through the doors into the hotel.

The rest of us exchange a confused glance and then follow her to the elevator. She's pushed the button. We're all waiting.

"Where did you go, dear?" my mother asks.

"I had to get close to it," she says.

I know she means she had to get close to her addiction, to test herself, to make sure she was strong. Sometimes I feel that way about Artie—mostly I know that I'm not strong enough and so I've had to keep my distance. Everyone else must be translating this in their own way. We're quiet. The elevator doors open. We all step inside.

"We were worried," I say, though I cringe, afraid this comes out overly maternal and chiding.

"I was worried, too," she says.

We step off the elevator and follow her to our door. She can't find her key, so we all wait for a moment. I don't want her to get out of this so quickly.

Finally, she says, "How can I sell my parents on the idea of me as a mother if I'm not sold myself? I can't talk to them about it. I'm not tough."

As Elspa starts to sob, my mother puts her arms around her. I slip the card key into the lock and we all step inside the room. John stands there awkwardly, not sure what his role is now—should he stay? Should he go?

And I'm wondering where my toughness has gotten me. Nowhere—only cut off, shut down. Elspa is the strongest of all of us. "Forget all of my strategies," I say, feeling a jagged tightness in my throat. "Forget I said anything. Speak from the heart. Tell them what you want. What you're afraid of. Tell them everything. Honestly. Don't shut yourself off. Feel it. Feel all of it!" For some reason, I feel furious. I feel like throwing the TV out the window and overturning furniture. "What good does it do not to feel anything? People lie to you and disappoint you." I'm shouting now, my eyes shut tight. "You find out your son-of-a-bitch husband is a serial cheater, and if that's not enough, next thing you know he's going to abandon you—just up and die. And if you don't feel that, then you won't ever feel anything. Bad or good, ever again. So, fuck it! Feel it—all of it!"

When I open my eyes, I find that I must have slid down the hotel wall because I'm sitting on the carpeting. They're all staring at me, stunned. There's a moment of silence.

"Okay," John says. "New plan. Feel all of it."

This breaks the tension. I wipe my nose and almost smile. Elspa laughs nervously.

"Can you go in there tomorrow and face them?" I ask. Elspa nods.

"Okay," my mother says.

"Good," Eleanor says.

Having felt everything at once, an upheaval of the heart, a cavalcade of hate and love and betrayal, I say, "The new plan."

After Elspa falls asleep, I walk to the bank of windows, look out at the restless harbor lights. I've been here on business a bunch of times, but only once with Artie—a day trip about two years ago. We whiled away much of the day in the aquarium, gazing at the blue poison dart frogs and the shy scarlet ibis. Artie argued politics with the yellow-headed Amazon parrot that, despite its investment in the environment, was a vicious Republican—at least according to Artie. The pygmy marmoset, which Artie said had a striking resemblance to his Uncle Victor, stared at us, cocking its little head, until we felt sure we were the ones on display and it was the observer. Later, we rented a paddle boat, toured the harbor, our thighs knotting up, and made out in it like teenagers, the boat dipping and bobbing.

I call Artie. I'm expecting the night nurse, but it's his voice. "Lucy?" he says.

"Were you waiting up for me?" I speak quietly.

"Yes."

"I feel different," I say, without any idea how to explain it.

"Different how?"

"I've been so wrong." I want to add: about a lot of things. I think of slapping John Bessom, but I can't tell Artie anything about John's lies. That's not my secret to tell.

"How? What's wrong?"

"I've been so practical about my emotions for a while now, trying not to be emotional. But it's not working. I can't make it through all of this and continue to try to feel even less. It'll be the end of me. I have to feel all of it."

"All right," he says. "Wait a minute. If you're feeling more, does this mean you're going to hate me more?"

"Maybe, but I might love you more, too."

There's a pause. He's taking this in. "When I said I was despairing, I was despairing mostly because of you. All other forms of despair are minuscule in comparison," he says. "And if there's anything I can do to help you love me again, let me know."

"Are you accepting the fact that you hurt a lot of women in your life? That's what I'd like to know."

"I can't ever accept the fact that I hurt you, that I was the kind of person who would ever hurt you. I'll never accept that." But I know that men are liars. Just in case I forgot, for a moment—just in case I'd had a lapse and trusted one again—John Bessom has set me straight. Still, I want to believe Artie. I start to cry—the silent kind of crying—just tears slipping down my cheeks. And unfortunately, I do believe him in some way. I know he loves me, has always loved me. Maybe I'm feeling some kind of relief, some strange kind of acceptance of Artie, of men. "Remember the pygmy marmoset at the aquarium?" I ask.

"Of course. Why?"

"It's just that I'm here. Thinking of that trip with you and the marmoset that you thought was your uncle."

"I've decided I might believe in reincarnation," Artie says. "When you're dying, you get to think of things like that a little more earnestly. Maybe that marmoset *was* my Uncle Victor. I want to come back as your lapdog."

"They tend to be yappy."

"I won't be. I promise. I'll be one of the few Chihuahuas to take a vow of silence. I'll be a monastic Chihuahua, or maybe a mute one. And I won't even leg-hump dinner guests."

I laugh a little. "Well, now you're making promises you know you won't be able to keep."

"Tell me something more. Anything at all. I just want to listen to your voice for a little while longer."

"I should go. That's really all I had to say—about feeling more."

"Don't go. Tell me something. A story. A bedtime story designed for a lapdog Chihuahua. Make something up."

I think of the opening lines to *The Beverly Hillbillies* theme song—*a story 'bout a man named Jed.* I suddenly feel like I've lost so much and I'm only bound to lose more. My throat aches.

"Or a lullaby," he says. "That would work, too."

"I've missed you all this time," I say.

"Is that part of your made-up story?"

"No," I say. "That's the truth."

"I've missed you all this time, too."

"Good night," I say.

"Good night."

Chapter Thirty-two

Waking Dreams Can Seem Less Real
Than Dreams Themselves

Elspa and I are standing on the grassy lawn while Gail works to secure the car seat in the back of my car. Rudy is holding Rose and her diaper bag.

Eleanor and my mother didn't want to go to the zoo. My mother pulled me aside and said she wanted time with Eleanor, to talk to her about being a widow. "I know what it's like to still be in love with a dead man," my mother said. "And she still loves Artie. It's going to hurt terribly when he's gone." There are things that I trust my mother with. She'll be good for Eleanor.

And John is gone.

He slipped a note under my hotel room door before Elspa and I woke up. It was addressed to the four of us. He explained that there was a work crisis back at home. He was taking the train. He was so very sorry.

I was relieved by the note at first, but then I imagined him with his scratched face, sitting on the train, and I wondered what kind of explanation he had for me. But I don't really want to hear it. Not really. I know I have to feel everything. But I can take one emotion at a time. And I can't help it; I'm tired of lying men.

But then I see it from a different angle. Artie wasn't the lying man, in this case. He was the man lied to. The joke has been on him, hasn't it? He's spent all these years taking advantage of women while carting around this wound of not being able to see his one and only son . . . but it wasn't his son. He paid for another man's child.

And so why did John Bessom spend hours getting to know Artie? Was it an act of kindness or has he really just wanted the money all along? Was he lying when he said that he'd always wanted Artie in his life? Was he part of the hoax and still part of it—trying to cash in one last time?

Gail says to Elspa, "There are Cheerios and peeled apple slices for a snack in the diaper bag, a sippy cup, and a change of clothes, in case she pees in her big-girl pants." There's something tender and intimate about the words *big-girl pants* that makes me feel for Gail for the first time. But then she rears from the car, takes Rose from Rudy, and says, "Are you ready to go to the zoo with Auntie Elspa and her friends? It will be okay! You'll see!" And this makes me sigh. Why does she have to call her *Auntie* Elspa? And why does she have to say it will be okay, as if Rose has been wringing her hands all morning wondering if it will be?

Rose is a sweetie. She smiles shyly and wriggles to get down and climb into the car into her seat.

"Look at her go," Gail says. "I've tried to teach her caution, but she'll hop out of my arms and go off with anyone, really, into any adventure—just like her mother, I suppose."

Gail is obviously baiting Elspa, but Elspa doesn't seem to notice. She's so happy to be going off with Rose, almost giddy. "We'll meet at Chez Nous at six for dinner," she says. "It won't be too long."

We all pile into the car, Elspa in the back with Rose. As we pull out of the drive, Elspa tries to wave to her mother, but Gail has already turned and is marching into the house.

The day is bright and clear. I haven't been to a zoo since I was a child. Elspa ties a balloon to Rose's wrist. She waddles with Rose near the penguins. Elspa and I squat with Rose to check out ants in front of the lions' cages. We eat peanuts. Rose pees in her pants near the giraffes. Elspa and Rose—in a new pair of pants—walk along pointing out birds.

I begin to lag behind. I take some time to stare at llamas, and finally I feel guilty about John—not for the slap, no. I feel guilty because he's missing out on this, and he was invested in this trip, wasn't he? On some level? And what of all those hours spent with Artie—the soft patter of their voices? Was that all fake? He was the one who'd drawn out Eleanor, asking her questions about her connection to Artie. I remember the way he listened to all the stories about Artie and me, and that moment when he found the lost kid in the Walk-through Heart. Was it all an act? Could it be?

Rose comes padding toward us. Elspa is running after her. Elspa catches her and swoops her up and makes her laugh. And then she sets her down. The sun is setting. Rose waddles a few feet away then gets distracted by the balloon attached to her wrist.

Elspa says, "If I had to, I would be able to be happy with this, too. This may be all I get—moments like this, scattered here and there." And this reminds me of Artie—all I have left with him are moments scattered here and there. I'm ready to go home.

Rose waddles to Elspa. She says, "Pick me up!" Elspa lifts her and holds her close to her chest. They walk over to a park bench and sit down. She pulls out the bag of Cheerios. Elspa feeds Rose, and Rose feeds Elspa.

As soon as we pull into the parking lot at Chez Nous, a Mercedes flashes its headlights at us.

"That's their car," Elspa says in a hushed voice. Rose is fast asleep, head lolled to one side of her car seat. We're restlessly silent.

Suddenly, I'm flooded with fears. What if this doesn't go smoothly? What if she can't see it through? And what if it does go smoothly? Have I really even thought of what life will be like with Rose in it? Am I prepared for any of this? Is Elspa really capable of being a good mother—not just in a zoo on a bright day, but every day, in the daily messy rigor of raising a family?

The Mercedes pulls up alongside us. The window buzzes down. It's Rudy. Gail is a dim figure in the passenger's seat, sitting completely still. "Good evening, all!" Rudy says. "How was it?"

"What's wrong?" Elspa asks, sensing something that I don't quite see.

"We'll have to cancel dinner. Your mother has one of her headaches."

Gail glances at us, two fingers pressed to her temple as if this provides the necessary proof.

Rudy steps out of the car, leaving the engine running.

"What?" Elspa says.

He opens the back door of my car.

"She's asleep," Elspa says. "Can't she just spend the night with me tonight? Let's not shift her now and then again when you get home."

I cough a little, hoping to let Elspa know that we're shooting for more than an overnight here.

"Rose is asleep now?" Gail says, alarmed. She gets out of the car now, too, and strides over to see Rose for herself. "Her sleep schedule will be completely off track."

"I need to talk to you two," Elspa says.

"We can talk tomorrow," he says. "Let's get this kiddo home to bed. Poor sweetie."

Elspa looks at me. Her eyes are wide and panic-stricken.

I grab hold of her arm, as if to steady her. "Don't give up now," I whisper to her. "Go on."

She stares at me a moment and then nods. She gets out of the car and stands there with Gail and Rudy, creating a triangle between the cars. "I need to talk right now."

I look at my hands in my lap, wanting to give Elspa privacy, but I glance up again and again. I want to be present, too, for support.

"We've got to get her home," Gail says.

"I'm her mother. Her home is with me."

Gail turns to Rudy. "I told you she'd try to pull something!"

"Don't do this," he says to Elspa.

Elspa looks strong and tall. Her back is stiff. "Do you want me to pretend I'm not her mother? 'Auntie' Elspa? Who came up with that?"

"Let's not get ugly," her mother says.

"I'm heading back tomorrow and Rose is coming with me," Elspa says.

"You can't handle it, Elspa," Gail says anxiously. "We've been over this. We've been dragged through it!"

"I can handle it now, though. I've changed. I've started over."

"Let me make this perfectly clear," Gail says, leaning in. "I'm not going to hand that child over to you. I am not going to have one failure turn into two."

"Am I a failure?" Elspa says. "Is that what you think of me?"

"It's a simple fact that you are incapable of raising a child," Gail says. "We've been through counseling. We know how this will play out in all of its disastrous variations."

Rudy touches Gail's arm. "Don't," he says. "Gail."

"Don't touch me, Rudy!" she shouts. "I know what I'm doing! She is not taking this child!"

Elspa reaches out and puts a hand on the roof of the car to steady herself, and before I know it, I've stepped out of the driver's seat and I'm saying, "This isn't about what you think about Elspa. This is about Elspa's rights. You don't have custody, and if you try to reach into this car and pick up Rose and leave with her, that constitutes kidnapping."

"Don't you threaten me," Gail says.

"Let's not get out of control here," Rudy says, trying to smile while glancing nervously at each of us.

"I need this little girl in my life," Elspa says, and now she softens, like she remembers the new plan—feeling everything. "I need her as much as she needs me. I'm afraid, of course I'm afraid. But I've done okay. And now I want to have a reason to be the best version of myself. And that reason is Rose, because that version of myself is Rose's mother. Every day." She pauses a moment. Everyone is silent. "I won't do it the way you have. Completely perfect. I'll make mistakes. But they'll be my own mistakes. You have to allow me that."

Gail freezes. She looks ashen. She grabs Rudy's shoulder and looks around the parking lot, wide-eyed. "I tried to create the perfect childhood for my children," she says. "But in the end, I failed you."

"No, you didn't," Elspa says.

"Why have you always disagreed with me on everything? I failed you," she says. Her eyes well up.

Elspa takes a step toward her mother to give her a hug, but Gail holds up her hand to stop her.

"No," Gail says. "I can't go through this." She turns to Rudy. "So, here it is. You said this would happen one day. You said I would have to let her go. And you were right. Is that what you'd like to hear?" She starts walking back to the car. "Let's make this break as cleanly as possible."

"We don't have to do this cleanly," Elspa says. "We just have to make our way. I'm not expecting it to be clean."

Gail stops and says, "I'm offering you all that I'm capable of." She gets into the car and slams the door.

Rudy stands there, staring at Elspa. He's stunned for a moment and then he tears up. He rubs his eyes, trying to regain his composure. He can't. He turns his back, revealing his shaking shoulders. When he faces Elspa again, he touches her hair, then kisses her gently on the cheek. "I've been waiting for this moment for so long. I knew you would come for her when you were ready. I've said it all along."

"You have?" she asks shyly.

He nods. "I'll be able to take care of it with your mother." He tears up again, and then clears his throat. "We have to be able to see Rose. Often. She's our little girl, too. We love her."

"I know," Elspa says. "I'll never be able to repay you. She needs her grandparents. I know that. There will be a lot of visiting. This isn't an ending. Tell Mom that. Tell her that this could be the start of a new relationship. A good one."

His eyes are wet and when he smiles, the tears slip down his cheeks, and then he turns and walks back to the car and gets in. The car sits, as if stalled, and then slips away.

Elspa and I stand there for a moment.

"You did it," I tell her. "You were amazing."

"I think I was," Elspa says, a little stunned.

And then we both turn and stare at Rose, still sleeping soundly.

Later, in the hotel room, Elspa lays Rose down on her bed. She takes off her daughter's shoes while she's still sleeping. I've called my mother, Bogie held under her arm, and Eleanor into the room to see.

"I can't believe she's here," I whisper.

"You really did it," Eleanor says. "You really did."

My mother smiles serenely. "She's breathtaking."

I sit down on my bed, feeling completely heavy and

spent. The day has been so gusty and wildly unpredictable. And I'm not sure why, maybe because my defenses are low now, or maybe because it seems like the right thing to be completely honest, but I find myself saying, "John isn't Artie's son." I didn't know I was going to say a word, but there it is.

Elspa's eyes open wide and she smiles. "So, he's on this trip because he's in love with you."

I have no idea why Elspa would make that odd connection. "He lied to me, Elspa. To all of us."

"Yes, but he did it because he's in love with you."

"That's ridiculous," I say. "No, no." I look to Eleanor and my mother for support, but they just look at me, shaking their heads, smiling a little. "Are you kidding me? You agree with her?"

"Mhmm," Eleanor says. "I do."

"She's right, honey," my mother says. "And he left because of you. And were you the one who gave him that scratch?"

"I don't have to answer that," I say. Even Bogie seems to be looking at me suspiciously.

Elspa shrugs. "It's the only thing that really makes sense. It's pure logic." She brushes some of Rose's bangs, damp with sweat, off her forehead. "Do you love him, too?"

"No," I tell her. "He's a liar. And he doesn't love me." I'm stunned because I'm not sure that I'm telling the truth. Could he love me? Do I love him, too? Of course not. I want to go on to say, *He's Artie's son—how could I fall in love with him?* But that's not true. It was never true. "I want to enjoy *this* moment." I point to Rose on the bed. She looks angelic. "Just look at her!"

Elspa tucks her in under the covers and curls up on top of the covers, face-to-face with Rose. "I can't believe she's mine," Elspa says, and she watches her daughter sleep. She runs her fingers over her features—sculpting her little girl's face.

Chapter Thirty-three

And Sometimes You Can Be Brought
Back to Yourself, Whole

We make our way home after a hotel buffet breakfast, which turned out to be a little extra sticky and gooey with Rose on board. She delights in her food, not just the taste but the sponginess of her French toast, the rubberiness of her eggs, the fattiness of her bacon.

In the car, Elspa keeps Rose distracted in the back by reading, singing, making up games with her fingers and string. Bogie is also used as a distraction. Rose likes to mimic his panting, and it's as if they're developing their own dog-child language—so many pants for yes, so many for no. I know Rose will bring the kind of lightness and playfulness we'll need to get through this next phase with Artie. Rose will help us make it through.

We make it home in two hours—a straight shot, no traffic. I walk quickly into the house.

One of Artie's nurses waves to me from the kitchen. "He has a visitor," he says.

I can't imagine who. One of the sweethearts? I decide

to ask her to leave. I have to talk to Artie privately.
"Thanks," I say, and walk directly upstairs. I know I could
probably make excuses for John Bessom's disappearance
from his life, but I've decided I have to tell Artie everything I know. Artie would want to know, even if it hurts
him. I don't know how he'll take it.

Artie's door is closed. I knock quietly and then open it
a crack. Artie is sitting up in bed. He looks thinner, and I
realize that when I'm away, I have a mental image of Artie
that I've refused to update—a healthier, more robust
Artie, not completely well, but much better, a version of
Artie on the mend. So it comes as a bit of shock that he
looks so ragged and pale and small. The oxygen tubes are
still in place—my mind had erased them.

He says, "I know the whole story now."

"What story?" I ask, wondering how in the world the
news got to him before I did.

"You have to hear him out," Artie says.

"Who?" I ask.

I open the door the rest of the way, and there is John
Bessom, sitting in a chair by the window. He looks exhausted, like he hasn't slept. His eyes are weary. The scratch
on his face is still there—angrier-looking than before.

"What are you doing here?" I ask.

"I'm coming clean," he says.

"What?" I ask.

"Let me tell you what's going to happen here. Lucy,
you're going to sit in the armchair," Artie says, "and the
kid is going to talk while you listen. That's it. The end. Do
you understand?"

"But . . ."

"No," Artie says. "You're going to sit in the armchair
and the kid is going to talk."

I move slowly to the armchair and sit.

"Go ahead," Artie says.

John clears his throat. He's nervous, fiddling with the edge of the curtain. "I always thought that Artie was my father, growing up," John says. "My mother told me he lived far away and couldn't visit because he was an extremely busy and important man."

"I *am* extremely important," Artie interrupts as a joke. He's still trying to disarm the situation. I know I must look confused and more than a little caught off guard. "That part was true."

"I found some old envelopes from Artie's monthly checks in a drawer in a hutch when I was around twelve, and I figured out by the return address that he lived not too far away. So I spent that summer spying on him. I'd catch the bus to his neighborhood whenever I could, and I'd hide out in the neighbor's bushes and watch him mow his lawn, talk to neighbors, have barbecues. I even had a notebook, trying to keep track of everything he did and everything I could hear him say. And I would go home and practice saying the things he'd said and walking like him." I try to imagine John Bessom as a twelve-year-old kid, crouched in someone's bushes, spending the summer trying to act like Artie. I have to admit it's really sweet— even though I don't want to admit to any of John's sweetness at present. John looks at Artie. "I didn't know then that he was spying on me, too—here and there—all of those years."

Artie nods. "I was."

John goes on. "But it was hard, too. I'd see him moving in and out of the house with other women." I glance at Artie and he shrugs sheepishly. "I was devastated that he didn't want to be with me and my mom. I admired him like crazy. Finally my mother found out where I was going, and she told me flatly that he wasn't my father, that my father was dead. 'Stop spying on the poor guy,' she said. 'He's a stranger.' " John looks like he's replaying this moment in his mind's eye, and I kind of hate Rita Bessom—not just for duping Artie, which was cruel even though it kind of served him right in the long run, providing a kind of balance of justice—but because she ripped Artie away from her son.

I look at Artie and then back at John. I'm not sure how I'm supposed to respond. This doesn't make everything all better. John Bessom was an accomplice all those years, and, worst of all, he lied to Artie on his deathbed. "I'm sorry about that," I said. "But still you lied to me. You lied to Artie all of these afternoons up here talking. Just to get his money."

"I never did it for the money," John says. "I had two reasons, I guess." He looks toward Artie as if asking for permission.

Artie nods. "Go on."

"First off," John says, "I never had a father, so why not Artie? Why not, at this awful time in my life, get some advice? I've never gotten advice, fatherly advice, in my whole life." Then he stops.

Artie smiles at him. "I never had a son, it turns out. Not really," he says. "So why not now, at this awful time in *my* life."

"And so we decided . . ." John says.

"We made a pact," Artie adds. "He's my son."

"And he's my father."

There's something sad in this, but so sad, it's tender. I realize that John has finally said it—finally called Artie his father. I hadn't expected it to turn out like this—to find out that Artie isn't his father and then to find out that, on this other level, he is. I take a moment to let it sink in. This is what I'd been wanting—this moment—for Artie and for John.

I gaze around the room, my eyes dart over Artie's pill bottles, the busted frame of the photo of Artie and me on Martha's Vineyard, the oxygen tank still noisy in the corner of the room. I want to know what the second reason is, too. I want to know if Elspa was right. Would he confess to this in front of Artie? "What's the second reason?" I ask.

"The second is more complicated. I came here and told Artie the whole story and this is the honest truth." He looks at Artie one more time to get his approval, and then, with the words spilling quickly out of him, he says, "I fell in love with you."

My chest tightens. I glance at Artie. He isn't angry, but there is a certain anguish in his face, a very slight contortion. I can tell that he's come to some new marker in accepting his death, that he's realized that my life will go on, and he has to let it, though the realization isn't without pain.

"I was drawn to you that first time you found me sleeping in the showroom, but then, during the tour, well, I fell in love with you," John says.

"No," I say. I close my eyes.

"Yes," he says.

I shake my head. "I can't tell when men are lying and when they're telling the truth anymore."

"That would be my fault, in part," Artie says.

"I helped out, too," John says.

"And you wanted the money?" I ask.

"I don't want the money," he says, and then he winces.

"I do need the money. I'd be lying if I didn't admit to that. But I'm not here because of money."

"You should settle for the money," I say, stiffening up. "I'll give you all of the money from that old fund Artie had for you. You'll be fine."

"I don't want to be fine. That wouldn't be sticking to the new plan. I'm supposed to be feeling it all."

"Artie," I say. "Artie, what do you want me to say here?"

"Nothing," Artie says. "He isn't asking you for anything."

John looks at me intently with his tired eyes. "I'm not asking you for anything. I can't explain it," John says. "It's like you woke me out of a dream, and I didn't know it, but you were the dream I'd been dreaming."

I sit there for a moment. No one moves. I'm trying to feel all of it—this kind of love. At first I press it down with a knot in my chest, but it doesn't work. The knot unravels and there it is again, untied, set loose. I feel like I've come back to some essential part of myself—love. I might love John Bessom. Can I let myself feel that much again?

"Artie," I say. "What about you? What can I do?"

I'm not asking you for anything either.

Now that I've felt love—or something close to it—for John, I feel like I can breathe again. I know I can bring this love to Artie. We need to love each other again, with all that love entails—even the hard things, like forgiveness and acceptance. I don't think it makes logical sense—that one love can bring back another love—but it's true.

Chapter Thirty-four

A Family Can Be Tied Together by an Unlikely Series of Knots

There's the unbelievable, glorious chaos of a three-year-old in the house. The refrigerator is adorned with crayon drawings; the counters are sticky with spilled juice; the dining room sofa covered in poppies has become a field for a herd of ponies with pink manes. There's a wee potty in the downstairs bathroom, a step stool at the sink. There are toys that sing and blink seemingly all on their own. Bogie has learned how to hide under the sofa in a far corner and to beg at the bottom of the stairs for someone to tote him up. The guest bedroom has been turned into a little girl's room, complete with a canopy bed from Bessom's Bedding Boutique, and the theme is frogs—Rose's idea. There are frog sheets and a frog nightlight and frog stuffed animals, which, it turns out, get along well with ponies of the pink mane variety. And there is Rose in the middle of everything—chirping, singing, dancing, stomping, pouting, laughing, roaring. She is this creature fully herself, so fully alive.

And, at the same time, there is a man dying in an upstairs bedroom.

As Artie grows weaker over the next few days, we're all there with him, trying to make him comfortable in the smallest ways—cooling his wrists with damp washcloths, plumping pillows, feeding him ice chips. The oxygen tank makes the room hotter, so we turn up the air.

John Bessom and I, we work together with a common goal. What was said in that room—the three of us—it hasn't stalled there. It exists still. But all our love at this moment, from every well and reserve within each of us, is being handed over to Artie. There isn't any left over. Not now. Not yet.

Still, sometimes I catch myself wondering what a life with John Bessom would be like—the same way I once thought about my life with Artie. I'm not as naive now, thinking only of the good things: beach vacations and our kids' birthday parties. I think of many different possibilities. I think of the beginning, when I first woke up John where he was sleeping on the floor model of a mattress, and the middle, which might include beaches and birthdays, and I think of the end, too. There's so much fierce emotion in an ending—or at least Artie's ending—that it has a lush beauty within all the sadness and loss. When I think of a life with John Bessom, Artie still exists. He's the intricate mechanism that's made this possible future. In a moment, my heart can feel like it's been ripped from me and in the next moment, it feels flooded with love—so much love that there's an uncontrollable current, a riptide.

I still like the night shift. I sing Artie every lullaby I know, and when I run out of lullabies, I sing Joan Jett songs in a soft lilting voice.

These last few days are each a kind of eulogy. I have

John to thank for that. I tell Artie the story of the bird in the shutters of our friend's guesthouse. I tell him about proposing to me with the crew shells gliding along the Schuylkill River and the pygmy marmoset at the aquarium. I tell him about praying for our future together at the Old Whaling Church in Edgartown. And sometimes, when he is too tired to listen to stories, I hold his hands and pray. And when I do, I always pray for abundant blubber—a richness not of money, but of a kind of happiness.

Early on, I stop praying for more time. There will be no more time doled out.

Artie asks me if my mother has any sayings that she never cross-stitched into a pillow revolving around the subject of the soul.

I can hear Rose downstairs talking to the television, a PBS show about cats. "I don't think so," I say.

It's become harder for him to speak. The projection of his voice is a strain, and so he whispers. "A soul should never be larger than a handbag?" he asks, looking down at Bogie asleep at the foot of his bed.

"Never let thine soul give in to gravity?" I say. "You don't want to show up in heaven with a flabby soul."

I want to know whether Artie has learned something—about himself or his soul. I feel like I've been through such a whirlwind of change, but he's the one who's been through the most. "And?" I say. "Will you?"

"Will I what?"

"Show up in heaven with a flabby soul?"

"Does my soul look fat in this body?" This is meant to be funny, but there's nothing fat about Artie now. He's gaunt. His cheekbones rise sharply from his face. Down-stairs, I hear Rose clapping her hands and now Elspa is singing along with the cat show.

"I guess I want to know . . . I'm not sure. I want to know if you've learned anything."

At this moment, Eleanor walks into the room. She's holding a tray of food that Artie will only pick at. "I'd like to know the answer to that, too," Eleanor says, "if you don't mind."

"Have *you* learned anything?" he asks Eleanor.

She sets the tray down, and it rattles a little against the wood of the bedside table. "I'm not here to learn some-thing. I'm here to *teach* you something."

"Really?" Artie says. "That's a waste of your time then."

"Listen, you're the one . . ."

"What do you want from me, Eleanor?"

I get up to leave. "I have to, um . . ."

"No, it's okay, Lucy," Eleanor says. "I know what I want. I want the world to be different. I want men to be sweeter. I want sincerity, honesty. I want to be able to be-lieve people. A little trust wouldn't hurt."

"Well," Artie says, matter-of-factly, "I love you, Eleanor."

"Don't be an ass," Eleanor says.

"I love you, Eleanor," he says again, working hard to speak loudly.

"Shut up," she says.

"I love you, Eleanor," he says.

And then I say it, too, caught up in the moment. "I love you, Eleanor."

She stares at the two of us, horrified. "What in the world are you doing?"

I'm not exactly sure of the answer to this question, but

luckily Artie is. "Giving you a chance to believe people again, if you want, or not," he says.

And now I know his reasoning, exactly. I say, "There isn't much you can do about the world and men and an overall lack of sincerity and trust. But the last thing you mentioned . . ."

"That's idiotic," she says, and then she turns, swinging her stiff leg forward, and marches toward the door, then stops. She pounds the doorjamb with her fist. "Goddamn it, I love both of you, too. Okay then? Fine."

And she walks out of the room.

"That was actually pretty sincere," I say.

Artie agrees.

In the middle of one particular night, Artie startles awake. His breathing is so labored now, each breath is forced out by his stomach. He's on a heavy dose of morphine to alleviate the sharp, deep pain in his chest. The oxygen tank in the corner is kicking up heat, but I also have the window cracked open—at Artie's request—and so the humidity seems to billow around the room like rolling fog. I'm the only one there, sitting on the edge of the bed. I haven't been able to sleep. I'm sitting on the edge of the bed where, once upon a time, Artie sat in a towel with shampoo still in his hair and confessed to me.

Hospice nurses have taken over. They give the morphine injections and oversee all his pills. But they do so much more than that. They are, perhaps, the most exquisite form of human being I've ever known. They've told me it won't be long now.

Between gulping breaths Artie says, "Listen." He reaches out and I hold his hand. "I'm afraid that . . ." His eyes fill with tears. "I'm afraid that I would have only broken your heart again."

I realize that I know this about him, that maybe I've known it for a long time. He would have cheated on me again. There's something inside him that he could never really trust. And would I really want some grand conversion, here, at the end of Artie's life? One that wouldn't ever be tested by the temptations of the real world? Is that what I've been waiting for?

No. Artie's come to the truth about himself and has given me a worthy confession—that he's afraid he'd have only broken my heart again if he lived. I prefer the truth. "I know," I say. "It doesn't matter now."

He says my name. "Lucy."

And I say his name.

It's as quiet and simple and plain as an exchange of vows.

And then he closes his eyes. He's gone.

The funeral, I'd handed it over to my mother completely, and it's everything a funeral should be, of course. My mother knows funerals. She's chosen all the right flowers, gorgeously displayed, the urn—Artie had requested cremation—and the photo of Artie on the beach, looking windblown and a little sunburned. Still, it all strikes me as more than a little surreal. Artie is gone. I understand that. I've accepted it, more or less. (My acceptance comes in waves.) But the funeral seems off—as if it should be reserved for the truly dead. Artie will never really be truly dead—not for me.

And as living proof that Artie is still alive, here are his sweethearts. They arrive slowly at first, trickling in one by one, mixing with Artie's business colleagues from the Italian restaurant chain. But then they start to arrive more quickly. A crowd has gathered, and now we're at standing-room-only capacity.

There is Marzie, dressed in a boxy suit, holding her motorcycle helmet. She's with a woman about her own age with long, windblown hair. They hold hands in one of the pews. The redheaded actress who was once a nun in an Actors' Equity production of *The Sound of Music* weeps dramatically, grasping the chair rail for support. Artie's former algebra teacher shows up, too, Mrs. Dutton, arm in arm with an elderly scowling husband—Mr. Dutton, I presume—wearing a crumpled bouton-niere. The mother and daughter who, much to their surprise, met in my living room, arrived separately and are sitting on opposite sides of the room. There's the smirking brunette from the first day, sitting next to the ever-on-edge Bill Reyer. She's glancing at him out of the corner of her eye.

Springbird Melanowski. I wait for her and wait, but she never shows up, not even to lurk in the back. For some reason, I'm disappointed in her.

And there are many women I don't recognize—old and young, tall and short, of various races and nationali-ties. In fact, the third row looks like an all-female United Nations meeting. I never thought I'd be glad to see a swarm of Artie's sweethearts. But I am. I'm glad they're here, each handing over some portion of love (and some measure of reasonable regret, even a couple of worthwhile grudges—Artie deserves those, too).

And, of course, there are Artie's sweethearts who have become my sweethearts, too: Elspa wearing a loose-fitting black linen dress, showing her tattoos; Eleanor sitting with a proper formality, though her eyes are smudged with mascara; and Artie's chosen son, John Bessom, who found his father and now is suffering, but the good kind of suffering, the one you're allowed to have only because you've really loved someone. He's sitting right next to me. Sometimes my elbow brushes against John's. He's been steady and patient, and, like each of us, consumed by what's happening now. All these sweethearts of mine sit beside my mother and me in the front row. But I know, too, that John's been waiting for an answer of some kind from me, some indication of my heart's leanings. I'm waiting, too.

And then there's Rose—she's sitting on Elspa's lap and wearing her shiny shoes, brushing the back of a stuffed corduroy frog with a plastic Barbie brush. I love her soft dimpled hands, the way she cups the frog gently and sometimes whispers to it, apologizing for tangles.

Lindsay is there, too. She arrives late and sits in the back, but she catches my eye. Her suit jacket fits perfectly, like she's finally gotten one tailored. She looks all grown up, taller even, and it's wonderful to see her—like seeing part of myself that I don't want to lose.

So this is the funeral—there are black dresses and flowers and an urn and everything is going fine until the funeral director starts in with a one-size-fits-all eulogy. He has a pomp of hair on top of his head, swirled like a cinnamon bun. He's talking about living life to the fullest. He's talking about Artie, whom he didn't know, but whom he admires because of "the legacy of love that he's left behind."

It's bullshit, of course. I look back over my shoulder

at the roomful of sweethearts—and the occasional businessman—and no one else is buying it either. They're squinting at the funeral director and whispering to one another. There's a good bit of glaring. Artie was Artie. They've come for something honest and true.

My mother pats me on the knee and smiles sadly in a way that's supposed to mean *You should smile sadly, too, dear. Do as I do.* This is not her fault. She's trying to lead me in the world as best as she can. But she's trying to lead me through the world as *she* knows it. And that world is foreign to me.

This is the moment when John leans against me, shoulder to shoulder. "What we need is an Irish bar," he says.

And he's right, of course. Why didn't I think of it? This has nothing to do with Artie. Not really.

After the funeral director finishes up monotonously, I nudge John. "Invite everyone back to that Irish Pub," I say.

"Right now?" he asks.

I nod.

The problem is I'm not sure how to start a wake. I have no agenda to pass around, no charts, graphs, no PowerPoint display. The sweethearts are here. No longer hushed by the funeral parlor's churchiness, they're loud now, ordering drinks, talking to one another and the bartender and the men who were here whiling away the afternoon watching a basketball game on the ceiling-hung TV.

Eleanor, my mother, John, and I are sitting at a table with Rose, who's drawing with crayons that John rounded up from the waitress. Elspa isn't here. When we arrived, she said, "I forgot something. I have to get it. Can you all watch Rose?"

"Is everything okay?" Eleanor asked.

"Fine, fine. I just forgot something important. I didn't know the day was going to take this kind of turn." She smiled.

We told her to take her time, that Rose would be fine with us. And she was out the door like a shot. I watched her through the window, running down the street to her car. I have no idea what she's forgotten, but she's right. The day has taken this dogleg turn. Artie's funeral is becoming something else.

"This feels more like it," John says. He's taken off his suit jacket, loosened his tie. He looks tired—these weeks have been hard on all of us—and rumpled—not unlike the first time I met him. I find myself drawing on one of Rose's sheets of paper, borrowing her crayons. I'm nervous. *This feels more like it.* I haven't been inside this bar since the first time I met Artie. It's exactly how I remember it: Irish and pub-ish. I remember how it felt, watching Artie here that night, all those years ago, as he told the story of catching the bunny in that suburban neighborhood, and later, how it felt just to be next to him. He was put on this earth so fully charged.

John has gotten us a round of drinks. Rose has a Shirley Temple with its bobbing cherry. She takes a sip. "The bubbles are in my nose!" she says, rubbing her cheeks. I'm not sure why, but everything is resonating deeply now. Rose with the bubbles in her nose seems like it's some grand comment on life—something optimistic and poignant and simple.

"How do you start a wake?" I ask John.

"I don't know," he says. "I guess someone starts talking."

I look at my mother.

"What?" she asks.

"You always have something to say," I tell her. "Why don't you start?"

"Talk about Artie?" she asks. "Something *nice*?"

"Something *true*," Eleanor says.

"Anything," I say, "just to get things going."

My mother stands up, walks to the middle of the bar, and then whistles through her teeth like a longshoreman. She holds up her hands and everyone turns and stares.

"This is a wake. I have to say that I'm opposed to these kinds of honest displays of emotion, as a rule. I like a generic funeral myself. But I've been asked to begin the wake with a few words about our Artie." She smiles at me as if to say: So far so good! "Now I like feminism except, of course, when it asks me not to wear a support bra. My question to you all is this: Why did we love him? Will his kind persist? In our current society, is he the kind of big lovable ornery beast who will become extinct? Will the next generation put up with such nonsense of the masculine variety?" She pauses here as if she's actually waiting for an answer—from whom? Rose? Is she the next generation? After a brief pause, my mother goes on. "I'm not sure that it matters. We love who we love—even when we hate them. The heart does what it pleases. And we all loved Artie, in our own ways."

The truth is Artie would have loved this speech. It's filled with sayings that my mother never cross-stitched into a pillow—gem after gem.

I find myself crying in a way that seems wholly new to me.

John raises his glass. "To Artie!" he shouts.

Everyone raises their glasses and drinks, and this is how it begins. The sweethearts tell stories about Artie—one of him sitting through a dog birthday party wearing a fur-trimmed pointed birthday hat (Artie would have hated a dog birthday party); one of him skinny-dipping in a community pool at night; and one—from Eleanor—of him dancing with her for the first time in her life. I'm surprised she's told this story, but I know it's even more important for her to tell than for everyone to hear. And maybe that's the way it is with wakes—everyone hauling in their stories and unloading them.

John gets up and says, "Artie Shoreman became my father on his deathbed. But no one was more alive, even while dying." He looks beautiful, choked up, but smiling. His eyes are teary, but he doesn't cry. "I loved him with all my heart."

Elspa reappears while one of the sweethearts is talking about Artie pretending he knew how to play the piano by clanging atonally, claiming a deep admiration for a new composer named Bleckstein. She hands me a tall cardboard box that still has shipping labels stuck to it.

"What's this?" I whisper. Now I've had a few rounds. My cheeks are flushed and sore from laughing. I'm a little drunk myself.

"Open it," she says.

The thing inside is covered in newspaper. I dig a little and then pull out a strange blue object. It's a sculpture—rounded at the bottom and then boxy, cylindrical, slightly veering up top. It takes me a minute to figure it out.

"It's Artie," she says. "Part of him. You said once that you wanted to see it. I had to call a few people to track it down and have it sent."

I start to laugh. The sculpture of Artie's penis. Here it is. "It *is* abstract," I say. "But I think you've captured something of Artie here. Some essence." And this word, *essence,* strikes me as even funnier than the sculpture.

Elspa starts laughing, too. "Some essence all right."

Eleanor, my mother, and John all look over. "What is it?" they ask.

I hold the sculpture up for them to see—hold it like it's an Oscar. "Artie," I say. "It's Artie, abstract. Maybe that's his best look."

I grab Elspa and give her a hug. We've come a long way together. This sculpture seems to report just how far.

Rose is holding up her drawing. "Look, look!" she says.

Elspa takes it in her hands and says, "Is this abstract, too?"

I look down at my own drawing. Here are my simplistic renditions of Elspa and Rose and my mother and Eleanor. I've drawn Artie, in his bellhop uniform again— the way John depicted him on the restaurant's paper tablecloth—with epaulettes and a suitcase. I've drawn John and me.

He's listening to the woman in the middle of the bar. She's a little drunk, too—maybe just about all of us are a little drunk now. She's slurring through something about Artie and that wakes are really for the living. I fold my drawing in half and then in half again and fit it into my pocket.

I look at John. He senses it and turns to look at me. I move my chair close to his. I only say, "Hi," and slip my hand into his, which is warm and soft.

He smiles and squeezes my hand. "Hi," he says.

This seems like a beginning instead of an end. I know I'll hand him the drawing at some point in the future—a new version of what the future might be. I look around the table—at John, my mother, Eleanor, Elspa, and Rose. And it looks like a family to me—close enough.

I don't know what I'll say when my turn comes. I have so many stories to tell. But I don't know that it matters, really, which one I choose, in the end. We each say what we have to say, and we will spend this long afternoon crying and laughing at the same time, so much so that I can no longer tell which one is the truest form of grief.

THE END

Acknowledgments

Oh, I want to thank so many people who helped me through the muddy waters. Justin Manask, thank you for coming in with the defibrillator paddles, bringing it all back to life. Frank Giampietro—a thank-you that's long overdue. I love your deep understanding of the female psyche. I owe you (and owe and owe). Nat Sobel—you are such a genius! Thanks for the boosting and the sound advice, as always. Swanna, thanks for your steadfast championing of this book. Thank you, Caitlin Alexander, for your brilliant eye and gentle care of these characters. Thank you, Florida State University. Go 'Noles! As always, I thank me mum and me pops, and the broodlings— my sweet and clever crew. And, Dave, my Starsky. I thank you for all I've got with all I've got.

About the Author

BRIDGET ASHER lives on the Florida panhandle with her husband, who is lovable, sweet, and true of heart—and who has given her no reason to inquire about his former sweethearts.